PRAISE FOR *Twist of Fate*

'*Twist of Fate* is beautifully written wi[th] natural banter and unforgettable chara[cters, a] delight to read.' —The Burgeoning B[ook...]

'A fun, magical transformation, fairy-tale–like story that sails along at a perfect pace.' —Cindy L. Spear

'Demonstrating her consummate storytelling skills, Karly Lane manages to write a wryly funny romance in *Twist of Fate* while at the same time delving into the nastiness of coercive control.' —Living Arts Canberra

PRAISE FOR *The One That Got Away*

'If you are looking for a read-in-one-session rural romance with a dash of mystery then this has it all! Perfect to read on the plane, train or beach-side holiday.' —Reading, Writing and Riesling

'I absolutely couldn't put *The One That Got Away* down . . . it had me totally consumed . . .' —Mrs G's Bookshelf

'Both tender and tragic, heartbreaking and triumphant . . . A wonderful life-affirming story I highly recommend—another riveting read from Karly Lane!' —Cindy L. Spear

PRAISE FOR *For Once In My Life*

'Lane's engaging storytelling instantly draws us into Jenny's world . . . a compelling, fast-paced and engaging read with heart and substance, perfect for summer reading.' —Better Reading

'If you are looking for a good holiday read, then definitely choose *For Once In My Life* . . . sit back and relax and enjoy the characters.' —Blue Wolf Reviews

PRAISE FOR *Time After Time*

'*Time After Time* moves from a small country town in Australia to the red carpet of London and Karly Lane has woven a story of dreams, fashion, fame and second chances.' —The Burgeoning Bookshelf

'Proving herself once again top of the game in this genre, Karly Lane brings us a tale that juxtaposes the high-end London fashion industry and a small-town community.' —Living Arts Canberra

'Lane vividly evokes Australian rural communities, and gives due recognition to its challenges, especially for farmers. With the warmth, humour and heart for which Lane's rural romances are known, *Time After Time* is an engaging read.' —Book'd Out

PRAISE FOR *Wish You Were Here*

'A comely rural romance that encapsulates the heart and emotions of Australian country life . . . You can't go wrong with a Karly Lane novel and this latest one was no exception.' —Mrs B's Book Reviews

'All the small town country vibes you could want in a closed door romance with a whole lot of heart.' —Noveltea Corner

'The magic of country atmosphere, a cast of incredible characters, true community spirit and a relatable romance . . . You can smell the way of life, feel the weather and breathe in the fresh air as Karly's inviting storytelling comes alive on the pages.' —HappyValley BooksRead

PRAISE FOR *A Stone's Throw Away*

'Fans will not be disappointed and new readers are likely to be converted . . . those looking for romance, suspense or contemporary novels will all find something to enjoy.' —Beauty and Lace

'With its appealing characters, well-crafted setting and layered storyline, *A Stone's Throw Away* is an entertaining read.' —Book'd Out

'Karly Lane has delivered a wonderfully immersive novel with a highly engaging plot, gripping suspense and compelling twists. *A Stone's Throw Away* is a story of courage, resilience and a passion for the truth.' —The Burgeoning Bookshelf

PRAISE FOR *Once Burnt, Twice Shy*

'Well written, and bravely done . . . *Once Burnt, Twice Shy* is Karly Lane's best yet, celebrating the power of community working to support one another in terrible calamity.' —Blue Wolf Reviews

'Karly Lane gives it her all in *Once Burnt, Twice Shy* . . . a story of faith, courage, strength and future prospects, Lane's eighteenth novel is a sizzling summer read.' —Mrs B's Book Reviews

'Heart in mouth stuff, readers. You won't be able to put the book down till you know what happens to Jack and Sam.' —Australian Romance Readers

PRAISE FOR *Take Me Home*

'Full of romance, humour and a touch of the supernatural, this is another engaging tale by the reliable Karly Lane.' —*Canberra Weekly Magazine*

'Such a fun read . . . Karly has smashed the contemporary fiction genre with *Take Me Home*.' —Beauty and Lace

'*Take Me Home* is a delight to read. I loved the change of scenery while still enjoying Karly Lane's wonderful, familiar storytelling.' —Book'd Out

Karly Lane lives on the beautiful mid-North Coast of New South Wales, and she is the proud mum of four children and an assortment of four-legged animals.

Before becoming an author, Karly worked as a pathology collector. After surviving three teenagers and now navigating the return-to-nesters, her resume has expanded to include her expertise as referee, hostage negotiator, law enforcer, peacekeeper, driving instructor, counsellor and early childhood educator.

When she isn't at her keyboard, Karly can be found hanging out with her beloved horses and dogs, happily ignoring the housework.

Karly writes Rural and Women's Fiction set in small country towns, blending contemporary stories with historical heritage. She is a passionate advocate for rural Australia, with a focus on rural communities and the issues currently affecting them. This is the twenty-fifth book she has published with Allen & Unwin.

ALSO BY KARLY LANE

North Star
Morgan's Law
Bridie's Choice
Poppy's Dilemma
Gemma's Bluff
Tallowood Bound
Second Chance Town
Third Time Lucky
If Wishes Were Horses
Six Ways to Sunday
Someone Like You
The Wrong Callahan
Mr Right Now
Return to Stringybark Creek
Fool Me Once
Something Like This
Take Me Home
Once Burnt, Twice Shy
A Stone's Throw Away
Wish You Were Here
Time After Time
For Once In My Life
The One That Got Away
Twist of Fate

KARLY LANE

Needle in a Haystack

ALLEN&UNWIN

SYDNEY·MELBOURNE·AUCKLAND·LONDON

This is a work of fiction. Names, characters, places and incidents are products of the author's imagination or are used fictitiously. Any resemblance to actual events, locales or persons, living or dead, is entirely coincidental.

First published in 2025

Copyright © Karlene Lane 2025

All rights reserved. No part of this book may be reproduced or transmitted in any form or by any means, electronic or mechanical, including photocopying, recording or by any information storage and retrieval system, without prior permission in writing from the publisher. The Australian *Copyright Act 1968* (the Act) allows a maximum of one chapter or 10 per cent of this book, whichever is the greater, to be photocopied by any educational institution for its educational purposes provided that the educational institution (or body that administers it) has given a remuneration notice to the Copyright Agency (Australia) under the Act.

Allen & Unwin
Cammeraygal Country
83 Alexander Street
Crows Nest NSW 2065
Australia
Phone: (61 2) 8425 0100
Email: info@allenandunwin.com
Web: www.allenandunwin.com

Allen & Unwin acknowledges the Traditional Owners of the Country on which we live and work. We pay our respects to all Aboriginal and Torres Strait Islander Elders, past and present.

 A catalogue record for this book is available from the National Library of Australia

ISBN 978 1 76106 934 5

Set in 12.4/18.9 pt Simoncini Garamond Std by Bookhouse, Sydney
Printed and bound in Australia by the Opus Group

10 9 8 7 6 5 4 3 2 1

 The paper in this book is FSC® certified. FSC® promotes environmentally responsible, socially beneficial and economically viable management of the world's forests.

*For all the generations of women in my family:
past, present and those to come.*

One

Lottie Fairchild stood barefoot on the front verandah of the little old cottage at the top of the hill and sipped her morning coffee. She loved this view, her hometown stretching from the top of the road down through the main street and along to where the old church sat, stoic and proud, at the other end. The church had once been the hub of the small town, in its church-on-Sunday era, until it suddenly wasn't and the parish decided to sell it off. Now the tourists flocked to it for its cafe and restaurant like the parishioners had once done for sermons. These days, the only sermon that took place in there was the occasional author talk that the book club managed to throw together.

The cool morning air smelled like eucalyptus and wattle, and Lottie breathed in deeply. Soon it would start to heat up, the sound of traffic would replace the call of magpies and the odd kookaburra laughing and the brief moment of serenity would be gone.

The little cottage, with its fresh lick of paint and the newly weeded garden her grandmother had planted years before, looked like something from another time. It was old—built when the first pioneers settled Banalla, around 1855, when small towns had started popping up all across the country, almost overnight, during the gold rush era. In the hallway was a framed photo of the house that had been taken in the late 1800s. It showed a horse and cart parked out front, and a family was posing on the front verandah. In the photo, the newly sawn timber hadn't yet been painted and there was a rustic, almost primitive look to the little place. Lottie loved staring at the image, imagining herself somehow thrown back in time.

She loved history—always had. She had a passion for anything old, which was why, when her mother decided to sell the family antiques store, Lottie had left her government HR job in Sydney and returned home to save it. She couldn't bear the thought of the store being run by anyone else—it had been her grandmother's pride and joy. Not to mention a dream come true for her. There hadn't been enough money in the business for two people, but for one it brought in a tidy income. Lottie had grand plans for growth over the next few years, going into larger furniture and more expensive collectables.

As she finished the last of her coffee, Lottie headed inside, the screen door giving the slightest of squeaks as it closed behind her. Over the few years since she'd been back, she'd been lovingly restoring the old house to its original condition—or as close as she could. The results were stunning, with the original timber flooring, doors and timber panelling finally able to shine through from beneath generations of paint—especially the last coat, a canary yellow her mother had decided would cheer up the place. Lottie loved her mum—she really did—but they were like chalk and cheese.

Lottie's gran, Rosemary, had been a raging hippie prior to marrying a handsome soldier she'd met while attending a peace rally in Sydney. Six months after her new husband had been shipped off to Vietnam, he'd been killed in action and Rosemary, pregnant and widowed, had returned to Banalla to raise her child. Hannah had, from all accounts, been a bit of a wild child growing up, and at eighteen she'd left home and headed for the city.

As a child, Lottie had never seen her mother as anything other than a city dweller. Hannah had only returned to Banalla to drop off and pick up Lottie when she'd stay with her gran during school holidays. Hannah had been a hard worker, working as a barmaid during the day and cleaning offices at night to provide for the two of them, but she had never given up the party girl life. Hannah had never been the stay-at-home and work-at-the-school-canteen kind of mum. She didn't believe in marriage and she rarely had boyfriends long enough to bring them home. Lottie's father had been a one-night stand back in the nineties. Hannah had never kept Lottie's conception a secret—she'd always been open about the fact her father had been some stranger who played no part in their lives—and the two of them had been just fine.

Hannah had been a social butterfly, constantly needing fun and new people around her. There was always a party at their place on weekends. Lottie didn't mind. Her mum always had plenty of friends with kids and she was never lonely. She only ever remembered happy times with people dancing, laughing and having fun, although, looking back now, some of that could be attributed to copious amounts of drinking and the odd joint that most of the adults enjoyed.

Hannah had always been a good mum. There were plenty of cuddles and bedtime stories, and the odd crazy adventure—spontaneous late-night road trips to watch the stars over a moonlight-bathed beach, sleeping in the back of their battered old station wagon, just the two of them. It was only once Lottie had gotten older that she sometimes felt more like the adult than the child. She started to turn down the late-night trips to the beach and camp-outs in favour of studying and worrying about a career. Hannah's free-spirited ways occasionally clashing with Lottie's more practical personality, and she and her mum had drifted apart for a few years.

When Rosemary became ill, Lottie visited when she could, between lectures and exams, but Hannah had come back to Banalla to take over the shop and ended up staying. For a long time, Lottie couldn't imagine her independent, city-dwelling mother back here in quiet little Banalla, but over the years, her mother had slowed down and become drawn to spirituality. She gave up the wild parties and instead, embraced clean living with a focus on healing.

Years later, when Rosemary passed, Hannah decided to sell the shop and follow her own dreams, buying a small property on the outskirts of town and creating a wellness retreat, Riverstone Serenity Retreat and Day Spa.

Lottie had never seen her mother happier. The only thing that worried her was the fact her mother was adamant she would never fall in love. It was about this point when she realised her mother's choices in the past had been somewhat . . . extreme. One day, as they were finalising the handing over of the shop, she asked her mother about it.

'The women in our family are cursed,' Hannah had told Lottie matter-of-factly. 'Or rather, our relationships are. You know the stories.'

'Yes, but cursed?' Lottie replied, sending her mother a doubtful look.

'It's true.'

'I know that's what Gran thought, but there's no such thing as a curse, Mum.'

Hannah gave a slight tilt of her head. 'Believe what you want, but the record speaks for itself. Women in our family have a habit of losing their husbands.'

Lottie started to scoff at her mother but then realised she was serious.

'Your grandmother was married for six months before she was widowed,' Hannah said, picking up the delicate teacup to sip her herbal tea, 'and *her* mother was only married a year. Not to mention the two generations before them. Every generation of women in our family has soon become a widow, left to bring up a child after their husbands have died.'

'That doesn't necessarily prove anything. My grandfather was killed in Vietnam and *your* grandfather was killed in a mining accident,' Lottie pointed out. 'Both were kind of high-risk occupations. All the way back through history, wars, disease and work accidents in a pre- O, H and S era meant that lots of people died young. Besides, your grandmother remarried and went on to have more kids, and her husband outlived her, if you recall.'

'Maybe, but the pattern can't be a coincidence.'

'Then I guess we have to hope all the bad luck has run out by now,' Lottie said with a shrug.

'Oh, I've made sure of it,' Hannah said breezily.

'You've made sure of it?' Lottie asked slowly.

'I'm not passing down the ring to you. I've planned that it will be buried with me, so you'll be fine.'

'Gran's opal ring?'

When Rosemary had passed away, in the belongings she'd left Hannah was her beautiful opal ring, which had been passed down through generations of her family.

'The common factor in all those tragedies was that ring,' Hannah said. 'Once it's been handed down to you, you find true love . . . and it gets taken away.'

Lottie remembered the ring. It was a huge blue opal, and she'd been fascinated by the way it changed colours in the light—the little flashes of colour almost seemed to move and swirl inside the gorgeous stone, and as a child it had somehow felt magical. It wasn't a piece you wore every day, but whenever her gran got dressed up or went out to a special occasion, the ring had always been on her finger.

That ring had always meant so much to Gran. But her mother had never worn it, and it was stored in the safe custody box in the bank, where it was apparently destined to remain.

'Your gran refused to believe it too, but I'm telling you—it's the ring.'

'A ring can't be cursed,' Lottie said, trying not to roll her eyes.

'I have a healthy respect for anything supposedly cursed. The same way I wouldn't use a Ouija board at a séance. Why tempt fate?'

Lottie didn't particularly care if she ever got the ring or not—if her mother wanted to be buried with it, then so be it, although she thought it a tad dramatic—but what did concern her was that her mother was so worried about this stupid curse that it had shaped her beliefs in love and relationships to the point that she refused to allow herself to fall in love. *That* was not healthy.

She hated the thought of her vivacious, beautiful mother spending the rest of her life alone simply because she believed finding someone to love would somehow kill them.

Two

The beauty of living so close to the shop was that it was a five-minute commute to work by foot. Days like this were the best—clear blue skies, not too hot and the hustle and bustle of the little town filling her with energy.

Located on the major highway connecting the coast to the west, and with its close proximity to two larger regional towns, Banalla was in a prime position to prosper. It was a thriving community full of art, culture, history and agriculture. An eclectic mix for a rural town, but it worked. The quaintness of its heritage buildings and the fact so much of its architectural structure had been preserved gave the little town a welcoming, homey feel. The rugged bushland setting, dotted with rocks and caves and endless plains of farming land, added a harshness to the beauty, like taking a step back in time to when this land bred a toughness in the people who lived here.

Lottie slowed her steps as she neared the large monument erected on the corner of the main street, taking in the detailed face of the man seated upon his rearing horse, surveying the town with a steely eye. Lottie always felt her breath catch and hold, as though at any moment the horse would drop back down and the rider would tip his hat and gallop off into the sunset. It was a romanticised notion that her saner self scoffed at. This was Gentleman Jack McNally, the infamous bushranger who held the record for the biggest stagecoach robbery in the country. As an amateur lover of history, she'd researched Jack intensively—she knew firsthand some of the more ungentlemanly aspects of the bushranger's life—first and foremost, that he made his fortune by stealing, but also that he'd kidnapped a nineteen-year-old woman, taken her on the run, gotten her pregnant and then abandoned her and the child.

The last part wasn't exactly common knowledge, but the hand-me-down story she'd been told through her family. That woman the bushranger had become infatuated with had been her five times removed great-grandmother, Emeline, and that connection was something her family had kept secret for a very long time.

Nowadays, it was less terribly scandalous than an interesting bit of family gossip, but up until only just before her mother's era, it had apparently been a very embarrassing glitch in their family tree.

As a child, when she'd heard the story told to her by her grandmother, she'd listened with wide-eyed fascination, her imagination propelling her back into the 1800s, imagining a young woman going about her duties on her father's farm and being swept up into the arms of a dashing bushranger. Of course, it hadn't happened exactly like that, but that had been the version she'd always pictured. To this day, the matter of the kidnapping remained contentious. The original, and official, story leaned heavily towards the innocent, virginal daughter of a respectable church-going sheep grazier being forcefully dragged from her family by Jack, brutishly raped and then left pregnant after his final shootout with the police and subsequent death. This had been followed by a rushed wedding to a suitable man from a local wealthy family and a baby born shortly after.

Years later, upon further research, Lottie uncovered a previously thought lost police report from an eyewitness who'd alerted the police to the gang's whereabouts before the shootout. He claimed he'd seen the woman being 'on very friendly terms with the bushranger and who had seemed completely at ease in his presence'. It painted a very different picture from the one that had ended up in the official report.

Instead of the research clarifying the facts she already knew, Lottie had been left with *more* questions unanswered. So she had decided to write a book about the women in her family, including their connection to Jack McNally. It was something that she'd never have been able to do when her gran was alive—or any of the previous generations, for that matter. But it had all happened more than a century ago. Surely now it couldn't hurt.

Needle in a Haystack

She sent the bronzed man one last look before leaving the past behind and returning to the day ahead.

7 April 1863

Jack felt the bay mare beneath him move slightly as she picked up on her rider's tension. She gave a soft snort and he heard the creak of leather and the jingle of metal from the men around him, patiently waiting on their own mounts for his signal.

The groan of the lumbering stagecoach and the steady clip-clop of hooves along the well-travelled dirt track grew louder and more distinct. Everything depended on this heist. If his information was correct this could be the hold-up that set him and his men up for the rest of their lives.

Fourteen thousand pounds was said to be on board the coach heading from Sydney and, in a matter of moments, it would be in his hands. No more living hand-to-mouth for him and his men. They could set themselves up somewhere far away from these mountains and live the life of the gentry. And why the hell not? This was a new country, with opportunities for any man to make his fortune.

A memory of his parents flashed before his eyes—cold, old and hungry. Working themselves into early graves just to put food on the table for their nine children while the rich landowners grew fat on the back of their suffering. His fists clenched the reins tighter and his horse gave a small nicker and moved sideways again. It was time to take back from the rich and distribute the wealth more fairly—between him and his men.

'Hold,' he said quietly as the sound of gravel under wheels grew louder. 'Hold,' he repeated, a little louder this time, as horses and men began to stir and the air around them grew electric. 'Now!'

His mount leaped from the dense bush beside the track as the coach came to a halt, its path blocked by the large gum tree the men had felled across the road only a few hours earlier.

Gunfire erupted. Jack ducked his head as a bullet whizzed past his ear and then he took careful aim and fired, dropping the armoured guard beside the stagecoach driver. He searched for his next target, a sense of calm descending upon him as it usually did once the fray began. It sometimes scared him, the level of detachment he could summon when the occasion called for it. He didn't like violence as a rule, but it had been a formative part of his life and he knew that, more often than not, it was the only way to make people listen.

Once the shooting stopped, he dismounted and walked to the closed door of the coach. He opened it, blinking in surprise at the pair sitting there—a woman, back rigid, face pale and lips firmly pressed together, and a well-dressed man holding a gun.

'Call your men off or I'll shoot,' the man said in a surprisingly deep tone that Jack hadn't expected from the rather toffy way he was dressed.

'You must be Compton,' Jack said, narrowing his gaze slightly as he put two and two together.

'I am. Now, call off your men.'

'The man himself,' Jack said, as he considered his next move.

'Sir, I'll kindly thank you to cease talking and call off your men this instant.'

'It looks like we're in a bit of a stand-off,' Jack said casually before moving his weapon to aim at the woman. 'But I'm willing to bet you won't want any harm to come to your wife. I take it this is your wife?'

Jack saw Compton's eyes widen. 'What kind of fiend threatens a lady?'

'Fiend? Well, now you've hurt my feelings. I'll have you know, I'm quite the gentleman when it comes to the ladies. But if you don't lower that weapon, I might just forget my gentlemanly tendencies.'

Slowly, the revolver lowered. Jack nodded for him to throw it to the floor, which Compton did.

'My apologies for the unexpected stopover, madam,' he said with a small smile. He hadn't been expecting a woman to be on the coach. She was somewhere in her mid-twenties, with creamy skin that had never seen a day's work, and she held herself regally, as though she were on a Sunday ride through the park. Her frosty glare amused him. He had no time for the wealthy and little care for her discomfort, but he did enjoy women and he prided himself on being a gentleman—something he'd always reluctantly admired about the gentry he'd observed as a small boy back in Ireland. 'If I may help you out of the coach, my men need to unload it of its burden. You stay there,' he directed at Compton as the man started to get up.

The woman he assumed was Mrs Compton hesitated briefly before realising she had no real choice. She descended, refusing the hand he offered her gallantly.

Jack grinned at the woman's bravado. He'd seen grown men curled up in balls, sobbing hysterical pleas to spare their lives and *fortune, which always disgusted him. This woman had more courage in her little finger than most men had in their entire bodies. His gaze fell on her long, sleek hands and he noticed the brilliance of an enormous blue stone that contained flashes of iridescent green and bright crimson, flecked with turquoise blue, and that was set in an intricate band of gold. Never before had he seen something as magnificent as the opal that sparkled before him. The stone itself was massive, the largest he'd ever seen. The colours were almost mesmerising, seeming to swirl and change hue before his eyes.*

'This ring,' Jack said abruptly, taking a firm grip of her hand, ignoring her attempts to tug it free. 'Where did it come from?'

'It's of no worth, except sentimental value. Just a pretty bauble my husband found when he first came here. I have far more expensive diamonds,' she said, lifting her other hand, but it was the opal that had entranced him.

'Jack! We have the money,' John called impatiently as he scanned the track behind the coach. 'Let's go!'

'Keep your diamonds, my lady. I'm not a complete brute. However, I will relieve you of this pretty trinket. I find it quite stunning.'

'No. You cannot,' she snapped, reefing her hand from his grasp with surprising force.

'Unhand my wife!' Compton said, bursting from the coach, catching Jack, who was still preoccupied by the opal, off guard.

It happened so quickly.

The man had produced a knife from his boot and lunged with surprising agility. Jack instinctively fired his weapon, watching the shock that spread across the other man's face, the blood seeping from his chest. Through the tunnel of silence that seemed to surround him, a woman screaming eventually penetrated the fog, snapping him into action.

He turned to the woman, noticing for the first time the swell of her belly, before seeing her anguished face crumpled with grief. There was no real regret for killing her husband, though he did feel sorry that she would now be left to raise her unborn child alone. But, unlike his own mother, left in the same situation when his father had died, the good lady would have a comfortable house and staff to ease the burden.

He took hold of her cold, limp hand, tugging the ring from her finger and slipping it into the breast pocket of his coat.

'You are a monster,' the woman said, lifting her gaze to his and holding it with an icy, almost hollow look.

'I'm not an unreasonable man.' Jack shrugged. 'Your husband made his choice. You should have just let me have it.'

'Well, you have it now. May it bring you and yours heartache and pain.'

Jack took a step back from the woman, whose crystal-clear eyes chilled him to the bone. A sudden unease washed over him, which he quickly quashed. 'I'm sure the pain will be easier to bear now that I'm rich. Good day,' he said, tipping his worn hat with his fingertips before swinging himself into his saddle and urging his horse forward. He resisted the urge to glance back over his shoulder, despite something determinedly trying to make him do so.

A few miles down the track, he was just starting to breathe easy when a volley of bullets whizzed overhead.

'McNally! Give it up!' came the shout from an unexpected second party of armed guards.

Jack's horse reared as he swore loudly, shouting orders for a retreat, and then it was hell for leather through the rough terrain, taking all his concentration to keep his head on his shoulders.

Three

Lottie unlocked the front door of the shop and began setting up for the day. She dragged out the larger items she displayed outside—this week, a nest of beautiful old suitcases that had just come in and a rocking chair she swore she was going to take home for herself if someone didn't buy it soon. She did that a lot—her little cottage was almost bursting at the seams with the things she fell in love with at work. She really needed to work on that . . . or buy a bigger house.

'Morning, sweet cheeks.'

Lottie glanced up as a familiar, rather flamboyant figure sashayed towards her, leaning in for a brief cheek kiss. Cherise, also known as Cher, was Lottie's best friend and neighbouring shop owner. She operated the swanky cafe-tapas bar Madame Dubois, a little slice of Melbourne in downtown Banalla. They were also unofficial cousins, thanks to their very first conversation in which the two had discovered a shared connection to Jack McNally. Cher had proudly declared she was a descendant of Kate O'Ryan, the sister of Jack McNally, and that she had decided to do a pilgrimage of sorts and return to her family's historical hometown. Once here, she'd fallen in love with the place and decided this was her destiny.

Cher changed her appearance like most people changed underwear. She had a closet full of wigs and outfits she'd collected during her years as an actor and singer and proudly donned them as part of the dining and show experience she provided in her bar. Today, she was a redhead wearing a red-and-white polka dot dress with a 1950s flared skirt and V-neck bodice that clung to her curvaceous, size twenty-eight body. Her make-up was an artform in itself. She looked stunning.

'Girl, have you checked your messages?' Cher demanded, her husky smoker's voice rising in a perfect imitation of Memphis Tennessee sassiness.

'Uh, no. I haven't had time this morning.'

'Well, I can see why. All that time it must have taken you to put on your make-up and pick an outfit,' she said, crossing her arms and kinking an eyebrow sarcastically.

A low blow, Lottie thought, *but not entirely unwarranted*. Lottie rarely wasted time with make-up—what was the point? It wasn't as though she were trying to impress anyone. She was working in a quiet antique shop, not some high-end department store, and there was nothing wrong with her comfy work uniform of jeans and a T-shirt.

'I'll have you know, I paid a lot of money for this shirt,' she said with a haughty sniff. 'It was full price—not even on sale.'

'Hmm.' Cher's expression spoke volumes to how underwhelming *that* bit of trivia was. 'If you'd just let me loose on a makeover, you'd be a new woman,' she said with a tsk.

'I'm happy with the old woman, thanks.'

'Well, that's what you'll end up being—a lonely, old woman. You're hiding yourself away like you're too scared to actually live.'

This was not the first time they'd had this conversation.

'Not everyone needs to be the centre of attention. I'm happy just the way I am.'

'There is always room for improvement.'

Cher had left her glitzy life in Melbourne, where she'd been part-owner of a prominent nightclub and had performed on stage in various theatrical performances and cabarets, searching for a simpler life after the breakdown of her relationship with her business and life partner. It was a complete one-eighty, moving from the glamour of a major city to the quiet, slower-paced Banalla, but Cher had managed to carve out a place for herself, and it was hard to think of life here before she'd burst onto the scene with all the drama and extravagance of a Broadway production.

She shouldn't have succeeded. The arrival of a six-foot-tall woman dressed in sequins and high-end fashion, custom-made for her curvaceous figure, who was unapologetically loud in every aspect—from the clothes she wore to the volume she talked—had many shaking their heads in disbelief. It hadn't helped that the renovation of the old haberdashery store, which had been vacant for years, was all done behind blacked-out windows. The gossip mills had run hot as to what kind of business could be going in. However, Cher had such enigmatic charm that she could sweet-talk the driest of stoic farmers and flatter the primmest of women. She'd had them all eating out of her hand within weeks and quickly became part of the community.

'Anyway,' Lottie said, changing the subject pointedly, 'what were you texting me about?'

'To see if you got the memo about the emergency meeting tonight.'

'What emergency meeting? Why?' Lottie asked, screwing her face into a grimace. The last thing she felt like doing tonight was attending yet another drawn-out meeting with the Chamber of Commerce. She picked up her phone and scrolled through her emails. Sure enough, there it was: URGENT CALL FOR AN EXTRAORDINARY MEETING was the subject heading in capitals. Daphney Hindmarsh had increasingly been the proverbial thorn in everyone's side since planning for the town festival had begun.

'No idea. Something about Daphney receiving a request from some author doing research for a book on Old Jackie boy,' Cher said with an uninterested wave of her hand. 'Apparently has something to do with the festival committee.'

'Why couldn't she just put it in the damn email?'

'Because then she'd have no excuse to get up and talk,' Cher said sarcastically. 'You know how she loves everyone's attention.'

Lottie bit back a grin at that. Cher was the pin-up girl for loving attention, which was probably why she and Daphney didn't get along. Although, in all fairness, Daphney *was* a pain in the arse and really did seem to have a thing for needing to be in control of absolutely every single detail of anything she was involved in. And she made sure she was involved in *everything*.

'Do you want to have dinner at the pub before the meeting? I, for one, will certainly be needing a few drinks before I can deal with the bullshit,' Cher announced.

'Sure, dinner sounds good,' Lottie agreed. Any excuse not to cook was always a good idea.

'Speaking of authors, how's your book going?'

'I'm not an author,' she automatically said, shaking her head.

'You will be,' her friend said matter-of-factly.

Lottie smiled at the certainty Cher always seemed to have whenever they spoke about her pet project. She wished she had that kind of belief in herself. 'I spoke to that cousin of Gran's I've been trying to track down, about the box of photos and bits and pieces she used to have. She said she was going to see if she could find it. I'm going to visit her on the weekend so I can take a look through it.'

'That sounds exciting.'

'Maybe . . . I mean, I hope there's at least something in there that I can use in the book, but I'm not getting too excited.' She'd been gathering information about all the women in her family and trying to put together a picture of their lives, but finding anything evidence-based, rather than purely handed-down stories, was proving difficult. Unlike doing a normal family tree, putting together a maternal-line family tree, tracing female ancestors as they married into different families, was a little more complicated. And this meant that photos, and other memorabilia and keepsakes, were held by distant relatives in many different families. She desperately wanted to find at least a few images of the women from her line as far back as she possibly could, but photos had clearly not been something her ancestors had been fond of—or, in the earlier cases, maybe they hadn't been able to afford them. Either way, there were very few images and it was frustrating, as she'd been hoping to have at least one of each.

The ring itself, which had originally been the focus of the book, had been photographed a few times with family members—namely her gran and her great-gran, both of whom had been wearing it in wedding photos, but before that, there was nothing. She was desperately hoping that one of the cousins of her great-grandparents may have something that had been passed down in old photo albums or scrapbooks.

'Well, I better get back. I'll see you tonight.' Cher kissed her cheek and wiggled her long, red-nailed fingertips in farewell before disappearing out the door, leaving only a lingering scent of Versace perfume.

The Royal was the oldest of the three pubs still operating in town, and the most popular. The building was a grand old structure, with wide verandahs on the second floor that shaded the street below. It had recently been renovated and given a facelift with a new coat of paint, making it look brand-new again . . . in an 1860s kind of way.

Stepping through the large front doors always felt like stepping back in time, and Lottie never tired of the sensation. Black-and-white photos of the town lined the walls—a testament to the town's origins—and the furniture, although new, was timber and understated, lending an original feel.

Lottie spotted the fanatical waving of her friend as she looked around the room. She waved back and headed to the bar to order a drink. Wineglass in hand, she weaved her way across to the table where Cher sat, nodding and greeting the locals she knew along the way.

'I think everyone on the committee had the same idea of getting smashed before listening to Daphney,' Cher murmured as Lottie took her seat.

'Smashed might be a tad exaggerated,' Lottie replied, eyeing the other tables casually, but noting that a few people had obviously been here early and were clearly not on their first round of drinks.

'There she is! The most beautiful woman in the room,' a voice slurred as Dougie Walters stopped beside their table, leaning heavily on the back of the chair across from Cher, ogling her voluptuous breasts, which were barely contained within the deep neckline of her dress.

'Hello, Dougie. I haven't seen you around for a few days,' Cher said with her usual unruffled grace.

'I've been in hospital. Bloody doctors pokin' and proddin' at me all day.'

'I hope you're better now,' Cher said politely.

'Still kickin', aren't I?' he replied, giving a hoot of laughter before breaking into a fit of coughing. 'Anyways, how about I buy you drink?' he continued unperturbed.

Lottie tried not to squirm in her seat. The man always made her uncomfortable, even though it was Cher he seemed besotted with.

'That's kind of you, Dougie, but I've already got one and my friend and I are about to order dinner.'

'Righto, love. I'll leave you to it, then,' he said, toasting her with his half-empty glass of beer. He pushed away from the chair and walked unsteadily back to the bar.

'I don't know how you're so patient with him,' Lottie said, watching him butt into a conversation with two men across the room.

'He's harmless. Just lonely, I think.'

Lottie wasn't even sure where he lived, exactly, he didn't seem to have any family around town and he was always at the pub. It seemed a sad kind of life.

'Hurry up and order. I'm starving,' Cher announced, before handing her the menu.

'Okay, geez. Give me a minute,' Lottie said, glancing down the list of choices but already knowing exactly what she was going to get. 'I think I'll have the—'

'Chicken parmigiana,' Cher cut in. 'I figured,' she said, holding up a table buzzer with a grin. 'Which is why I already ordered. I was just showing you the menu so we could play the game of pretending you'd order something else.'

'I like chicken parmigiana,' Lottie said defensively.

'I know,' Cher said, with a roll of her eyes.

They settled back in their seats to wait for the table buzzer to go off. Lottie scanned the room and noticed a nearby group of four people she didn't recognise. They were clearly out-of-towners visiting, since they were all unsubtly eyeing Cher with varying expressions of surprise and curiosity. In their defence, Cher was an unexpected force of nature to find in a small rural town.

Cher's resilience around other people never ceased to amaze her. She never took offence when people stared, whether at her size or her attention-grabbing fashion. It didn't seem to worry her. She used her brashness and theatrical personality to defuse any situation and the locals were all used to her now. Sometimes, Lottie suspected, Cher quite enjoyed the attention from newcomers now that she was pretty much accepted by the majority of the community. Where was the fun in that? 'Not everyone is meant to be a moth, my darling,' Cher had told her more than once when she'd tried to talk Lottie into a makeover in the past. 'Some of us are destined to be bold, beautiful, butterflies that light up the room like a rainbow.'

When Cher had realised the town lacked a theatre group, she'd quickly set about rectifying the situation. It was quite the talk about town once the flyers went up, with locals doubting there'd be enough talent about to create such a thing, but, gradually, Cher managed to coax out a surprising number of closet theatre buffs, like Bob, the local plumber, who had surprisingly wonderful comic timing, and Nigel, the mechanic, whose wife had dragged him along to an audition where he'd floored everyone with his remarkable deep-voiced rendition of 'Gaston' from *Beauty and the Beast*. The group had grown in confidence and over the last few years, under Cher's experienced guidance, had put on a number of productions that raised money for charities.

As something of an introvert, it wasn't always easy having a best friend who was so flamboyant and outspoken, but Lottie was in constant awe of Cher, and wouldn't have traded her for all the tea in China.

Four

Daphney Hindmarsh entered the room in the rear of the pub, which was set aside for corporate functions—although no one could recall the last corporate function held there. The closest thing was the Chamber of Commerce meetings the first Tuesday of each month. She strutted in, her long flowy skirt swishing around her high heels, a benevolent smile she'd learned in her Miss Banalla Show Queen days plastered across her face as she greeted her loyal subjects. Behind her trailed her ever faithful sidekick-cum-committee secretary, Lisa.

The usual suspects were gathered around the table; Shorty, Terry, Christine, Carol and Janelle, all Banalla born and bred, along with some of the new blood—the blow-ins, as the locals sometimes referred to them—newcomers from the city who'd made a tree change. They sat together on the opposite side of the table: Skye and her partner, Tori, who ran the organic vegan cafe; Corbin, who owned a landscaping business; Elijah, who had opened and been the instigator of the town's very successful art gallery and cafe; and Solene, who ran the health food store.

The mix of new and old should have been a recipe for disaster, and may not have worked in some small towns, but the committee had been dwindling and in dire need of new members, so the willingness of the newcomers to be part of something to better their community had been welcomed with open arms. It hadn't gone without the occasional disagreement—after all, change in any capacity was always going to meet with some kind of resistance—but, on the whole, everyone wanted the same thing: give Banalla a new lease of life, keep it relevant and ensure the businesses in town had the opportunity to thrive.

The committee had taken on a huge role in organising this festival. They had a number of subcommittee members, who were usually not the most reliable at turning up to meetings but did lend valuable hands when the need arose for extra volunteers, which they'd be needing on the day. From a tiny idea, the festival had suddenly morphed into a massive undertaking, and if they managed to pull it off, it would be something the whole town could be proud of.

'I'm sorry to have called you all here tonight so unexpectedly, but I have some exciting news to share that simply couldn't wait until our next meeting,' Daphney said, beaming and clapping her hands together like an excited kindergarten teacher in front of her class. She paused, waiting expectantly.

'The suspense is killing us,' Cher said with great irony.

Daphney shot her an unfriendly look. 'I was going to let you try and guess,' she twittered. 'But I can't wait that long. You might recall earlier in the year, I suggested we send out a few feelers for a guest speaker to come along to our festival. Well, I did, and today I received a confirmation,' she announced. 'Professor Damian Loxley from the University of Sydney has agreed to come along as guest speaker!'

'Why are we having a professor speak at the festival?' asked Terry Fuller, a gruff man in his early sixties from a local farming family.

'Because, Terry, Professor Loxley is an expert on early colonial history and in particular the bushranger era. He's also in the process of writing a book on, among other things, Jack McNally, so he was planning a research trip out here anyway. It was meant to be,' Daphney said simply. She went on to list an impressive résumé of published works and accreditations, as well as a list of fictional works based on major historical events. There was no doubting the man's credentials, but Lottie wasn't so sure replacing their original plan of a celebrity with some stuffy professor would draw the crowds they were hoping for.

'Are we supposed to pay this fella for the privilege of coming out here to tell us all about our local history?' Shorty Norton asked. Shorty was at least six-foot five and built like a brick wall.

'This is one of the things we need to discuss,' Daphney admitted. But she rushed on. 'We have money set aside and I'm recommending we use some of it to secure this speaker. It's very rare that a man of this calibre would even consider attending a festival like this.'

'So he's lowering his standards to rough it for a day or two? Nice of him,' Terry muttered.

'He was kind enough to waive an appearance fee, so I think it would only be fair that we pay for his accommodation and host a dinner the night before the festival in his honour.'

'How much is that gonna cost?' Shorty asked.

'Once we vote on the decision tonight to accept his offer, I'll find some prices and options, but it's considerably less than if we had a celebrity accept,' Daphney snapped.

'Did you ask *any* celebrities?' Cher asked.

'I sent out a number of invitations, yes.'

'And none of them accepted?' Cher prodded.

'No. They were all booked out.'

'So basically, this professor guy was the bottom of the barrel and the only one to show any interest?' Cher surmised.

'Does it even matter, Cherise?' Daphney sighed impatiently. 'The point is, this works out perfectly. He is the ideal person for the job.'

'He's just not famous enough to attract any of the publicity we were supposed to be trying to get,' Christine pointed out, disappointment heavy in her tone.

'I was hoping we'd get that Grant Denyer fella. I reckon we'd get a few people comin' along to see him,' Janelle said.

'I wanted Larry Emdur. He's so dreamy,' Carol put in.

'We wanted Sam Armytage. Now, *she* would have brought in the crowds,' Shorty said, and Terry nodded his agreement with more enthusiasm than Lottie had seen in quite some time.

'Well, we got Professor Loxley instead,' Daphney said briskly.

'Come on, everyone, let's just remember we're all on the same team,' Skye the twenty-something-year-old inserted calmly. 'I'm sure Daphney has done her best.'

'Thank you, Skye,' Daphney said somewhat stiffly, her gaze falling on the younger woman's dreadlocks with a slight twitch. Two more opposite women in a room you could not have possibly conjured up. 'I could only work with what I was given. Let's just vote and get on with it. All those in favour?'

A slow, less-than-enthusiastic show of hands went up around the table accompanied by a low mumble of discontent. Daphney looked across at Lisa and gave a brisk nod. 'Please note that the majority has voted in favour of accepting Professor Loxley and that terms of the offer will be finalised at the next meeting and a letter of offer sent out. That concludes this extraordinary meeting. I'll see you all here next week.'

As usual, Daphney wasted no time, gathering up her paperwork and striding out of the room while her minion, Lisa, hastily gathered her things and scampered along behind.

The rest of the committee lingered over their drinks and socialised for a few more minutes before calling it a night.

'She's lost the plot! I can't believe we get stuck with some nobody history teacher, old fogey instead of a celebrity . . .

even a minor one would have been fine,' Cher muttered as they walked out of the pub. 'I told Daphney I had contacts who could have helped but she point-blank refused my offer.'

'Well, I hate to admit it, but she probably has a point,' Lottie said. 'Someone with a historical degree would really suit a festival about a bushranger a lot better than a celebrity.'

'Who cares? People don't want to hear about that stuff, they want to get a photo with someone they've seen on TV,' Cher said. 'You won't hear stories about the day I went to Banalla and met boring old Professor Doodlebug and got this photo, will you?'

Lottie grinned and shook her head. 'I guess not.'

The planning for the festival had started years before, in the lead-up to the anniversary of Jack McNally's death one hundred and sixty years before. Then Covid had struck and the festival had been put on hold. Now they were finally going ahead with the festival plans, but it wasn't the nice round number of one hundred and sixty; it was now the one hundred and sixty-third anniversary, which just seemed an odd number to be celebrating. Still, it was what it was. They had funding for the event, and it needed to happen.

It was their usual practice for Cher to drop Lottie at her house after a meeting, despite Lottie protesting that she could walk home. She supposed old city habits died hard, despite the fact Banalla didn't have much of a crime rate. Lottie stopped beside the massive, candy-floss-pink ute and waited for Cher to unlock the doors.

As far as statements went, this vehicle pretty much shouted from the rooftops that the owner was anything but understated. From its massive tyres and pink bull bar to the hot pink numberplate that read HOTTIE, everything about it perfectly suited its owner.

'Anything promising on the dating front?' Cher asked after starting the huge ute.

'Nope.'

'Have you even opened your dating app recently?'

'No, I haven't,' Lottie said firmly. 'I told you last time, I'm done with all that.' She'd only joined an online dating service in the first place to shut Cher up. She'd had nothing but creepy, rude men who seemed to want nothing more than casual hook-ups and an incessant need to send photos of their genitals to her. *No thank you very much.*

'You haven't even given it a chance.'

'There's not even anyone on there remotely close enough to date anyway.'

'Only because you refuse to look at anyone who lives nearby.'

'I don't want strangers recognising me if they happen to come into the shop. How weird would that be?'

'That's the whole point of doing online dating, to actually meet people. Usually nearby,' Cher said, rolling her eyes.

'And what if I meet someone and they turn out to be sleazy? I'd run the risk of bumping into them whenever I was out and about in Armidale or Tamworth. How awkward would that be?'

'I seriously don't know what I'm going to do with you,' Cher muttered, shaking her head.

'It'll be fine. We'll just grow old together and end up in the same nursing home. We don't need no man.' She grinned.

'Speak for yourself, sweetheart.'

'Oh, lovely,' Lottie said, taking off her seatbelt as they pulled up outside her house.

She watched Cher's tail-lights disappear up the road as she closed the front door. She didn't need a man in her life complicating things. She was happy being an independent businesswoman with her own house and people she loved surrounding her. She *didn't* need *no man*, she told herself determinedly, adding a defiant nod just to drive home the point.

Lottie glanced at her ringing phone and saw her mother's name on the screen. 'Hi, Mum.'

'Did you catch the sunrise this morning? Absolutely stunning,' her mother said, continuing without waiting for a reply. 'So, what was the big emergency meeting about?'

'Oh, that,' Lottie said rolling her eyes. 'Daphney finally had someone accept the invitation to be the festival keynote speaker.'

'Really?' her mother's interest picked up notably. 'Anyone interesting?'

'Not really. I mean, that's not true,' Lottie corrected herself quickly. 'They got a history professor to do it.'

'Oh.' There was definite disappointment to the sound.

'To be fair, it makes sense to have someone knowledgeable about history to open a festival based on a historical figure, I suppose.'

'Yes, but . . . I mean . . . we wanted someone famous, didn't we?' her mum replied bleakly.

'Yeah, that was the idea, but apparently Banalla isn't really a celebrity drawcard kind of place.'

'What a shame. Oh well, I'm sure the festival will still be a big success. I'm almost finished making up the last of my tea blends for the stall.'

Her mother's tea was stocked in a number of local cafes and was a big hit with the wellness groups. 'That's great. The stall registrations have gone through the roof. I think the last count was about eighty. The market day alone will draw lots of people to town.'

'Absolutely.'

The committee had worked tirelessly to get the market and food stall part of the festival up and running. They wanted to make sure that local producers were able to showcase all the amazing produce and artists Banalla had to offer. They had local musicians booked to play venues throughout the day, with wine and beer tasting from nearby vineyards and the town's own boutique brewery. Not to mention the jewel in the festival crown: the re-enactment of the infamous stagecoach robbery. Lottie knew there were quite a few locals who rolled their eyes at the whole idea, but secretly she was really looking forward to it. They'd secured a stagecoach, horses and driver from Queensland, which had depleted the bulk of the committee's funding which, Lottie suspected, had largely been responsible for the lack of monetary enticement needed to lure a celebrity. Local riders had been persuaded to dress up as Jack and his gang of lawless sidekicks, happy with payment in alcohol and a free feed at the pub afterwards. Of course, the re-enactment wasn't going to take place out in the original location—a few kilometres out of town—but in the centre ring of the showground. It wasn't really going to be the same, but still, there were horses involved, so that should make it worthwhile. Everyone loved an event that included horses.

'I think it'll be a fantastic day. The whole town seems to be buzzing and it's still a few weeks away.'

'The place does have a definite vibe happening,' Lottie agreed. The council had been noticeably out in force, mowing, landscaping and giving the parks and showground a facelift in preparation for the festival. She'd never seen so many fluorescent yellow work shirts around town at one time. So that the *whole* town would benefit, they'd decided to spread the venues all around, including the local hotels and restaurants, as well as having buskers along the main street so visitors would be able to enjoy shopping at local retailers as well as the markets. As a result, the main street was looking extremely festive. The majority of shops had got involved and been throwing themselves into creative window displays.

'Oh, I've got another call coming in. I'll talk to you later,' her mother said and promptly ended the call, leaving Lottie to finish her coffee before she headed to the shop.

While being on social media throughout the day would be frowned upon by most employers, in this case, Lottie was technically working. She listed a lot of her stock online and also ran an online store for some of the smaller items that could be reasonably posted to buyers. It took up a large portion of her day, but it was proving quite successful.

Managing the online side of her business had its own dangers and temptations, though, and as she finished filtering through her various platform messages, Lottie accidentally clicked an article about the discovery in the UK of a painting that had been purchased for twenty-five pounds at garage sale and turned out to be worth over *five million pounds*. An hour and several related articles later, Lottie's eye caught sight of the time and she shook her head. Her finger was poised over the close screen button when a heading caught her eye.

Missing Gems: Twenty Jewels That Were Lost and Yet To Be Found

An attached slide show automatically began playing and showed an exquisite diamond necklace. She quickly clicked on the link to open the full story.

Lottie scanned the article, which talked about the mysterious disappearances of various pieces of jewellery, ranging from necklaces gifted by royalty and brooches smuggled from Europe during wars. There was an alarming number of museum pieces that had simply gone missing, and the stories behind them were like something out of a spy movie, but there were also other interesting stories, such as those about pieces that had belonged to wealthy socialites who had sunk with ships during storms.

As an antique dealer, she was often approached by relatives offering various pieces of jewellery and other bric-a-brac from deceased estates. She liked to think she had a keen eye for detail and for selecting quality pieces, and she had a jeweller in the city she often took pieces down to for appraisal. It was her dream to discover that one of the pieces she'd purchased was worth a small fortune, but to date, it hadn't happened.

Still, reading this article gave her hope that she might strike it lucky. She glanced at the small but pretty collection of jewellery in the glass cabinet on the counter and smiled wistfully. *Not today, but who knows . . . maybe one day.*

Five

Lottie finished dragging the last of the outside display items inside before locking the door. She stood back for a moment to admire the window display she'd been working on for the last few days.

Since she had quite a few bits and pieces lying around in the shop to make use of, she'd tried to recreate the kind of bush camp Jack and his gang would have used. The garbage bags of leaves she'd collected the weekend before and the large log she'd managed to drag back to her car from her mother's property looked fantastic as the bush backdrop, and was almost worth the near hernia she'd given herself.

There was a swag rolled up next to a log fire that she'd taken far too long to arrange decoratively. She'd had to experiment with red cellophane and some battery-powered tea lights to create a realistic look. She had an old lantern and a billy can for boiling tea, as well as some hessian sacks full of provisions. She'd added an old newspaper from the era and made copies of the original wanted posters for Jack and his gang that had circulated around the region at the time. Overall, it set a reasonable feel for the part of Jack's life that had largely been spent hiding out between robberies, making him and his men very experienced bushmen.

She was heading to another meeting at the pub. Daphney had been in overdrive lately, and the number of emails coming through seemed to match the stress levels of their fearless leader.

'I have a few concerns,' Daphney started without preamble. Lottie sensed everyone around the table brace themselves.

'I opened the festival's Facebook page this morning and saw an enormous advertisement for the cabaret show.'

Lottie felt Cher straighten in the seat beside her. *Oh God, this is not going to be good.*

'Cherise, I really don't feel this cabaret show of yours is suitable for the festival,' Daphney said, rubbing her fingertips lightly against her temples.

'The show has *everything* to do with the festival. It's a tribute to Kate O'Ryan.'

'Yes but . . . I don't see how a musical—' she pursed her lips and drew out the word '—can properly do justice to the historical aspect of the festival.'

'Daphney, may I remind you that I am in fact a descendant of Kate O'Ryan. If anyone has a right to decide what to do to honour her, it's me. Which I have done. With this show.'

'I just don't see—' Daphney started to protest before being cut off.

'You don't have to see. The committee isn't contributing any funding to the show and I don't have to get your approval to host it since it's in my bar. I even made it for the Friday night so it wouldn't clash with the festival plans. So why bring it up?'

'I'm just concerned that it might . . . *cheapen* some of the more historical aspects—'

'Cheapen?' Cher echoed in a calm, softly controlled voice.

Oh fuuuuuuck.

'Let's go back, weren't we focusing on the program?' Lottie suggested quickly, sensing the exchange rapidly deteriorating into something unpleasant.

'Which is partly why I've brought up the subject of this show,' Daphney insisted. 'I'm suggesting we *remove* it from the program listing.'

'What?' Cher demanded, leaning forward in her chair.

Lottie caught Janelle's eye, then Christine's. They both looked as surprised as she felt. The rest of the table exchanged furtive glances, while Shorty's previously bored expression had perked up, possibly hoping for some kind of jelly-wrestling match to eventuate, and a few people shifted in their seats.

'You said yourself it wasn't funded by the committee. As such, I don't think it's appropriate to list it on the program as though the committee is endorsing it.'

'I'm part of the committee,' Cher said stiffly, giving a toss of the long blonde hair she'd worn, giving off Margot Robbie vibes.

'Maybe we should all take a step back—' Solene started gently before getting cut off.

'But your show is not,' Daphney retorted. 'You decided to go it alone and put this all together without any prior consultation with the rest of us—'

'Do you have any experience with putting together a theatrical production, Daph?' Cher asked bluntly. Lottie suppressed a wince at Cher's use of the diminutive; they all knew Daphney hated it.

'I have some theatre experience,' she said in a tight tone that signified Cher's comment had hit its mark.

'That would be volunteering at the primary school for their end-of-year Christmas concert, I'm guessing?' Cher asked sounding mildly bored.

'Ladies,' Terry cut in, turning paler when both scowling women turned to him. He cleared his throat quickly. 'I can see this is getting a little heated. As Solene tried to say, perhaps we need to take a step back for a moment.'

'I don't think that's necessary, Terry. A simple show of hands is all that's required here,' Daphney said, tilting her chin slightly to look down her nose at Cher. 'Those who are in favour of removing the cabaret show from the program, say yea,' she said, stretching her hand into the air and looking around with a confident air . . . which slowly began to deflate as she noticed the lack of other raised hands. 'You can*not* be serious?'

'This festival was supposed to be inclusive. We all agreed on that,' Elijah stressed, his dark eyebrows rising, making his rather long face seem even longer.

'That's true,' Skye agreed, turning to Tori, who sat quietly beside her. 'After all, that's been the main focus of everything the committee has been promoting—that Banalla is a progressive and inclusive town.'

'For *cultural* aspects,' Daphney said.

'Inclusivity isn't simply about culture,' Cher put in. 'It's about not excluding any parties or groups and making *everyone* feel valued. Do you think you're being particularly inclusive right now, Daphney?'

There was an awkward pause before Daphney spoke, ignoring the question. 'I can't *believe* the rest of you are agreeing to this. It's making a mockery of this whole festival.'

'That's your opinion, and you are welcome to voice it. However, majority rules and the nay vote has spoken on this matter,' Terry said calmly. 'Shall we move on to the next point of business? I'd like to wrap this meeting up and get home.'

'Fine,' Daphney bit out, snatching up the notes in front of her. The meeting continued, albeit in an uncomfortably strained atmosphere.

'Can you believe the nerve of that woman?' Cher snapped as they left the pub after the meeting ended.

'I know,' Lottie soothed. 'But everyone had your back in there, so that was good.'

'She called my show *cheap*!' Cher continued, outrage still simmering. 'Cheap!' she repeated, turning to face Lottie. 'There is *nothing* cheap about my shows. My shows are *classy*!'

'They are,' Lottie agreed. 'You know what she's like. Just ignore it and move on.'

'Easy for you to say, no one just insulted your business.'

Okay, fair point. 'I just think if you let her get under your skin, it's the same result as if she'd managed to shut down your show. Don't waste your time giving her a second thought.'

'I'm writing in an extra character,' Cher said with a devious narrowing of her eyes. 'I'm writing in a whore named Daphney.'

Oh great. 'Do you think that's wise?'

'Probably not. But it would be absolutely hysterical and more than a little satisfying. I'm going home right now to make the changes. I'll need to find an extra person. Who do I know who's slutty enough to pull that kind of character off?' she asked herself thoughtfully, as though mentally flipping through her contact list.

'Cher, I really don't think—'

'I know the perfect diva!' she said, brightening. 'Ruby Red. She's a bit of a biatch—can't stand her, really—but she'll be perfect.'

Lottie gave up trying to talk her friend out of her quest for revenge, realising she was too far gone, if the expression of evil genius currently on her face was any indication.

'Okay, well, goodnight,' she said sarcastically as Cher began walking away, clearly forgetting she was Lottie's ride.

'What? Oh. Yeah, night, honey, talk tomorrow,' she said, giving a limp wave over her shoulder.

Whatever Cher had in store for Daphney, it was sure to cause a commotion. Still, it wouldn't happen until the festival, so that sounded like a problem for another day.

Six

That weekend, Lottie made the four-hour drive to her grandmother's cousin Marie's place. She found it rather relaxing. She listened to music as she admired the passing scenery, forever amazed by the ever-changing landscape. From the wide-open spaces of Banalla, scattered with rocks and jagged outcrops to the rich, fertile countryside of the mountain country, where rainforest and waterfalls ruled, then down towards the coast, where glimpses of the jewelled sea could be spotted as she travelled along the highway. She loved the ocean—what wasn't there to love? It was beautiful—but her heart belonged to the highlands. There was just something about them that pulled her back there.

Still, she could enjoy a brief visit to the coast, even if it was a day trip—albeit a *long* day.

She didn't know Marie well—they'd only met maybe twice in her entire life—but she'd grown up hearing about her and the family through her grandmother relaying any news over the years, as grandmothers tended to do.

The address she pulled up in front of was a modest white fibro house with a pretty garden full of colourful flowers and a rather extensive collection of gnomes lining the pathways, the front steps and the edge of the front verandah. They ranged from cute *Snow White*-themed ones to the more risqué, with a few being downright obscene. Lottie gingerly picked her way through them to the front door and knocked.

'Here she is!' Marie's greeting caught Lottie off guard; with that same soft, countrified accent, she sounded almost identical to Gran. *She even looks a little bit like Gran.* Lottie blinked back her surprise.

'How was the trip?'

'Fine. It didn't seem to take that long, actually.'

'You must have had an early start,' Marie continued. 'Come on in, I'll put the jug on.'

Lottie followed the older woman down a hallway towards the rear of the house to a small kitchen area with a round table covered in an assortment of magazines, opened mail and knitting. 'Take a seat,' Marie offered, reaching across to remove the knitting and some of the clutter and place it on a smaller table nearby. 'How's your mum? I haven't seen her in years.'

'She's good. Busy with the new day spa and business.'

'Day spa,' Marie said, shaking her head slightly as she busied herself with the coffee mugs. 'Sounds fancy, doesn't it? Good on her. I'd love to catch up with her again one of these days, but I don't do much driving since Brian passed away. He used to do most of the driving. I'm getting too old now for long trips.'

'I'm sure Mum would like to hear from you,' Lottie said diplomatically. Her mother wasn't particularly close with any of her extended family. Most were like Marie, second cousins and quite a bit older. Few stayed in contact.

Lottie politely drank her coffee and tried to keep up with the family gossip, but really, she was more interested in what Marie had found that related to her research. Finally, after finishing her coffee, Marie announced she'd better get the things to show her and heaved herself up from the table. She disappeared down the hall, reappearing a few moments later with a box that she placed on the table in front of Lottie.

Lottie lifted the lid of the box and placed it on the table. A slight musty, old-house smell wafted up from inside. It was a familiar scent—her shop often had a similar smell for the first few minutes every morning when she opened the front door. It was the smell of memories and long-forgotten treasures.

Inside were a number of black-and-white photographs and Marie leaned across to explain who the people in them were. Basic information was written on the back of each one, but Lottie was grateful to hear the stories about each of the people in the images. 'This is Hattie, Emmeline's daughter,' Marie said, holding up a photo of a young woman in her early twenties wearing a simple white dress with long sleeves and a high collar. Marie handed her the photograph and Lottie studied it carefully. Hattie's hair was swept into a bun on the top of her head. The yellow-brownish tint of the image made it impossible to tell what colour her eyes or hair were but there was something familiar about the way her head was slightly tilted that reminded her of Gran. She'd read and typed Hattie's name into her computer countless times over the years, but this was the first time she'd seen a photo of her and she couldn't deny that it made her a little emotional.

Underneath the photos was a bundle of photocopied papers and Lottie carefully lifted them out, her pulse rate leaping as she noticed a date in the top corner.

'I think those will be of interest to you too. I don't know what happened to the original letters, I only have the photocopies, and they aren't the best quality, but they were from Emeline to her cousin, Adelaide. The originals would have been very old by the time the copies were made, so they're a bit hard to read, but very interesting if you have the patience to decipher the handwriting.'

Lottie picked up the first one and took a moment to admire the elegant, minuscule penmanship. The original letter would have most likely been written in black ink but, as Marie had warned, the copy was faded and quite difficult to read. Emeline's slanted, looping handwriting, although beautiful, seemed almost unreadable at first glance, though Lottie could pick out a few words here and there.

'These are brilliant, Marie.' Lottie glanced up and smiled at the older woman. 'I'm so excited to start reading them. This is exactly the kind of stuff I was hoping to find.'

'Well, that's good. I'm glad I could help. None of my siblings or grandchildren were interested in family history, and I only have a little bit on your line of the family tree, because I seemed to be the only one who wanted to save it. I was so happy when you told me about your book and I realised I could give it to you.'

Marie put the jug on for another cuppa and they went through the rest of the photos. This time, Lottie made sure to take notes as Marie talked through the pictures. There was only the odd one or two people that Marie was a little hazy on, but Lottie hoped she'd be able to find some more information once she was able to do some digging of her own.

As she drove home, her mind was already racing with ideas.

As far as information went on Emeline, there wasn't a great deal. She seemed to pretty much vanish after the hullabaloo of her kidnapping. There was one article Lottie found that mentioned the safe return of William Grant's daughter two days before Jack was killed in the shootout, then nothing. It seemed odd, but then, Lottie supposed, there'd been so much going on at the time, maybe it was simply overlooked . . . or had been played out that way. If the gossip was true that not everyone believed Emeline had been taken against her will, and that maybe she and Jack had really been lovers, she could understand why such an important family would want the whole thing to just blow over quietly.

Lottie found a newspaper announcement about her marriage to Henry Oldsfield, the son of another wealthy family in the area, only a few weeks after her return home. Maybe it was just another way to protect reputations—a show of support to end rumours of the Jack and Emeline romance. Whatever the reason, it seemed extremely fast.

Her phone rang, with Beyoncé belting out the lyrics of 'Diva'.

'How did it go? Find anything juicy?' Cher asked when Lottie answered.

'Not as juicy as a signed confession that Jack McNally fathered Emeline's child, unfortunately, but there are lots of gorgeous letters and photos that will be perfect for the book. It was well worth the trip.'

'That's great news!'

'What about you? How was the weekend?'

'The show on Saturday night went fabulously. A huge crowd. I'm still recovering from the Melbourne crew who came up to perform. I think I'm getting old, darling. I don't seem to bounce back from a night of drinking and dancing like I used to.'

'Happens to the best of us,' Lottie chuckled. 'I'm sure you were still the last one off the dance floor though.'

'Of course,' Cher agreed haughtily and Lottie could imagine her fluttering those incredible false eyelashes and giving a flick of her wig.

They said goodnight and Lottie walked back into the lounge room, where she'd spread out the contents of the box onto the floor. She hadn't gotten through everything yet, but she already knew exactly which stories she wanted to put with each of the images. She decided to get busy and start scanning everything so she could work on her project. She wouldn't be getting to bed early tonight, but she didn't mind—the book ideas were flowing and she wanted to jump on this surge of inspiration.

Seven

A loud revving motorbike engine interrupted Lottie's peaceful reading after a busy morning of customers. She frowned as she watched the rider, dressed in a black jacket and safety gear, slowly reverse his large bike into a parking spot in front of her shop, before he cut the engine and quiet returned once more.

She went back to her book. She'd only planned to skim it, thinking that as a committee member she really should at least be familiar with their guest of honour's work so they'd have something to talk about at the pre-festival drinks and dinner that had been organised at the last festival meeting—the second one for the week. She *wouldn't* be missing the meetings once the festival concluded.

However, she'd found the book fascinating, so much so that she'd gone to the library to see if they had any other books he'd written. Happily, they had. This current one was titled *A Wide Brown Land*, a novel based on detailed research. It had a mix of both fictional and real-life characters that brought the history of the early settlers to life in a way a mere textbook never could.

A short while later, she heard someone entering the shop and reluctantly put the novel down, stood and approached the man, who had started looking around. 'Good morning.'

He lifted his gaze from the set of metal scales he'd been admiring and returned her greeting. He was tall, dressed in jeans and chunky black leather biker boots, his wide shoulders stretching out a comfortable-looking grey T-shirt. Her smile wavered slightly as she glanced outside to the bike and saw a black jacket draped over the seat.

For the briefest of moments, Lottie felt the urge to girlishly drop her gaze, but managed to suppress the impulse by reminding herself that she was a grown-arse woman who ran her own business. *I don't even like bikes.*

She realised she was still staring at him and felt a blush begin to creep up her neck. Lottie cleared her throat and forcefully pulled on her professional face. 'Can I help you with something? Are you looking for anything in particular?'

'I'm never actually *looking* for anything, but that doesn't normally stop me from finding something I *need* to have,' he said, brushing a hand through darkish brown hair that was cut shorter at the sides and a tad longer on top.

'I totally understand. Hence why I now own an antiques store,' she said.

'Really?' He smiled broadly, and Lottie found herself returning it. A small flutter went through her stomach. *Stop it.*

'Well, kind of. I bought the business off my mother. The women in my family tend to do hand-me-downs. This shop was my grandmother's before that.'

'That's a real family legacy.'

Lottie gave a brief shrug but smiled. 'It'd be nicer if it was a legacy that made a fortune.'

'Ah, well. If it's a labour of love, that's probably far more satisfying than a job you don't like.'

'That's true.' She couldn't argue with the logic. 'I'll leave you to browse then. If you need any help, just give me a yell.'

Lottie went back to the counter and picked up her book, flicking her gaze to the man in her shop every so often, telling herself she was just checking if he needed help. *I'd do the same for any non-gorgeous customer.*

'Any good?'

Lottie looked up at the unexpected intrusion. 'Sorry?'

'The book.' The man nodded his head towards the book in her hand. 'You seem engrossed.'

'Oh. Sorry, I didn't realise you were waiting.' She quickly placed the book down and stood, feeling guilty at being caught out reading at work, even if she *was* the boss. 'Are you a reader?'

'I am, although I don't get to do as much of it as I'd like to.'

'Well, if you like history, I can definitely recommend this one.' She held the book up to show him the cover and saw his eyes widen briefly. His casual attitude suddenly changed and he looked uncomfortable. 'Not into history?' she asked, trying to gauge his reaction.

'Uh, actually . . . I am. It's kinda my thing,' he said, looking awkward.

'Well, I'm really enjoying this.'

'I'm glad,' he said then cleared his throat. 'This is really embarrassing, but, uh,' he shoved his fingertips into the small coin pockets in the front of his jeans and hunched his shoulders, 'I wrote that.'

Lottie stared at him, blinking as she tried to process what he was saying.

'The book. I'm Damian Loxley.'

No. Way.

He shuffled his feet slightly on the other side of the desk before giving a small grimace. 'I know, it probably sounds like I'm lying, but it's true. I just arrived in town to scope out the festival planning and do a bit of research for my new book.'

'Holy sh—' Lottie cut herself off. '*You're* Professor Loxley?'

'I am.'

He could have been kidding about being the author of the book she was reading, but how would he have known that there wasn't any author photo on the inside back cover? She hadn't gotten around to googling him, she'd had too much else going on to remember, but she had been meaning to look him up.

'You don't look like a professor,' she found herself blurting, instantly wishing she could take it back. 'I mean, it's just that I thought you'd be older . . . somehow,' she said, thinking back to the meeting when 'the professor' had been announced as the guest speaker and everyone had assumed he was . . . well, older.

'I get that a bit,' he confessed, much to her relief.

For a moment, they both stared at each other until the silence stretched uncomfortably. 'Uh, well . . . welcome to Banalla,' Lottie said, sticking her hand out to shake. 'I'm on the Chamber of Commerce and the festival planning committee, although, clearly I'm just a behind-the-scenes minion or I probably would have recognised you . . . or knew you were coming out here early,' she added.

'I didn't tell anyone I was arriving. This is mainly a research trip, and I was going to check in with the event planners closer to the festival, in case they needed me to do anything.'

'Oh. Okay. Well, that sounds interesting . . . the research stuff.'

'Yeah, it's always my favourite part—the fieldwork, getting out and actually going to the places I write about. The book research is good too, but it's more paperwork, and inside . . . so . . .'

Lottie was relieved he seemed as uncomfortable about the whole exchange as she was feeling.

She took in his wide forehead and a jawline somewhat defined by the trimmed stubble around his lower face. He was built more like a rugby league player than a professor—or at least, not like any of the professors she'd ever had.

'I'm Lottie Fairchild,' she added, realising she hadn't actually introduced herself.

'Nice to meet you, Lottie. That's not a name you hear very often nowadays,' he said.

'It's short for Charlotte. Most people shorten it to Charlie, but my mum always liked to be different, so I'm Lottie.' She shrugged.

'It suits you,' he said, then added quickly, 'I mean, you work in an antiques store and you like history . . . Lottie's an old-fashioned name . . . It just kind of makes sense . . .' His words faded off.

She smiled shyly. 'Happy coincidence, I guess.'

He cleared his throat and seemed to be busy looking anywhere but at her.

'So are you staying in town? Do you have your accommodation sorted out?'

'Yeah, I booked into the motel in the main street.'

Lottie gave a small frown. She was sure Daphney had mentioned they were going to put him up at the Stag and Horn, located on the outskirts of town, but modern and with a few more stars than the Wild Colonial Inn. 'I'm pretty sure the committee was going to cover your accommodation. You shouldn't have had to book your own.'

'Oh, no. That's fine. I didn't mention I was coming out this early. I don't expect them to pay for this. I'm mainly here for my own research.'

'Are you sure? I can call Daphney and—'

'No, honestly. It's fine,' he interjected quickly, like a man who had spoken to Daphney and wasn't keen to repeat the experience. 'I was planning on staying under the radar a bit. I need to get a bit of work done before the festival.'

'Oh. Okay.'

'I only mentioned who I was because of the book. It would have gotten a bit awkward if you met me later and realised . . .'

Yeah, because this was so not awkward . . . She knew she was super uncomfortable around people, but this guy might even be worse than her. 'I'm glad you did. It's a great book.'

'Thanks.'

They stared at each other for a moment until Lottie opened her mouth to break the silence . . . at the same time he did.

'Is there anything you're interested in—'

'Would you like to have coffee—'

They both stopped and continued to stare.

Did he just ask me out for coffee? 'Uh, sure,' she stammered.

'You don't have to. I mean, I'm sure you're incredibly busy,' he quickly added, words tumbling over each other.

Lottie gave a small chuckle. 'Yes, I'm inundated with customers,' she said ironically.

He gave her a brief smile and shuffled his big, booted feet slightly.

Oh my God, he's nervous! The flutter in her stomach returned, and she made a decision.

'It's almost closing time,' she said. 'Maybe a bit late for coffee, but would you like to meet in about an hour or so for a drink? I know a place just up the street.'

'Sure,' he said, sounding relieved. 'I need to go back to the motel for a bit anyway, so I could meet you there.'

Lottie told him where to meet and watched him leave the store, her view interrupted by an older couple who walked into the shop a few moments later. She heard the bike start up and just managed to catch it as it pulled out onto the road and headed uptown.

Was she seriously about to meet a man for a drink? Like a date? She quickly pulled the brakes on that train of thought. It wasn't a date, she was just being friendly.

No, it was definitely *not* a date.

Damian stood out the front of the place up the street that Lottie had given him directions to. MADAME DUBOIS read the elegant sign on a darkened window. This was not the kind of place you'd expect to find in a small rural town. It had definite Moulin Rouge vibes, with its black-and-red décor, showgirl pin-ups and Parisian-looking art decorating the front wall of the premises. He tentatively pushed the front door open to go inside.

This wasn't the only unexpected thing he'd discovered since arriving in Banalla.

Lottie Fairchild. The name made him smile. He'd loved how her hazel-green eyes lit up when she talked about her store, the way her straight, coppery hair framed her face then fell below her shoulders.

His sisters had always teased him about how oblivious he was when it came to women, but he wasn't that gangly teenager anymore, and he'd picked up on a definite interest from Lottie. He'd been told he'd been hard to read before, and now wondered if she'd realised the interest was mutual.

He ordered a beer and found a table with a good view of the front door, then allowed himself a bit of time to take in his surroundings. He felt a little out of place in his jeans and was glad he'd ducked back to his lodgings and swapped his T-shirt for a clean button-up shirt. Earlier, he'd stopped in a few of the shops and had been surprised by the price tags on the clothing stocked in one of the many boutique clothing stores in the main street. The leather boots he'd been admiring would have set him back almost a week's wages.

The clientele filling the tables around him were well dressed—not in designer cocktail wear, but in, he suspected, equally expensive rural wear. The men were mostly wearing moleskin pants, boots and button-up shirts in various tones of beige and tan. The women, bar a few exceptions in long dresses and boots, were dressed similarly—not exactly the rough and tough image of rural farming folk he'd been expecting in a small country town. Then again, he suspected the pub across the road would probably be where the straight-from-the-paddock-to-the-pub crowd hung out, rather than the swanky place this seemed to be. Nope, this had not been what he'd been expecting from Banalla.

Eight

Lottie pushed open the door of Madame Dubois and waited a moment for her eyes to adjust to the dark interior before searching the tables.

'Hi, Lottie. You looking for the boss lady?' Lenny, the bartender-cum-manager-cum-maintenance man, asked from behind the bar.

Lenny used to be a boxer back in the day and had worked with Cher as a bouncer in her previous business. He'd moved up to help Cher run the bar. Behind his almost-bald head, flat nose, thick arms and tattoos, Lenny had a heart of gold, and he had been a loyal friend to Cher for too many years to count.

'Hi, Lenny. No, I'm actually here to meet someone—' She stopped as she caught sight of Damian. 'Never mind, I found him,' she said, turning back to smile at the man.

Damian looked up as she walked towards him and a flicker of awareness went through her body. This was ridiculous. She'd only just met him. She'd never had this kind of reaction to a man before—at least, not this fast.

'Sorry I'm late, I had a last-minute customer come in just on closing time.'

'No worries, I only just got here myself,' Damian said smoothly, putting his phone back in his pocket. 'Did they at least buy something to make it worthwhile?'

'They did, actually,' she smiled. 'I had a gorgeous Dutch marquetry side table that had only come in a few days ago, and they snapped it up without blinking at the price tag.'

'How much was it?' he asked.

'Four and a half thousand,' she said, still a little giddy. She'd picked the piece up for an absolute steal from a deceased estate. The delicate floral inlay was stunning and the reddish-brown walnut timber was in excellent condition, but it was all the little compartments and hidey-holes inside that had fascinated her. That kind of craftsmanship was a lost art nowadays. It was just beautiful and she'd really, really wanted to keep it for herself.

He let out a low whistle. 'That's awesome,' he said, looking impressed. 'I did see that there earlier, but I clearly don't have the eye for detail that you or your last customer does.' He chuckled. 'Or the bank account,' he added. 'Do you often get sales that large out here?'

'Now and again. We get a lot of collectors coming up. The weekend tourist crowd is a bit of a mixed bag, but a lot of the boutique cafes and shops bring in the higher income, semi-retired demographic who've moved up from the city and seem to have money to spend. I've been dabbling in some more pricey stuff to appeal to that market.'

'Seems to be paying off?'

'So far,' she agreed. 'I'm still dipping my toe in the deep end, but I'm seriously thinking it's the way to go. It's just a bigger risk to buy in the more expensive items.'

'I can imagine. But that's really cool.'

Lottie flashed him a smile, enjoying the fact he seemed genuinely interested.

He reached over and picked up the menu. 'So, what's good here?' he asked.

'Everything,' Lottie assured him.

'That's a big call. I take it you come here often?'

'I may be a bit biased. My friend owns the place, but the food really is amazing here.'

'Then you should order for both of us. I put my complete trust in your hands.'

'Who's putting what in whose hands?' Cher's honey-dipped voice came from behind Lottie. 'Am I interrupting something, my darlings?' She placed two brightly coloured cocktails on the table in front of them. 'I've brought along some new ones for you to try,' she said, then rested one hand on the back of Lottie's chair as she sized up her companion.

'Cher, this is Damian Loxley. Cher is the owner and creator of Madame Dubois,' Lottie said.

To give Damian his due, he didn't bat an eyelid at the sudden appearance of a woman bedecked in a red-and-gold sequined evening gown and Dolly Parton wig and make-up. He simply nodded politely and told Cher how much he admired the bar.

'I said to myself, "Cher, what does this town need?" And it was completely obvious . . . it needed a swanky nightclub tapas bar and theatre. So here we are,' she said, waving an elegant hand in the air.

'I can see why that was the first thing that came to mind.'

'Loxley . . . why is that name so familiar?' Cher mused, sending Lottie a quizzical glance.

'Damian is our guest speaker for the festival,' Lottie explained, sending Cher a pointed look.

Her friend's eyes widened for a moment. '*You're* the professor?'

'Guilty.' Damian shrugged.

'You're . . . *the professor*?' Cher repeated, staring at him in blank disbelief.

'Why doesn't anyone ever seem to believe me when I say that?' he asked quietly.

'Because you don't look like any professor I've ever known. I think it's about time that lil' Miss Cherise Dubois headed back to university,' she said in a suggestive tone that made Lottie roll her eyes. 'Aren't you a little early, honey? The festival is weeks away.'

'I'm here to do some research for my new book, thought I'd combine it into one trip.'

'Oh! How exciting. Lottie's writing a book too,' Cher said, beaming across at her proudly.

'You are?' Damian asked, sounding surprised.

Lottie shifted uncomfortably in her seat. She appreciated Cher's enthusiasm but why did she feel the need to broadcast Lottie's work to the world? 'It's just a family history thing.'

'Family history's the best. Is it local?'

'You don't get much more local than the Fairchild family.' Cher nodded. 'Our little Lottie here has *quite* the scandalous family connection to Gentleman Jack himself. Tell him,' Cher prompted.

'Well, there's no actual proof . . . it's only really speculation . . .' Lottie started.

Cher interrupted impatiently. 'Her—what is it, five? Six? Times removed great-grandmother?—Was the *innocent*,' Cher wiggled her eyebrows suggestively, 'grazier's daughter who was *allegedly*,' she said, using her outrageously long, lethal-looking red nails to mimic quotation marks, 'kidnapped and held hostage when Jack was on the run from the authorities after the infamous coach hold-up.'

'That's part of my research, the events that happened leading up to and after the robbery,' Damian said. 'You're a relative of Emeline Grant?'

'She's more than that. She's a descendant of Jack McNally himself,' Cher announced.

'Well, that's the bit that we don't have actual proof about,' Lottie added quickly. Unlike Cher, Lottie preferred not to overplay the I'm-related-to-someone-famous card. It just felt a bit over the top, especially since there was no *official* link back to her family tree.

'But it's common knowledge,' Cher interjected.

'That Jack had a child?' Damian nodded slowly.

'You . . . you think the story has merit?' Lottie asked.

'I mean, records back then weren't always an exact science. It often took a long time for people to register births . . . if at all in some of the more remote places. There was also ample opportunity to be a little hazy with the dates in the case of children being conceived out of wedlock and whatnot. I've read the newspaper reports about the kidnapping, and it's easy to understand why a respectable family might go to great lengths to create a sympathetic story to protect their reputation or that of a very eligible young woman.' Damian seemed to study Lottie thoughtfully for a moment before he spoke again. 'Is this what you're writing about? That angle?'

'That's a small part of it. I'm doing all the women in my family tree. Tracing back their histories and stories from each generation and their connection to Banalla,' Lottie said. 'The town itself plays a big part. The women always came back here, that's what made me curious in the first place, the fact that in every generation, the women always ended up back in Banalla.'

Cher nodded solemnly. 'There's a whole cemetery full of them.'

'And Cher has a connection to Jack too,' Lottie pointed out, partly to take the attention off herself. 'She comes from Kate O'Ryan's line.'

'Kate O'Ryan?' Damian repeated, turning his head to look up at Cher again. 'Jack's sister?'

'The same,' Cher said cheerfully.

'Wow.' He eyed them curiously. 'So, technically, if you have family connections with Kate, and you possibly have connections to Jack . . . that would make you related. Distantly, of course.'

'Yep. We came to that conclusion too. I think that's why we've become best friends,' Lottie said.

'You *had* to become my best friend. I'm your cousin,' Cher said cheerfully. 'If we'd grown up in town together, our mothers would have *made* us play together.'

'Yes, well. I prefer to call you my best friend—that way I *choose* to be around you,' Lottie said with a smile.

'Aww, bless your little cotton socks. Isn't she the sweetest thing? Really, she only keeps me around as her best friend because I give her free food and cocktails.'

'I keep you around because one day, I might need to borrow a sequined evening gown.'

'Sweetheart, I live for the day I get to finally give you a makeover,' Cher drawled before turning to Damian. 'Anyway, back to you, professor. You're in town for a while then?'

'Thought I may as well come out here before the festival and get some work done on my new book.'

'Isn't that nice, Lottie?' Cher murmured.

'Yes. It sounds very interesting.' Lottie hoped her expression wasn't showing how uncomfortable Cher's blatant interest in the newcomer was making her. Lottie knew exactly what her friend was thinking. The same thing happened any time an eligible man appeared, which thankfully wasn't exactly common: matchmaking.

At least Damian seemed completely oblivious to the cogs turning in Cher's mind. 'If you don't mind, I'd really love to sit down and go into all this in greater depth one day when you have time? With both of you,' Damian added, glancing between them.

'You can go as deep as you like, honey child,' Cher said in a sultry tone that instantly made the professor swallow nervously.

'Uh . . . great. That's . . . great,' he stammered.

'Shall we order something? I'm starving,' Lottie cut in swiftly.

'Good idea.' Damian nodded.

'I'll send over the house specialty,' Cher announced, fluttering her fingers as she turned to leave. 'On the house, of course,' she tossed over her shoulder. 'Enjoy, darlings.'

'Well, I guess that makes deciding easier,' Damian said, putting down the menu.

'It's actually what I would have suggested myself. It's really good,' Lottie assured him, sipping the purple cocktail cautiously 'This is delicious,' she said, nodding at the lime green drink across from her. 'Have you tried yours?'

'I'm more of a beer man, myself,' he said, eyeing the concoction warily, but he took a sip, and gave a small shudder. 'It's a bit sour.'

Lottie grinned, 'I'll get you a beer instead.'

'No, I'll get it. Do you want something else?' he asked, rising from his seat.

'I'm fine with these, thanks,' she said easily. She was a little bit of a cocktail buff and Cher's were the best around.

'Cher is . . . unique,' he said, after returning with his beer, as they watched her sashay around the room and interact with the customers. 'Not the usual character you'd expect to find in a place like Banalla.'

'She's a character and a half,' Lottie agreed. 'She's theatre royalty back in Melbourne and she travelled all over the world in her earlier years, New York and London. All the big theatres.'

'And this place . . . *works* here?' he asked, looking around to take in the opulence of the swanky bar.

'I know. Seems crazy, right?' Lottie nodded. 'It's all Cher, though. She lives and breathes the theatre. She just has this passion for everything she does. Throughout the year, she brings up actual productions that are playing in Melbourne as fundraisers. People come up here from the coast and all over the place just to rub shoulders with the bigwigs in theatre.'

'She's certainly a force,' he said, watching her put another table in stitches before sauntering up on stage to talk to a man seated at a piano.

'It's funny. We're complete opposites,' Lottie said, smiling softly. 'She loves the limelight, I prefer to stay in the background. She's the most confident, self-assured person I've ever met. She has a way of disarming people despite the fact she's completely over the top and outrageous. But she has a huge heart and people end up seeing that. You can't help but love her.'

'She clearly champions you and your writing.'

Lottie wrinkled her nose. 'I'm not really a writer. It's more like I need to have these stories written out so I can try and make sense of them. I'm usually pretty logical, but when you're brought up in a family that likes to tell stories about curses and fated lovers . . .' She shook her head. 'I guess I just want to make sure there's a written history of it somewhere.'

'Curses?' he echoed.

'Well . . . kind of. That's what my mother calls it.'

'Now I'm really invested.'

'There is no curse,' she said firmly, 'which is what I hope to prove to her, by telling these women's stories. It's just a long line of tragic events.'

'Maybe we could help each other out,' Damian said.

Lottie frowned. 'How do you mean?'

'Well, I came here to get some local background history. Maybe between my research and yours, we can find a few missing pieces of each other's puzzles?'

Lottie stared at him across the table. He thought *she* would be able to help *him*? A professor? She smiled. 'I don't know how much use I'd be to someone like you, but *I* could certainly use any help I can get.'

The piano music interrupted their conversation, and they listened as Cher's smoky voice filled the room with a sultry classic.

'Wow, she's really good,' Damian said.

'She's great,' Lottie boasted proudly. 'So what's your new book about exactly? Or is it a secret?'

'No, no secret.' He flashed that sexy, slightly off-centre smile once more. 'I'm focusing on the era around the last of the bushranger activity in the area. Exploring the background of Jack McNally and others, and also looking into an old cold case.'

'What cold case?' Lottie asked, pausing to thank the waitress who had appeared with an enormous wooden serving board of tapas delights.

'It's an unsolved mystery from the late 1800s. A missing woman with nobility ties to England. She simply vanished without a trace.'

'Sounds intriguing,' Lottie said as she reached for a golden croqueta. The board boasted the best of the tapas on offer at Madame Dubois, which included various tortillas, chorizo, chicken and beef skewers, croquetas, meatballs and garlic prawns. 'And how does that tie into the rest of the research about bushranger activity out here?'

'Her husband was one of Jack McNally's victims from the stagecoach robbery. I'm not really hoping to find anything on her out here per se, but I was hoping to visit the property her husband owned and look more into his past, see if there's any clues that may have been missed back then. That's the thing with research—you never know what one tiny, seemingly insignificant piece of information may lead you to.' He stopped abruptly, looking a little embarrassed. 'Sorry, I tend to get carried away once I start talking about my work.'

'No need to apologise. I find it fascinating.'

'Well, anyway, it'd be good to have a look at any of the research you might have ... I mean, if you were okay with that, of course.'

'Sure. Like I said, it's mainly just family tree stuff, but you're more than welcome to it.'

'Great,' he said, looking pleased. He turned his attention to the food on the table. 'This looks amazing.'

'It's the best,' Lottie agreed as they tucked in.

Later, exiting the bathroom, Lottie found herself waylaid by her best friend. 'Girl! Where did that delectable specimen of a man come from?'

'I have no idea. He walked into the shop and we got talking, and he told me who he was.'

'Well, Daphney was clearly keeping this under her hat,' Cher said, peering past Lottie's shoulder to ogle Damian. 'I find it hard to believe she isn't here, demanding to be the one to entertain him.'

'I don't think he planned on telling anyone he was coming this early.'

'Can't say I blame him. Once her ladyship hears he's hit town, the poor boy won't have a moment to himself.' Cher tsked softly, her focus coming back to Lottie. 'He certainly seems into *you*.'

'Oh, whatever,' Lottie dismissed, rolling her eyes. 'He's just interested in my research.'

'Honey, that is not all that man is interested in, let me assure you.'

'I just met him.'

'Ever heard of love at first sight?'

'Now you're just being ridiculous.'

'Well, okay. Maybe not love, but attraction? Sexual chemistry? Baby, I can feel the sparks flying. That boy is iiiiiiiiin to youuuuuuu,' Cher said, snapping her fingers and pouting her ruby-red lips as she slipped back into her favourite imitation of a Southern drawl.

'Righto. I'm going now.' Lottie nodded, backing away.

'Mark my words. You got yourself an admirer.'

'Oh, for goodness' sake,' Lottie muttered as she headed back to the table, and Damian.

Nine

The air was a little cooler at night now, as the months crept from summer to the beginning of autumn. Soon it would be boots and jacket weather, Lottie mused as they stopped outside the bar.

Damian looked around. 'Where did you park?'

'I walk to work. I just live up the top of the hill.'

'I'll walk you home.'

'You don't have to do that. Honestly, it's just there.' She pointed towards her little cottage at the end of the main street.

'It's also dark. I could use the exercise to stretch my legs. It was a long ride today. It's no trouble.'

Lottie suspected he wasn't going to take no for an answer, and it would be nice to have the company. 'Have you been to Banalla before?'

'I passed through one time when I was on a trip out west, but that was a long time ago.'

'It probably hasn't changed,' Lottie said, wryly.

'I don't remember it being so . . . vibrant and busy. You don't see that in a lot of smaller towns anymore. It's great.'

'We've always had a strong community drive, but things really began picking up once we attracted new people to town.'

'Like Cher,' he pointed out with a smile.

Lottie smiled back. 'Yes, and others.'

'It's not typical of small towns to really embrace new things, though, is it?' he asked.

'I guess not. I mean, I personally don't like change. I guess that's why I'm drawn to antiques and history, but I think it helps if people have a shared goal. In this case, it was about keeping Banalla's heritage, but still embracing new opportunities. We've managed to find a balance between an eclectic mix of art and culture and the more traditional things. There's a lot of compromising on both sides, but we make it work here.'

'This festival is a great idea. The fact that Banalla has such an interesting connection to our early history, it's worth trying to preserve that.'

'It's had its moments. At one stage, it looked like it might not happen. The town was divided on the idea of celebrating a criminal. It's stirred up quite a lot of emotion.'

'He certainly was colourful,' Damian agreed. 'And I can understand people wanting to look at the whole thing logically. In today's terms, we wouldn't have a statue in the main street of a criminal who robbed people at gunpoint or killed policemen, but I think we have to remember that it was a whole different political landscape back then. McNally had come from Ireland where he and his family and neighbours were impoverished, removed from their homes—many faced starvation, some were sent away and enslaved.'

Lottie nodded thoughtfully. 'And they came here expecting better, and it was worse. It's a bit hard to trust the government authorities when they're doing nothing to protect you and yours.'

'Yeah, there was major distrust of any kind of government or law enforcement. The rich were the enemy—even more so the rich *English*.'

'People love to barrack for the little guy,' Lottie said thoughtfully. 'I think the majority of people from Banalla still consider it a fascinating part of our local history. That's what I like to think. We're celebrating our history, warts and all, more so than the man himself.'

'That's a good way to look at it.'

They walked in silence for a few steps before Lottie asked, 'So, tell me, what's so interesting about this missing woman you're researching?'

The spark in his eyes sent a small shiver of awareness through her body, an unexpected but not unwelcome reaction.

'You probably shouldn't get me started or I'll still be talking till the early hours of the morning.'

Not the worst idea in the world, she found herself thinking.

'But if you insist,' he said. 'Her name was Lady Catherine Compton. I was actually originally looking into her husband, Alexander Compton.'

'The gold-mine magnate who was killed in the coach robbery?'

'Yes, I found a throwaway mention of his wife, and I kept thinking about her for some reason. There are records showing she arrived from England a few weeks before the robbery. Jack and his gang killed Compton, along with two guards and a number of troopers, but there was never any mention of a woman on board the coach, and no mention of a wife in the coroner's inquest or the various newspaper stories about the funeral. In fact, it was noted that, for a prominent businessman, he had no relatives at all among the mourners. Catherine just vanished from the records.'

'Vanished?' Lottie frowned.

Damian stuffed his hands in his pockets. 'There's a record of her being on board the *Mary Elizabeth* and arriving in Sydney, but nothing after that. Then the husband is killed and his newly built house and thriving business get sold off.' Damian shook his head. 'It's sad, really. He built up his business here then returned to England to marry. When he came back, he wanted to finish building her a mansion before he sent for her. Only something went wrong and she never ended up even seeing it, let alone living in it, or starting their Australian dynasty.'

'That is sad.' *All that time, waiting to start a life she'd never get to live.*

'Yeah. I mean, his story alone is fascinating. The second son of a lord, a family history that rose to wealth from royal favour back in Henry I's reign, so he came from a very long-standing noble family. He decided to head to the Australian colonies to make his own way, since his older brother would be inheriting the family fortune, and moved up here when he heard about the gold rush. So he's an interesting character to write about, only . . . I don't like leaving things unfinished. For his life to end the way it did and with no idea as to what happened to his missing wife . . . I just can't let it go, you know?' he asked, looking over at her.

'I can understand that,' she replied. 'Could she have decided she didn't like it here and gone back to England?'

'There's no record of her being on any return voyage. Her family did send out a private investigator of sorts to make enquiries about her whereabouts after they were informed of Alexander's death, but he apparently couldn't find anything. It's like she literally disappeared off the face of the earth.'

'And you think there could be some kind of helpful information up here?'

'Maybe. I've got piles and piles of research—copies of correspondence to go through, newspaper archives and I'm in the process of searching wider, through old records from her family and known associates. But I figured it couldn't hurt to try looking about while I'm up here.'

'Well, it all sounds really interesting,' Lottie said, coming to a stop outside her little cottage. 'This is my place.'

'Wow. Nice.'

'Yeah, I love it. Thanks for a lovely evening and walking me home,' she added, suddenly feeling a little tongue-tied.

'No worries. Thanks for letting me ramble on all evening about my work.'

'It was really interesting. I'm keen to see what you turn up while you're here.'

'Well, if you're still keen later, I can always use another set of eyes going through the research material.'

'Really? That sounds amazing. I'd love to help.'

He chuckled, and she couldn't help but stare at the gentle crinkle he always got around his eyes when he laughed. 'It is, until your eyesight starts to go and your butt gets numb from sitting too long as you decipher old handwriting.'

'Well, I look forward to it. I guess I'll see you around. I'm usually always at the shop,' she added then felt stupid. 'I mean, if you needed to find me . . . for anything,' she tacked on awkwardly. *Stop talking, you fool.*

'I'll see you soon, then. Night.'

She watched him turn away to retrace his steps back down the hill and found herself smiling. Some days could throw the most unexpected things in your path.

As she wandered into the cottage, Lottie found herself thinking about the mysterious missing wife of Alexander Compton. How *did* a woman like that disappear without a trace? She hoped Damian had something in all that research that would answer that question.

Ten

Damian slowed near a two-storey, red brick and lime mortar building and pulled into a side street before reversing his bike into a park. The historical society had restored the old flour mill and turned it into a museum which showcased not only the art and culture of the area but also the local history of the gold rush era. A whole floor was dedicated to Gentleman Jack McNally.

He'd been itching to see inside ever since arriving, keen to immerse himself further in the history. He wasn't expecting to discover anything mind-blowing about McNally—after all, he'd been researching the bushranger and the era for years—but he was a lover of museums. He had an appointment with the library the next day to go through microfiche and look through their impressive local archives, which he hoped might throw up something unexpected to give him a new line of enquiry to follow in the Lady Catherine Compton cold case. But today, he was more of a tourist, here to enjoy a display of the small town's most infamous son, Gentleman Jack.

The invitation to be a keynote speaker and open the festival had been unexpected, to say the least. He knew he wasn't the first choice, which only mildly stung. The committee had originally approached celebrity historian Mike Gearsley, who Damian had known for years. They had both been lecturers and often went to the same conferences, as well as sharing shelf space in bookshops with their various publications, though that was where the similarities ended. Mike had become somewhat famous in the last few years, getting his own TV series and developing a massive social media platform. He was a nice enough bloke, genuinely suited to presenting and being in the public eye with his eccentric, over-the-top enthusiasm—kind of like the Steve Irwin of history. He'd had to turn the offer down because of a schedule clash, but he'd asked his agent to contact Damian and see if he'd be interested.

While Damian wasn't at all keen to take his career in front of the camera, the opportunity to visit the place he was currently writing a book about had been too tempting to turn down.

A bell rang as Damian pushed open the heavy, timber front door of the museum. The shuffle of feet from a room behind a front counter sounded moments before an older woman came into view, wiping crumbs from the corner of her mouth. 'Oh, hello. You caught me finishing my morning tea.' As she continued dusting herself off, he noticed she wore a badge with *Marge* scrawled across it.

'Sorry about that,' Damian said.

The woman waved a hand dismissively. 'I've got all day to fill in here. Between you and me, this is my second morning tea of the day.' She winked at him with a conspiratorial chuckle. 'What are they going to do? Fire me?'

Damian grinned back. Volunteers were worth their weight in gold, and he suspected Marge knew it. After he paid his admittance fee, and Marge finished telling him what the museum had on offer, he set off around the first floor to view the paintings, hung on the wall in chronological sequence, depicting the lead-up to the last shootout between Jack, his brothers and the police, where the gang was killed near an isolated dry creek bed aptly named Little Water Creek.

Damian had already planned to visit the location, which was marked as a heritage site, even though he understood that it was only a paddock with an eroded, dry creek bed.

He wandered through to a room of artefacts that had been found underneath the current building when they'd been restoring it—old leather shoes, buttons and coins that had fallen down between floorboards. To many others, it was stuff that might seem rather mundane, but to Damian, it was fascinating. Little pieces of the past that had quite literally slipped through the cracks of time.

He took his time exploring, soaking up the smells and sounds of the old building. Over one hundred and sixty years of industry was soaked into the floorboards and walls. The sound of his boots echoed on the dark timber floorboards as he walked through to the main exhibition.

Many poems and stories had been written about Jack McNally over the years. The museum had a number of the more popular ones on the walls, along with first edition books and newspapers in glass cabinets. Jack himself was known to have written a few—historians had managed to uncover some he'd published in newspapers under fictitious names, but they were rare.

In the centre of the room was the highlight of the collection: a glass-topped coffin-like exhibit with a lifelike replica of the body of Jack McNally as he'd appeared when he was put on show after his capture and death at the age of twenty-five. It was rather melodramatic, and more than a little bit eerie, especially in this dark, cold room. Damian felt goosebumps break out along his arms. Even though it was just a dummy made up to look like Jack, there was something unsettling about the fact the man had died not far from this very spot, in the early hours of the morning after the shootout, in the rooms of the local doctor.

Next to the glass-topped cabinet was a rickety old timber table with large stains still visible along its centre. This had been used in the courthouse to hold Jack's dead body while on display to the public.

Needle in a Haystack

There was an excerpt from a book on a sign:

Macabre as it sounds, Jack McNally was the equivalent of a celebrity, and the public had a fascination with anything and everything bushranger related. It was also something the authorities wanted to publicise—the death of a wanted criminal. The man who for so many years had eluded and often humiliated them had finally been brought to justice.

Damian looked down at the glass cabinet and tried to imagine what it would have been like for the townspeople on that day, back then. To the wealthy, Jack was undoubtedly a threat, often stealing livestock and holding up travellers. For the everyday person, though—especially the many expatriates of Ireland and Scotland for whom the wounds the English had inflicted were still raw—men like McNally and his gang were heroes. The fact the authorities had put his body on display and were touting their victory far and wide would likely have been met with extreme distress and sorrow. He'd been one of theirs—the underdog fighting the system and refusing to allow the old feudal ways their ancestors had been forced to live under to continue here. To Damian, Jack was just a man, barely older than a boy and forced to grow up outside the rules of polite society. From small child to adulthood, his life had been a fight to survive. He wasn't simply a man who robbed people and killed police, he was the product of a different time—a harder, crueller time, impossible to understand through today's social lens.

If he was a monster, then the world he lived in had turned him into one.

Damian moved through to the next area, dedicated to the town's gold-mining past which had once played an integral role in opening up this part of the country and bringing settlers further west. There was an impressive display of artefacts from the many Chinese immigrants who followed the gold trail.

Along the wall were a number of black-and-white photographs depicting the Compton gold mine when it was in its most productive era. A group of men stood in front of a crude-looking cave-like hole amid large rocks and rubble, the sleeves of their shirts rolled up, dirt-caked faces serious.

A portrait of Alexander Compton hung nearby. Damian had seen the photograph before, with everything in it screaming of wealth and privilege, from the way he dressed to the shape of his perfectly straight nose, despite the fact he was building his empire in the rough bushland of New South Wales. He stared at the camera with an aloof expression. Some might even say arrogant, but Damian saw a steel-like quality in his eye—a determination. From his research, Damian knew he'd been a shrewd businessman, relentless in chasing his dream to establish his fortune in a new country. He knew of his desire to prove himself to his father and family, having been destined to a life of second-best by fault of birth. He thought about the man's diaries, which gave a far more interesting depth to the stony-faced man in the portrait, and on the words he himself had already drafted about the man's life:

Unlike other men of his privileged station in life, Alexander Compton had no qualms about getting his hands dirty, quite literally heading into the mine alongside his men to assess and inspect. He wrote about his daily life and the people he had contact with. He seemed to have a great respect for his advisers—the men he'd employed to oversee the mining—who had the experience he'd lacked in the beginning. Some of these men he'd met in the gold fields, where he'd gone to try his luck and make enough money to start his own business. He also wrote about the other driving force behind his desire to make something of himself: Lady Catherine Shoebridge, his childhood sweetheart. The two had grown up together in neighbouring families, but from a very young age it had been decided that Catherine, the only child of Lord Winston Shoebridge, would one day marry Alexander's older brother, Henry, to unite the two families. Alexander had asked her father for Catherine's hand in marriage only to be rejected. He was the second son and would not inherit any titles or land and therefore not what Shoebridge wanted for his only daughter. Heartbroken, Alexander vowed he would make his fortune and claim her hand in marriage, heading to Australia with the sole purpose of becoming wealthier than his brother.

Within seven years, Alexander had achieved his goal—and returned to England to claim his bride.

In preparation for bringing Catherine to Australia, Alexander had undertaken the construction of Frolesworthy Hall, the grandest homestead in the entire New England area at the time. It had nine bedrooms, a grand ballroom, numerous receiving rooms, servants' quarters and a sweeping staircase the likes of which had never been seen before in the bush community of Banalla or surrounding areas.

Damian stopped in front of a large framed photograph of the homestead, taken only months after it had been completed. It truly was magnificent.

From the diary entries, Damian knew the photo had been taken for an article in a prestigious newspaper that Alexander had commissioned to feature the house and write a story on his meteoric rise and wealth. Maybe it had been an attempt to further solidify the fact he'd made his own wealth and was successful without the backing of his family or their vast fortune. This seemed to be a consistent theme in many of the entries Alexander wrote—an almost burning obsession to rub his triumph in the face of Winston Shoebridge and everyone else who'd ever written him off as nothing more than the spare to the heir.

This was also Alexander's downfall, Damian mused. When his mine hit a larger-than-expected payload, it was reported far and wide. It came after a particularly tumultuous period, where Frolesworthy was being built and his workers at the gold mine had gone on strike. A newspaper article at the time had reported Alexander had sent a consignment of gold to Sydney and was returning with bags of cash intended for wages and payment of builders. Jack and his men were alerted to the fact a coachload of cash was due to arrive in Banalla—easy pickings, if you knew a certain place to ambush it. Which, it turned out, Jack did.

As Damian stood before the photo of the house now, he couldn't help but feel a sadness for the ambitious man. After all the years of blood, sweat and tears, tragedy would strike only a few short months after this photo was taken. Alexander Compton's entire empire would come crashing down, and the woman he'd built it for would never be seen again.

Eleven

Damian removed his sunglasses from the neck of his T-shirt and slid them onto his face as he walked out into the bright sunlight. He paused at his bike, looking each way up the wide side street. He liked the quieter pace of this small town. No one seemed to be in a hurry—they just went about their business, stopping to chat to people they knew here and there, while loyal working dogs sat patiently in the backs of utes, waiting for their owners to return. If he used his historian imagination, he could almost visualise this town as it might have looked back in Jack McNally's day. The streets would have been dirt, and the cars would have been horses, but the layout would have been the same. Even a few of the houses and buildings would have been here. However, back when the town was first settled, there would have been a lot more lean-to type structures and tents until building materials and supplies were able to be transported for more permanent buildings. Still, the bones of the town that remained were the same.

A ding on his phone caught his attention and he checked the screen as a new message popped up from his siblings' group chat. He let out a quiet moan.

Kaitlin: So? How did it go?

Jess: Ohh, yes! Updates!

Damian: We just had a drink.

He knew he should have just kept his mouth shut yesterday afternoon when he'd been talking to his eldest sister Kaitlin, but he'd been trying to get off the phone to go and meet Lottie at the bar and he'd accidentally let it slip. His three sisters were like sharks—once they caught the scent of something interesting happening in his love life they wouldn't give up.

Kaitlin: And?

Damian: And nothing. I walked her home.

Jess: What was she like?

Damian: She's nice.

Kaitlin: Nice? Like Susan the librarian nice or like Vicki the crazy-eyed accountant nice?

Damian: Vicki wasn't nice.

He suppressed a shiver of horror at the mention of the woman he'd once dated a few years earlier, who'd been the closest he'd ever come to having a stalker.

    Jess: You thought she was nice at first.

    Kaitlin: Hence why we now screen your dates—because you have no clue when it comes to women.

    Damian: Stop screening my dates. Don't you two have husbands you can go and annoy or something?

Both his older sisters were happily married and had busy lives, yet still somehow managed to find time to try and meddle in his.

    Emilly: Wait, wait . . . I'm catching up . . . Okay, I'm caught up. So she was nice?

Emily was his younger sister by two years and lived the closest to him—only a few blocks away. They usually managed to catch up for coffee once a week, but nowadays she had her hands full with eighteen-month-old twins, so coffee was usually done either in her small apartment or at the park.

    Damian: Yes, she was nice.

    Kaitlin: So she's into antiques and road trips.

    Damian: What? How did you know that?

Needle in a Haystack

Kaitlin: 😳 Hello? Social media.

Damian clicked on the link his sister sent through, and Lottie's smiling face beamed up at him from the screen. He wasn't a social media fan and apart from the odd bit of promotion for his books he avoided it where possible.

Damian: I didn't even tell you her last name!

Kaitlin: I didn't need it. You told me her first name and I just did a search of the town, and voila!

Damian: That's unsettling.

Emilly: Aw, she's cute!

Jess: She really is. I like this one. You should invite her for Christmas.

Damian: Christmas? I literally met her yesterday.

Kaitlin: Yeah, calm down guys. She could be a nutcase.

Damian: She's not a nutcase

Kaitlin: That's what you said about Vicki.

Jess: That's true. You did say that.

Damian: I've got to go.

Jess: Wait! Are you seeing her again?

Damian: Probably.

Emilly: I'm proud of you!

Kaitlin: Me too. Look at you finally getting into this dating thing—and all by yourself too.

Jess: Must be the T-shirt. Were you wearing it?

Damian typed back a not-so-polite reply and put his phone away. His sisters had thought it hilarious when they found a T-shirt that said: *If you're flirting with me, please let me know and be extremely specific. Seriously, I'm clueless.* He used it as a rag to wipe his hands on when he did an oil change on the bike.

He started his bike and rode slowly to the intersection of the main street. Then his gaze fell on the antiques shop a little further up.

He hadn't been able to stop thinking about Lottie Fairchild, and he wanted to see her again. Badly. He wanted to admire that smile lingering on her full lips that had done strange things to his concentration. When was the last time a woman had captured his attention in this way? Maybe never.

Work and research dominated his life—it was the way he liked it, even though his mother and sisters often warned him that if he wasn't careful he'd end up a grouchy old professor with only a pile of dusty books to keep him company. That had always been a slight exaggeration—clearly an active imagination ran in his family. He went out on dates, occasionally.

In truth, mostly it was only when he needed a companion for an awards night or some compulsory university dinner. It had proven difficult to find a woman who shared his love of history and wanted to tag along on the numerous weekends away for conferences, or explore the remains of historic places of interest—often hidden in bushland and in remote rural areas long since forgotten.

Damian wondered if Lottie would be the kind of woman who would enjoy those kinds of things. Something told him that she would. She seemed to share his passion for history, which was a good start.

His stomach grumbled quietly and he glanced up, checking the weather—a necessary evil when riding. He was relieved to see the cloudless blue sky. His plan was to head out to Frolesworthy Hall, the estate that had once belonged to Alexander Compton, but first, he needed to find something to eat. He hadn't had breakfast and it was almost lunchtime.

He hadn't planned to stop in such close proximity to a certain antiques store . . . well, maybe he had—just on the off-chance he might catch a glimpse of Lottie and have an excuse to stop in and say hello. However, when he walked past, he saw she was on the phone and he decided not to interrupt, heading into the bakery.

The smell of freshly baked bread and pastries filled his senses, and his stomach growled once more—louder this time, in case he tried to ignore it again.

'Hey darl, what can I get you?' asked a round-faced, blonde-haired woman behind the counter.

His eyes were already busy devouring the offerings in the glass display case. He decided on the breakfast pie and a vanilla slice, pointedly ignoring the judgemental eyebrow his conscience was lifting at his selection and the reminders that he'd been promising to start eating healthier. *One more day won't make any difference.*

He made small talk with the woman about the weather as she packed up his food, finding out her name was Judy and she'd lived here all her life, before paying and saying goodbye. He headed towards the park at the end of the street to eat.

There was a motorhome parked nearby and he gave a nod to the couple as he walked past to a table in the sun. He thought of his own parents, who were currently somewhere in Western Australia and enjoying the freedom of taking each day as it came and stopping to explore wherever the fancy took them. One day he hoped he'd have a chance to do the same thing.

The warm sun on his back and the delicious food in his stomach made Damian stop and appreciate where he was. He'd lived in the city all his life and he loved it. There was always somewhere to go, something to do. He enjoyed people watching and exploring places he'd never been, despite growing up there. There was always something new to find. He didn't particularly enjoy the hustle and bustle, but he liked watching it, finding a quiet place to sit and observe everything around him. Which was exactly what he did in this quiet little park, with the grass lush and green, freshly mown and with the garden beds neatly maintained. He could see the little town behind it, moving at a slightly faster pace—traffic flowing through the main street, visitors strolling along, taking their time as they stopped to look in the windows or browse at their leisure. The locals were the people dodging said visitors, moving with purpose, ticking jobs off their to-do lists and stopping occasionally in the middle of the footpath to chat to other locals, causing the trickle of oncoming people to part and walk around them.

The squawking of cockatoos high up in the gum trees accompanied the chortle of a family of magpies hopping about on the thick blanket of grass, dipping their beaks in search of worms.

I could live here, Damian thought idly. Until recently, he'd never considered living anywhere but where he'd spent the last forty-one years of his life, but lately, he'd caught himself thinking about doing something new. He was proud of the work he'd been part of in his current job at the university, but he'd accomplished what he'd set out to do and now his real passion was his writing. He wanted to focus more on his books, which had always had to fit in around his work life. He'd been tossing around the idea of taking a sabbatical from teaching to focus completely on writing, and a change of scenery wasn't a completely unrealistic idea. In fact, the idea had merit.

Damian dropped his rubbish in the bin and wandered away, still deep in thought. When he finally looked up, his breath hitched slightly at the sight of Lottie, only metres away, watering a potted plant out the front of her shop.

'Hi,' she said as he reached her side.

Suddenly, he couldn't seem to make his mouth connect with his brain. 'Uh . . . hey.'

'I thought that was your bike.' She smiled and his stupid heart rate spiked like he'd just received an electric shock.

Lottie had wondered if he'd stop by the shop again. She'd accomplished a lot while trying to distract herself from thinking about Damian all day. There wasn't a skerrick of dust to be found inside after she'd dusted every surface, the windows had been cleaned and she'd even remembered to water the plants out the front.

'Do you want a ride?' he offered now as he caught her looking at his bike.

'A ride?' Lottie asked, surprised. 'On your bike?'

'Yeah . . . I mean, if you don't want to it's okay,' he backtracked quickly.

'No,' she said hastily. 'I mean, I *would* like to go for a ride.' She found herself feeling a little too excited at the prospect of sitting behind him on a bike. 'Do you have anywhere in particular in mind?'

'Well, I was planning to go out and look at the old remains of the house Alexander built. Frolesworthy Hall. Have you been there?'

'Yeah, but not in a while.' In fact, the last time she'd been out there, she'd probably been about seventeen. She'd gone out there with a group of friends on a whim and ended up making out in a car with Michael Chambers.

'I'd like to get some photos.'

'When were you thinking of going?'

'How early do you close?'

Lottie found herself eager to pull the door shut behind her right now. 'It's been pretty quiet today,' she admitted. She hadn't had a single customer in the store all morning, not even to browse.

They did have the odd slow day. They had a few busier days too, when the tour buses came through town doing daytrips from surrounding nursing homes on outings. The cafes and pubs always did well, as did the thrift shops and craft stores. It was mainly the more affluent weekend visitors who spent up in the boutique and specialty shops. And there hadn't been any buses scheduled for today. 'I'm pretty close to the owner, so I can take an early mark.'

'Would, say, an hour be okay?' he asked, glancing down at his watch. 'I need to get fuel and sort a couple of things out. Then I'll come back and pick you up.'

'Sure.'

He sent her a grin before returning to his bike and climbing on. It wasn't till he rode away that she began to have serious doubts about what she'd just agreed to. It was definitely *not* like her to spontaneously jump on the back of a motorbike with a man she barely knew—albeit a very sexy man—and go gallivanting about the countryside.

Her ringing phone interrupted her scattered thoughts.

'I'm just calling to get the tea on Mr Sexy Pants from last night,' Cher said, sounding eager to settle in for a gossip session. 'How did it go?'

'It went fine. He walked me home.'

'Aaaaand?' she prompted.

'And nothing.'

'Nothing? Like actually *nothing*?'

'Yep. He went back to his motel.'

'I had more faith in you, Charlotte Fairchild,' she tutted, disappointment flooding through the phone.

'I only just met the man.'

'So? He's the first bloke to come to town with all his own teeth for goodness' sake! You don't just let that walk away.'

Lottie shook her head and gave a despairing chuckle.

'Did you at least make plans to see him again?'

'Yes, actually. I'm going for a ride on his bike this afternoon.'

There was a moment of silence before Lottie heard an approving grunt. 'I'm loving this bad boy professor thing he's got going on. It's refreshing.'

'I don't think he's deliberately set out to achieve a certain style,' Lottie said dryly.

'It's pure genius, really. A dorky, hot, motorbike-riding bad boy . . . you couldn't actually make that shit up, because it sounds like it wouldn't work. Yet the boy has managed to pull it off spectacularly,' Cher said with appreciation in her low tone.

'I'm actually having second thoughts about going,' Lottie admitted as her doubts resurfaced momentarily.

'What? Why?'

'Well, I don't really know him that well. And motorbikes are kind of dangerous . . .'

'Would you just live a little for once in your life? Sheesh, woman. This is the kind of stuff you tick off a bucket list. Ride off into the sunset with a hot biker dude: tick,' she said firmly. 'Slow dance with a cowboy at a honky-tonk: tick,' she continued.

'That one isn't on my bucket list.'

'Neither was the biker, I bet,' Cher said. 'That's what I mean. Get out there and start living, girl!'

They hung up as a customer finally came into the shop and Lottie found herself pondering her friend's advice. Maybe Cher was right. It wouldn't hurt to have a bit of excitement in her life. She wasn't too sure what else she'd put on a bucket list, but ticking off at least one thing had to be a start.

Twelve

True to his word, Damian was back at the front of the shop an hour later, carrying an extra helmet. Unclipping it from where he'd secured it around his arm, he swung his leg off the bike and walked towards her. 'I saw this in a shop up the road yesterday. I'm hoping it fits. Otherwise, I can go to Armidale and see if I can get one.'

'I didn't even think about a helmet,' she said, staring as he passed it over to her. In her defence, she'd never ridden a bike before. At least she'd worn jeans today. She pulled her hair back and clumsily tugged the bulky helmet over her head, tilting her chin up when he asked her to, then feeling the breath lock in her chest as he stepped in closer to secure the strap. The moment was gone after he lifted his hands and placed them on her helmeted head, tugging rather unromantically to make sure it didn't slip around too much.

'Couldn't have done better if I'd known your size,' he said. 'I also have this—it's an old one of mine I keep in the saddlebag.' He pulled out a black jacket from a compartment-type bag attached to the side of his bike.

Lottie shrugged into it and attempted to zip up the front, finding it quite difficult to do with a heavy helmet weighing on her head.

'It's not perfect, but it'll do,' he said, moving her hands aside and taking over to do the zip up to almost under her chin. 'You ready?'

To feel like the Michelin Man? Then yep, she was ready. 'What do I do?'

He got back on the bike and started it, then held his arm out to her. 'Climb up onto the back,' he said, raising his voice over the motor.

Lottie tilted her head down to try to find the foot pegs he'd swung out for her and gingerly took hold of his arm to climb on behind him. He turned his head back as far as he could. 'Lean when I lean. Just follow what I do and you'll be right. Hold on,' he called.

She quickly grabbed hold of his waist, bunching up his jacket beneath her hands. Taking off was terrifying yet exhilarating, and she had no time to process either sensation before they were heading out of town, the wind loud inside her helmet and the roar of the bike powerful beneath the seat.

Lottie had never felt so . . . *free*. With nothing around her, the road and the other vehicles around her were frighteningly close, making her feel incredibly vulnerable . . . and yet completely uninhibited. This was how she imagined flying would feel—the noise and the wind rushing around her body. Tucked behind Damian's big body, his warmth somehow penetrating through the layers of protective wear and into her own, she felt safe. Protected.

The paddocks beside the highway flashed past, and she kept her eyes on the scenery and not the giddying sensation of watching the bitumen pass beneath them. She had an unsettling moment as she realised that if she fell off this thing, it would be very bad—protective gear or not—before she quickly banished the thought and found herself staring at the back of Damian's neck. She could see the tiny hairs on his neck, trimmed in a short cut, that worked their way up to the base of his head. His skin was tanned, exposed to the sun whenever he was out and about on his bike, she supposed. She had the insane urge to lift her hand up and touch it, but self-preservation thankfully held her hands firmly buried in the fabric of his jacket.

Eventually, she heard the bike slow down and she looked up to find they were approaching the turn-off to the road that would take them out to Frolesworthy. This road was narrower and it wound its way between endless sheep paddocks with large boulders and scattered outcrops of rocks until it reached a small intersection with an old white signpost that pointed towards Frolesworthy Hall.

Over the years, the hall had been owned by a few families, but the upkeep of such a large house and its surrounding buildings was expensive. Neglect led to decay.

Eventually, a new home was built on the property and the old hall abandoned. The property owners continued to raise beef cattle, but the parcel of land the hall stood on was left open to the public.

As they reached the entrance to the long driveway, Damian slowed down and they made their way along the potholed track.

The two-storey building would have been an impressive sight in its heyday. Lottie had seen the photos in the museum and was sad the house had been left to slowly decay. Today, only the outer frame of the Edwardian mansion still stood. The sandstone bricks formed a bland rectangular shape, with a curved tower-like structure at the front. A bushfire that had ripped through the area fifteen years earlier had burned away all that had remained of the timber verandah and balustrades that had once surrounded the house on both floors that she remembered seeing years earlier. It reminded Lottie now, of a tired, grand old dame, just marking time at the end of a long and colourful life. There were a number of other buildings in similar disrepair further away—the remains of large chimney stacks and the mill that had been used in the gold mine from which Alexander had made his fortune.

Damian turned off the engine and for a moment, they both simply sat and took in the building. It was quiet except for the tick of the hot engine and the calls of the birds who sang out from the tops of the handful of tall trees surrounding the house and its overgrown garden and outbuildings. The wind whispered through the foliage, but there were no sounds of modern-day life—no traffic or tractors working in the distance. If you ignored the fact they were sitting on a motorbike, they could have almost stepped back into the late 1800s.

The creak of Damian's leather jacket as he moved his arm to help her dismount broke the stillness. After spending so long with her arms wrapped around his waist, feeling the heat of his body on hers, it felt strange to suddenly no longer have it. She breathed in the heady scent of leather and an earthy, masculine scent he was wearing that shot through to parts of her that had become extremely sensitive after spending the last half-hour on the back of a bike.

'It would have been amazing to see it in its prime,' he said, sounding wistful as he hung his helmet on the handlebars and reached to take hers. Their fingertips touched and for a moment, Lottie found she couldn't look away. Her heart gave a small out-of-kilter beat and she swallowed quickly, dragging her gaze from his as she realised her breathing felt heavier.

'It's such a shame it wasn't saved,' she said, forcing herself to look at their surroundings.

'It's a crime, really. The stories this place could tell.' He took out a large camera from a black bag on the rear of the bike, holding it easily in one big hand.

They walked inside, where only the stone walls and the tiled floor remained, as well as a few of the inner walls that divided the rooms downstairs. Lottie was saddened to see the traces of graffiti on the walls. The grand staircase leading to the floors above had also been lost in the bushfire, so there was no longer any way of reaching the second storey to see the view. *There was nothing for miles around*, she thought, remembering standing all those years ago on the top verandah and seeing the flat, open land encompassing the old house. She stepped aside to allow Damian to walk past and his body brushed against hers. Familiar heat again disturbed her sleeping senses, waking them up as if from a long slumber. His fingertips gently grazed her hand, making her skin tingle with awareness.

They headed out the back of the building to what would once have been a kitchen garden and orchard, but now was just barren dirt. Only part of the original wall of the garden was still intact.

Damian clicked photos as they moved through the grounds, and they ended up following an old road of cobblestones that had been laid long ago and were still visible.

They decided to take a closer look at the stone buildings scattered around the main house, spaces that once would have been stables, a blacksmith shop and supply store rooms to support the gold-mine workers and their families. This place had once been almost its own little town when Alexander built his gold mine—albeit a short-lived one.

Lottie watched as Damian crouched and adjusted his camera lens to take a photo of something he found on the ground. The black T-shirt he wore stretched across his wide shoulders and lovingly wrapped around his torso. The denim of his jeans encased muscular thighs, and the memory of her own sitting extremely close behind them made her skin tingle. He stood up slowly and turned, catching her looking at him, and she swallowed nervously, trying not to look like he'd just caught her lustfully recalling how tightly their bodies fitted together.

She feared the blasé expression she was trying for had come off as more of an uncomfortable wince, and she quickly looked away.

Damian slowly lifted his camera and clicked off a few more shots of the crumbling outbuildings then lined up Lottie through his lens as she strolled ahead through the ruins, trailing her fingertips along the warm rocks of a nearby wall. He wondered if she was imagining how life would have once been here, like he was doing. She wore a faraway look, her eyes lowered and her lips slightly parted in a not-quite smile—something more like wonderment, or contemplation, maybe. He took a few more photos as a growing desire to touch her again began to build inside him.

She'd felt so good behind him on the bike. He could still feel her warmth against his back and remembered how his hand had itched to run across her thigh so tightly pressed against his. He rarely took anyone on his bike, and he'd forgotten how intimate it was. He'd never *wanted* to take anyone on his bike before—now, he couldn't wait to do it again with her.

The late afternoon sun steamed through a gap in the rock wall behind her, framing her in golden light, and he snapped one more photo—unable to resist—before lowering the camera just as she glanced up and his heart did a weird flip inside his chest.

He didn't know what was going on . . . but he knew he was in trouble.

This place feels so melancholy, Lottie thought. Maybe it was just her, knowing how hard Alexander had worked to build all this for his bride, only for her to never have seen it. The life he'd dreamed of creating, the children he'd most likely envisioned, the generations of Comptons he'd hoped to fill this house with . . . none of it had ever happened. Had it been worth giving up his life in England to get so close to having his dream, only for it to slip through his fingers at the end?

As they walked side by side, lost in thought, Lottie stumbled over a loose cobblestone. Before she could even gasp, she found herself pitching heavily forward into a freefall, and her heart leaped to her throat as her body braced for impact. In that instant, a pair of strong arms suddenly wrapped around her body, warm and firm. Her fall halted and she was gently drawn upright and set back on her feet. Her heart now began to thud painfully as she turned slightly and found her face close to Damian's.

His lips felt warm against her own as he tentatively touched them in a gentle kiss, and a bolt of desire shot through her entire body. Lottie felt her lips part beneath his, and he kissed her more deeply. She wasn't sure how long they stood there; time seemed to have almost stopped. She'd been kissed before—she was a grown woman for goodness' sake, and hardly a nun—but this . . . This was like nothing she'd ever felt before.

When they eventually pulled apart, they were both breathing heavily. Lottie could only stare dumbstruck into his gorgeous chocolate-coloured eyes as she fought to catch her breath. He seemed equally surprised, if his silence was anything to go by, and the knowledge made Lottie feel somewhat better. *It's not just me, then.*

'Wow,' he finally said.

It hadn't been the reaction she'd been expecting from a guy who made his living out of words.

'Yeah,' she agreed. She shifted a little, stepping back as he dropped his hands from where they'd still been holding her moments before.

'Are you okay?' he asked.

'Well, I mean . . . I don't think I've ever been kissed like that before,' she said, finding herself stammering slightly.

'I . . . uh, meant your ankle. You lost your balance . . .'

Idiot! 'Oh, yeah. I'm fine.' She gave an awkward cough. 'Thanks.' *Just kill me now.*

'But I completely agree. That was some kiss.'

Lottie squirmed under his amused gaze before clearing her throat. 'Well, it's getting a bit late and the kangaroos will come out soon. We probably don't want to be riding back into town when they do.'

'Good point. I just want to get a few more photos. I'll be quick.'

Once he'd walked away, she allowed herself to breathe deeply once more. She'd been wondering what it would be like to kiss him since they'd met. Now she knew.

But what did they do now? He was only here until the festival. Was starting something with someone who lived so far away something she really wanted to do? Maybe he wasn't interested in anything long term anyway. Was she okay with that? She couldn't say she'd ever had a proper relationship before—not a live-in one, anyway—but the men she had dated and liked had lasted for a few months at least. This was all new territory. Was it all just an impulse from one of Cher's bucket lists? *Sleep with a hot biker: tick.* The idea of a casual affair with Damian didn't really sit right somehow. What would happen if she couldn't do casual?

What if she wanted more?

The ride back into town seemed to take longer than the ride out, maybe because there was a new awkwardness hanging over them. It wasn't even really awkward—more like neither of them seemed to know what to do now that it had happened. She wondered if he was regretting it. Maybe he was worried she would want something more than he was willing to offer?

And what *did* she want? To be honest, she was still in shock that it had happened—and so naturally. But what if she'd been reading him all wrong and now he couldn't wait to get rid of her?

Damian pulled up in front of her house and reached an arm out to help her dismount. Lottie struggled with her helmet, finally pulling her head free and quickly running her fingers through the tangle of hair left in its wake. *Real classy.*

She fumbled with the helmet as she attempted to hand it to him, but he shook his head. 'You keep it with you . . . for next time. If you want to ride again after today?' he tacked on, eyeing her closely.

'I'd like to,' she said honestly. 'It was fun.' She'd never imagined how exhilarating it would be. Why hadn't she found this sooner? Clearly, she hadn't been hanging around the right kind of people—namely, someone with a motorbike.

He seemed relieved by her answer. 'Good. Then you keep the helmet and the jacket. For next time.'

'Okay. For next time,' she said almost shyly. 'Thank you for today.'

'Thanks for playing hooky and coming out with me. Good thing you have such an understanding boss.'

Lottie grinned a little at that. 'She's good that way. Well, I better get going.'

'Yeah. Me too. I'll see you later,' he said sliding his helmet on effortlessly.

She stepped back as he started the engine, watching as he pulled away before heading inside. The idea of ruining whatever it was they might be discovering felt like a lot less of a big deal now.

Thirteen

7 April 1863

Jack cursed once more as another bullet whizzed by his head a little too close for comfort. The traps were proving far more tenacious than he'd given them credit for. They'd been trying to shake them off for close to an hour, and now found themselves almost back to where they'd left the stagecoach. A mob of wallabies scattered ahead—startled by the gunfire and men on horseback.

'We've been running around in flamin' circles, Jack!' Paddy snarled. 'We gotta make a stand.'

Jack agreed. Seeing a small clearing ahead, he gave the order to dismount. They'd barely had time to take cover behind an old log before the bullets started, thick and fast. Clearly the men had been prepared for the possibility of a robbery—after all, it was McNally territory. Jack's men were outnumbered and outgunned from the outset; still, they had the advantage of being on familiar ground, and they knew the land well. If they could just keep the police off their backs for a breath, they'd be able to disappear into the bush like ghosts.

An unexpected movement caught Jack's attention and he scanned the coach off to the side. Something moved on the ground beside it. Thinking it might be a survivor of the robbery keen to rejoin the fight, he aimed his gun towards the shadow, preparing to fire, but stopped when he saw that the figure was not a man, but a woman—the beautiful wife of Alexander Compton. Narrowing his eyes, Jack tried to focus, swearing softly as he watched her writhe, her face contorted in agony and her hands clasping her stomach.

The baby.

All around him, bullets flew and men yelled, but Jack's whole attention was on the woman on the ground, a gunshot wound to her side, sitting beside the body of her dead husband as she prepared to give birth to a child.

'Jack!' Paddy yelled, breaking through the rush of blood inside his head. 'We have to go.'

'You go ahead,' Jack said, making a split-second decision. He bounded to his feet and ran across the clearing to where the woman lay. As he got closer, he saw blood had stained the bodice of her dress just below her waist. Her eyes were closed and her head slowly moved from side to side as she gave a low, pained moan.

'What are you doin'?' He heard John calling frantically from behind him. 'Leave her.'

The shots continued as the other men refused to leave without him. Then, after what seemed like an eternity, the gunshots stopped.

Jack tentatively lifted his head and saw the prone bodies of the policemen.

'We've got to go before more traps turn up!' Paddy yelled.

'I'll be right behind you,' Jack snapped, looking over his shoulder at them before bending down and scooping the delirious woman into his arms. She weighed next to nothing. Her slight form jerked against his chest as he carried her towards his horse. She was such a small thing, it was no wonder it looked as though she was having trouble with the delivery.

Kate will know what to do.

He passed her into Paddy's arms then swung onto his horse, leaning back down to lift her up and settle her in front of him, trying not to hurt her more. Paddy was staring at him as though he'd lost his mind. Perhaps he had. Jack wasn't sure why he couldn't turn his back on this woman—especially when his and the lives of his men were so clearly at stake—yet something refused to let him leave her there alone.

'Easy does it,' he said to her in the low gentle tone he used on his horses. She gave a soft whimper and his heart squeezed with regret. He hadn't wished this on her. He would have preferred not to have killed her husband, but he certainly never intended to harm a woman or child.

He wasted no time urging his mount forward. It wasn't an easy ride ahead, and he had doubts that she would survive the trip, but he owed it to her to at least try. If not her, then at least the innocent babe she was about to bear. It hadn't asked for any of this to happen.

'You kissed him!'

'Would you keep your voice down?' Lottie hissed.

'Oh, please. Doreen Miller is deaf as a post and Pearl and Tilly are too busy fawning over Edward Miles to listen in on our conversation.'

'Why are we meeting here again?' Lottie asked, giving the old cafe a quick glance.

'I'm checking out the competition.'

'What competition?' Lottie asked confused. The old cafe lived up to its name, but not in a rustic-chic trendy kind of way. Sitting by itself at the top of the main street, this place was just plain *old*.

'Donald and Louise have leased the whole business. Apparently, he's a chef.'

'A *chef*?' Lottie asked, kinking an eyebrow doubtfully. The only cooked food they'd ever sold here, to her knowledge, was Chiko rolls.

'Right?' Cher agreed, matching her dubious expression. 'Still, in this business, it pays to listen to the rumours.' She was sporting a black pixie hairstyle, a red lace-up bodice and black tailored trousers, looking very Liza Minnelli-ish from *Cabaret*.

Lottie picked up the menu, recalling the last time she'd been here. Today, there was no sticky plastic cover, and she opened it with a little more optimism.

'New gourmet pie range,' Cher read across from her. 'Pepper brisket, mushroom brisket, mac and cheese, Rajdhani butter chicken, brisket and bacon, chorizo, jalapeno and cheese, Philly cheesesteak.'

'Well, those are all new,' Lottie said with a somewhat-impressed nod. In fact, everything written on the menu was new.

A tall, skinny young man with a thin moustache walked from the kitchen carrying a plate, placing it in front of Doreen.

'Oh my God, that smells amazing,' Lottie whispered.

'Excuse me,' Cher said as the man headed back to the kitchen, 'who *are* you?'

'Who are *you*?' he shot back haughtily.

Lottie gave a snort at the look on Cher's face. She was usually the one with the sassy attitude.

'*I*,' she emphasised pointedly, 'am Cher, owner of Madame Dubois and co-founder of the Theatre Des Moines club in Melbourne. No doubt you've heard of it?'

'Nope,' he said dismissively, making to walk away.

'Just a minute, I'm talking to you.'

'I'm busy. You ordering something? Or are you just gonna take up my booth space?'

Cher's mouth dropped open . . . literally.

Lottie had to smother a giggle at the sight. 'We're still deciding. Everything sounds amazing,' she cut in to defuse the moment.

The man lifted his chin towards the front counter, where a young woman sporting some rather intriguing piercings sat filing her talon-like nails. 'Order at the counter when you make up your mind,' he said before walking away.

'Who the hell-o Dolly does he think he is?' Cher bit off angrily.

'With that kind of ego, I'm assuming he's the new chef.'

'Well, he certainly won't go far with *that* kind of behaviour,' Cher said, narrowing her eyes, with their luscious false eyelashes—the black, everyday-wear ones, without the sparkles.

'Actually, he reminds me of someone,' Lottie murmured, returning her gaze to the menu.

'Oh, puleeeze! I am *always* polite to my customers.'

'Hmm,' Lottie said without comment.

'Everybody loves me because I'm friendly, damn it!'

'Yes, so approachable ...'

'I *am* approachable. I just don't suffer idiots.'

'You are a very fine performer and a savvy businesswoman,' Lottie agreed lightly.

'I did not come into this town with an attitude like that.'

'You came to town with *some* attitude,' Lottie corrected, recalling the gossip mill nearly self-destructing over her arrival. Cher had definitely been a Banalla first.

'Not *that* much,' Cher muttered, sending a glare in the direction of the kitchen.

'Let's just order.'

'Fine,' Cher finally agreed with a pout.

After they'd placed their orders with the indifferent woman at the counter, they settled back in the booth. 'Back to other breaking news,' Cher said, never down or distracted for long. 'Tell me everything about the sexy professor and that kiss. I bet it was dreamy.'

Lottie had hoped that particular conversation had been forgotten, but it seemed not. 'It was . . . nice,' Lottie said, mustering as much dignity as she could.

'Nice?' Cher repeated, flatly. 'Honey, looking out your window at a sunny day is nice. Kissing a sexy man should not fall under that same umbrella.'

'It was . . . better than nice,' Lottie conceded. There was no point trying to close the subject when Cher was like a dog with a bone.

'I should hope so. With all that outside packaging, it would be such a waste if he turned out to be a dud root.'

Lottie closed her eyes briefly, drawing strength. She should be used to the fact that every time Cher opened her mouth, there was always the chance something outrageous was about to come out.

'So, what's the problem?'

'There's no problem as such,' Lottie said, trying not to shift uncomfortably under her friend's eagle-like gaze. 'It's just . . . well, what's the point? He's here for the festival and then he'll be gone.'

There was a moment of blessed silence.

'Sometimes I really worry about you,' Cher said, breaking it. 'How did you survive living in the city as long as you did? I swear, sometimes you're like a little country bumpkin who's never left this one-horse town.'

'I survived perfectly fine, thank you very much,' Lottie said mildly. 'Just because I haven't got an impressive bedpost notch count doesn't mean I'm naïve.'

'I blame your mother's distrust of men and love.'

'No one's to blame for anything,' Lottie said.

'Tell that to your love life.'

'There's nothing wrong with my love life. And my mother doesn't distrust men. She just has a weird fixation on a family curse.'

'Hmm,' Cher murmured with a very disapproving Southern drawl.

'Oh, for goodness' sake, stop looking at me like that. *I* know it's not true.'

'I'm not saying you believe it. All I'm saying is you were brought up by a woman who was adamant and very vocal about never falling in love. You've had no male role models in your life,' she argued, 'and all that has to have made an impact, whether you realise it or not. Subconsciously, it has to have had some influence on you.'

'It's not like I haven't had any experience with men,' Lottie said defensively.

'True, but not recently.'

'I've been on dates.'

'When?' Cher challenged.

'The other . . .' Lottie stopped for a moment to do the calculations in her head. 'A few months ago, I went out with Jason Foster,' she said, lifting her chin defiantly.

'Five or six months ago. And remind me, how did that happen?' Cher asked coyly.

'You forced me,' Lottie snapped.

'I *arranged* it,' she corrected. 'When was the last time that *you* initiated a date with someone?'

'That's really not relevant,' Lottie said, glancing around the room, hoping their order was about to come out.

'A year,' Cher answered her own question. 'It had been *a year* since you'd last gone out with a man when I arranged that date with Jason. You're a young, vibrant woman with needs,' she said, her voice rising as enthusiasm for her favourite topic took hold; namely, interfering in Lottie's love life. 'It's not natural to suppress them the way you do.'

'My needs are perfectly fine, thank you very much,' she grated out.

'This man has been dropped in your lap,' Cher argued. 'It's a sign from the gods. Even the universe is sick of watching you waste away among your precious heirlooms. If you don't be careful, you'll end up exactly the same way—old, dusty and sad.'

'My shop is not old, dusty *or* sad, thank you very much.'

'Okay, maybe that was a tad excessive. But you know what I mean.'

'I know exactly what you mean. I should just throw caution to the wind, sleep with a complete stranger for as long as he's in town and then go on my merry way when he leaves without a backward glance.'

'*Exactly.*' Cher beamed.

Lottie rolled her eyes. 'I was being facetious.'

'I know,' Cher drawled. 'But it's exactly what you need to do. Take a chance. Who says it has to end once he goes home? People meet like that all the time, you know.'

'It seems like a waste of time. I'm not interested in a long-distance relationship.'

'Then have a really awesome fling. The point is, if you never take the opportunities that cross your path, you'll end up regretting it. You'll end up like your mother,' she added.

'Funny, because right now, *you're* beginning to sound suspiciously all new age-y and stuff,' Lottie said, raising an eyebrow across the table. 'And, for the record, I'm not saying I don't want a relationship. I'm just pointing out that this one would be difficult, with the distance and the timeframe.'

'I'm serious, Lotts,' Cher said, softening her tone as she used her nickname. 'You have too much to offer. You hide it away in that little shop, with all your old things and love of history. The past is all well and good to obsess over, but not when it stops you living in the present.'

Had she really been doing that? Or was this just Cher being her overdramatic self? Lottie took her business seriously, and it did take up a lot of her time—it was her livelihood after all, as well as her passion. She loved antiques and she took great pride in the fact she didn't just go to a bunch of garage sales and take second-hand junk. She *selected* everything in her store. Lottie spent hours searching for pieces. Both her online store and her shopfront had return customers, some who she even bought specifically for, thanks to getting to know her clientele.

Although part of her wanted to dismiss Cher's observations, another part considered her friend's advice. It *had* been a long time between dates, but that was because Banalla was rather remote and had a somewhat limited number of eligible men in certain age groups. *You could always cast your net wider*, a little voice inside her pointed out, *if you really want to find a man.*

The arrival of their meal—the plates placed a little too firmly on the table to be polite—distracted Lottie from her thoughts.

'Thank—' Lottie's words were cut off as the man from earlier turned his back abruptly and walked away. 'Well, that was rude.'

'Ridiculous,' Cher said, fuming as she stared after him. She snatched up her cutlery and cut rather aggressively into the pie in front of her. 'I don't care how amazing he thinks he is—' she said, shoving the fork into her mouth and preparing to continue her rant, but she paused. 'Holy mother of God,' she ended on a low moan.

Lottie kinked an eyebrow in surprise before tentatively sampling her own pie. 'Oh wow,' she said as delicate flaky pastry melted on her tongue and delicious, richly flavoured beef fell apart in her mouth. 'This is amazing.'

'It seriously is.' Cher nodded, then glanced over at the counter, where the lanky, tattooed man stood watching them with a smug grin. 'But I will be damned if I tell him that to his face,' she vowed.

Lottie gave a small chuckle. 'I'm pretty sure he already knows how good his pies are.'

'Cocky bastard,' Cher muttered, returning her attention to her food. 'I'm going to do some digging and find out exactly what this guy's story is.'

There was no more time for talking. The food was amazing, and Lottie was once again astounded that their small town had somehow managed to produce yet another hidden gem that word of mouth would undoubtedly make the next culinary stop for foodies from far and wide.

'Ladies,' the man's voice floated across to them as they reached the door. 'I take it everything was to your satisfaction?'

Cher turned with a dramatic flounce. 'It was passable.'

To his credit, the man only flashed a knowing smile, which only fuelled Cher's irritation. She pushed through the set of French doors without looking back.

Interesting, Lottie thought as she followed along behind. She'd never seen anyone ruffle her friend's feathers quite that way.

There was never a dull moment in Banalla.

Fourteen

'Damn it!' Lottie said, leaning back in her chair. She'd been working on her online store, but the internet had chosen today to have a hissy fit and kept dropping out before she could finish uploading photographs. She jumped slightly when a voice sounded from nearby.

'Am I interrupting?'

She sat up quickly in her seat and instantly began gathering the scattered contents of her messy desk into a lopsided pile. 'Damian. Hi. No, not at all. My internet is playing up. The joys of regional Australia and unreliable internet.'

'I haven't had any trouble with mine so far.'

'You've been lucky then,' she muttered, closing her laptop and standing up. 'What are you up to today?'

'I just thought I'd bring you some files that might be of interest. These ones have lots of stuff about Banalla in its heyday, during the gold rush era.'

'Oh wow, thanks.' He'd mentioned he'd drop in some of his research material, but she wasn't sure he would remember.

'I also wanted to see you again,' he said simply. Lottie felt her breath catch a little as he continued. 'I haven't been able to stop thinking about yesterday.'

She felt his gaze on her face almost as though he'd touched her. 'Me either,' she said, battling the urge to look away.

'I'm usually pretty disciplined when it comes to work, but I'm struggling today.' His voice lowered and he stared at her mouth. 'All I can think about is kissing you again.'

A small shiver ran through her body. 'Then maybe you should,' she said softly.

A slow smile spread across his face before he leaned down and kissed her once more. The same stab of longing and zap of electricity raced through her veins. *This is crazy.*

'Safe to assume yesterday was *not* a one-off experience then,' he murmured as they pulled apart.

Lottie let out a small, shaky breath. 'Nope.'

'Maybe we should try again, though . . . just to make sure,' he suggested, his voice settling again into that low, gravelly tone that made her stomach flip.

'Better to be safe than sorry.'

'That's always been my motto.' He grinned before his lips once more created havoc within her mind and her body.

Over the next few days, it became a routine for Damian to come in at some point through the day. They'd read through documents and old newspapers online, Damian in search of anything relating to Lady Catherine Compton and Lottie for anything she might be able to use in her book. They would read tidbits out to each other, giving voice to theories, both probable and far-fetched. The passion with which he spoke about his work, and his determination that stories and lessons of the colonial past not be lost, was sweet in a way that didn't match his whole bad-boy vibe.

And the kissing. Oh heavens, it was her new favourite thing. Lottie wasn't an overdramatic person, and she'd never bought into the whole romance novel sex scene, with rockets launching and fireworks going off, but every time that man touched her, she swore she experienced some kind of chemical–physical out-of-body experience.

So far, they hadn't gone beyond kissing, allowing the heavy attraction between them to simmer. Lottie found the building anticipation frustrating, yet tantalising.

It was quiet in the shop and Damian had not appeared so Lottie, motivated by his enthusiasm for his work, had decided to do some work on her own book. She'd been making her way through the box of assorted things Marie had given her, bits and pieces kept over the years that had once held some sort of value—the odd postcard sent home from a relative, a novelty in a time when travel for a holiday was something most people couldn't afford, meaning it was quite the big deal to receive a postcard from someone abroad—or, in this case, even an exotic place such as Coolangatta. Lottie smiled at the image of a woman dressed in modest swimwear with a significantly less glitzy Gold Coast than it was now in the background.

But it was the letters relating to Emeline that she found the most interesting. There were only two that Emeline had written to her cousin, Adelaide. Both were extremely difficult to read due to the poor quality of the photocopy and the faint, cursive writing that had been popular at the time. The handwriting was beautiful, without a doubt, but all the elaborate loops and intricate swirls made it incredibly painful to read.

Going by the dates, the letters had been written when Emeline had been in her early thirties. She seemed to be at odds with the rest of the women in Lottie's family and the so-called curse. While, as far as Lottie could tell, the opal had started with Emeline, she didn't follow the same trajectory as the rest of Lottie's ancestors. While her husband had died, it was a good few years later compared with the other women, who'd mostly lost their husbands very soon after getting married, and usually before they gave birth to their first child. This was something Lottie liked to point out as a small hitch in her mother's unshakable belief in the family curse. Not that her mother let that get in the way of a good story.

The earliest of the letters seemed to be the first correspondence between the cousins for a long time, judging by the number of questions Emeline was answering, presumably in response to a previous letter. She filled her in on her daughter, Hattie's, achievements—it seemed Hattie had inherited her mother's riding ability, which Emeline's husband had thought was unladylike and tried to discourage, but she was growing into quite a spirited young lady who liked to question her father's authority regularly, often putting them at loggerheads. Lottie smiled at that. It seemed tweens and teens went through the same rebellion, no matter the era. There were more pages of updates on Emeline's life. She had apparently enjoyed a rather quiet life, happy to be a mother and wife and live vicariously through her daughter, followed by lots of questions about Adelaide and her children and various unfamiliar family members.

Lottie was intrigued by the letters, and also frustrated. She wanted details. She wanted to know what had really happened between Emeline and Jack. Had she really been the unintentional pawn in Jack's attempt at escape? Or was there some truth in the family gossip? Had she been unfairly labelled as Jack McNally's young lover or had she really been in love with him and gone with him, willingly?

Why didn't Adelaide ask these questions?

The second letter at least made mention of a few more relevant things, but still didn't give much more clarity on the situation. Although Adelaide must have brought up something in her responding letter, because Lottie reached a section of the letter that seemed unusual.

In regard to the *unfortunate incident* you mentioned in your letter, dear cousin, I have put that well behind me. I am fortunate to have a loving husband who is a good provider and wonderful role model to Hattie. My daughter shall grow up in a good home, loved and secure. When she is older, I will leave her the one thing given to me by her father, a symbol of our love that she may keep and treasure, as I have.

Lottie frowned as she reread the paragraph. Emeline didn't actually say Henry was Hattie's father; she said he was a good role model. Furthermore, she didn't say Henry had given her whatever the special thing was that she was leaving to Hattie, just that she had been given it by Hattie's father . . .

Was Lottie simply wanting these words to be ambiguous? Was she reading more into them because she wanted some kind of proof that Jack had fathered a child to Emeline? Had Emeline shared her secret with Adelaide and was simply being overly careful in what she wrote?

Lottie gave a small, frustrated groan. She had Emeline's words right here on this page—a handwritten letter by the very person who knew the answers Lottie desperately wanted to know—and they only held more questions.

9 April 1863

Jack sat on his horse beneath the shade of a tall gum tree as he eyed the homestead below. The Grants were a moderately wealthy family, one that he and his men had robbed a few times in the past—occasionally relieving them of a mob of sheep to sell further afield. That's when he met Emeline. He'd seen her briefly in town a few times in the past, before he'd become too famous to frequent town. She was barely sixteen the first time he saw her, with long rusty-red hair, huge brown eyes and skin like fine porcelain. The moment she locked those shy eyes on him, he knew he was going to marry her.

Of course, that had been almost three years ago, back when he'd had hopes of maybe making a life for himself farming. But his family reputation had preceded him and that fire in his belly—the one that raged at injustice and the system of the rich only getting richer off the backs of the poor—was too loud to ignore. He'd found more lucrative ways to make a living, though none as impressive as the haul he'd just taken from the stagecoach. That was a work of art. He was now rich beyond his wildest dreams, and the knowledge that he could buy this property outright from Emeline's father, as well as pretty much any other land in the district that he desired, warmed his body, filling him with bravado and pride. Now people would respect him. Sure, he could gain their respect through fear when he pointed a gun at them, but this kind of respect was like an aphrodisiac. They'd look at him like he was nobility, like he came from somewhere. Like he was someone. He could give Emeline the life she deserved—better than even her father could give her. He could take her away from all this and together, they would build their own dynasty.

Movement at the stables caught his eye and a slow grin spread across his face. He could always count on Emeline being a creature of habit. Her daily ride was made rain, hail or shine. He knew *how much she loved riding, her long hair loose and flowing behind her like a flag as she galloped across the open plains towards the river. He gave a click of his tongue, and his horse moved down the hill. He could already smell the lavender of her soft hair, feel the warmth of her lips against his own and breathe in the scent of her salty skin. His body hardened at the thought. God, he'd missed her. It had been close to three months since he'd seen her but now, in mere moments, he would feel her melt against him again.*

Her horse sensed his presence before she did. She pulled the mare around and came to an abrupt halt, staring at him in disbelief. 'Jack?' she whispered, her eyes wide and bright before suddenly her lip quivered.

He'd dismounted and was at her side within moments. 'What is it?'

'Oh, Jack . . .' she sobbed, and now he felt real panic begin to set in. 'I had no way of finding you.'

'Why did you need to find me?' he asked, searching her face.

'My father . . . he . . . I'm engaged,' she blurted.

'What?' He was more surprised by the news than upset. 'To whom?'

'Henry Oldsfield.'

Now the surprise gave way to rage. 'The judge's son?'

She nodded her beautiful red head as more tears fell. 'There was nothing I could do. I tried to argue with my father, but he wouldn't listen.'

'Well, there's something I can do,' he snarled. 'If Oldsfield isn't alive, they can't make you marry him, can they.'

'Jack, no.' She slid down from her horse, like she'd physically stop him. 'You can't kill him. He doesn't want this any more than I do, I don't think. It's our families that want the marriage. My father has always wanted me to marry into the Oldsfield family.'

Jack knew exactly why he wanted his daughter to align with the judge's family. His plans to go into politics were widely known. Having a judge in the family would be extremely handy for his future aspirations.

'Then we'll just have to ruin their plans won't we?' Jack said, flashing her a wolf-like grin. He knew she hated that there was no real love where her father was concerned. He was a cold man, hell-bent on his own ambitions. She'd told him her mother was no better, even more ruthless than her husband when it came to the possibility of a life in the city and high society instead of out here. The prospect of getting exactly what he wanted and depriving them of what they desired was too enticing. 'We'll get married beforehand.'

'What?' Emeline stared at him with a look of almost horror.

'I love you, Emeline,' Jack said softly.

'And I you. But my father would never—'

'Your father won't have a say in it,' he said with a shrug.

'But he'll never let you win, Jack. He has money and connections—'

'I have money now too. We can build a life of our own, bigger than anything even your father could wish for. I came to take you away. Come with me now.'

'Now?'

'Right now. We can just leave, start somewhere new.'

'But my family—'

'We'll make our own family. Do you want to be your father's pawn forever? Marry me, Emeline,' Jack said gently.

'Yes, Jack,' she whispered, fresh tears filling her eyes, happier ones at the thought of their future of endless possibilities. 'I'll marry you.'

Fifteen

Lottie carefully placed a sticky label on the centre of a jar and pressed it down. With market day fast approaching, she'd dropped by after work to give her mum a hand finishing off some of the packaging for her herbal teas. The vast array of different teas always amazed her. The packaging also set her mother's handmade teas apart. She made designer test tube–type sample teas as well as glass jars in a variety of sizes and beautifully presented gift and pamper packs. Her attention to detail made the whole display a gorgeous feast not only for the eyes but the other senses too, the fragrance of so many ingredients filled her mother's mixing room, it was almost like stepping into a warm, loving hug.

Her mother's work room had once been an old stable, and its stone walls were over a hundred years old. She'd converted it, as well as a number of the other outbuildings that had come with the property, restoring them and turning them into functional spaces—accommodation, work rooms and yoga studios. This was Lottie's favourite, though; the whole front section of the building where once timber doors would have been had been replaced by large glass windows that allowed sunlight to seep into the room. On cold winter days, it created the perfect place to work in beautiful warmth, no matter how bitterly cold it was outside. Large timber tables ran down the length of the room, where her mother worked her magic and packaged the teas she made, and shelves lined the walls, holding large bins of every imaginable herb, flower and essence necessary to create her tea orders each week.

'Are you going to tell me who this mystery man you've been seeing is?' Hannah asked, breaking the companionable silence.

'What man?' Lottie asked, trying for an innocent tone. She should have known word would have already spread, yet it still amazed her the speed at which gossip always travelled in town.

'The one you were spotted on a date with, and then again on the back of a motorbike heading out of town,' her mother continued serenely.

'I was *not* on a date with him,' Lottie retorted. 'He's the guest of honour for the festival. I was being hospitable.'

'And the bike ride? Was that just being friendly too?'

'He wanted to see Frolesworthy. I played local tour guide.'

'Hmm,' her mother said as she carefully measured out some beautiful blue dried leaves and scattered them into a bowl. 'Careful. It almost sounds like you enjoyed yourself.'

'Now you sound like Cher,' Lottie said, trying not to show she was discomfited by her mum's teasing.

'Well? Are you going to tell me about him?'

'There's nothing to tell. He's a history professor. He's here early to do some research for his new book. He's . . . nice.'

'Nice?'

'Oh, for goodness' sake, not you too,' Lottie muttered under her breath. 'He's very interesting and good-looking and I like spending time with him.'

'So . . . you're seeing him?'

'It's not like that,' Lottie said, absent-mindedly running her finger across the timber tabletop. 'He's interested in my research for the book, and I said I'd help him with his.'

'Well, that sounds promising.'

'I wouldn't read too much into it,' Lottie said.

'It's good to be cautious,' her mother replied like she'd agreed with her, and for a moment, Cher's words came back. Had her mother's attitude to love somehow influenced her? She'd never thought so. Lottie had nothing against falling in love and getting married . . . she just hadn't ever found the man she wanted to do that with. *Hadn't found? Or haven't allowed yourself?* a little voice that sounded suspiciously like Cher seemed to ask. The question gave her pause.

'Have you been seeing anyone lately?' she asked now.

Her mother blinked in surprise. 'What a strange question.'

'Why? You're still young. You're attractive, independent and own your own business. Surely you get lonely, Mum?'

'I'm too busy to get lonely.'

'I don't believe that.'

'Why on earth would I want to get mixed up in a relationship at my age?'

'You're hardly over the hill.' It was true that her mother had just turned sixty, but no one ever believed it. She barely looked to be in her fifties. She had flawless skin and the grace of a ballerina, long legs and even though she'd let her hair go grey, it was dark grey and had natural highlights which, instead of making her look older, only added to her beauty. Lottie often wished she had got her mother's height, grace or complexion.

'I'm old enough to know I don't want to mess up my life by adding a man to it.'

'Don't you want companionship? Someone to grow old with?'

'I have plenty of company. I also have male friends I can call when the urge arises—I'm a big believer in a healthy sex life, darling. Just don't confuse great sex with the need to make it a long-term commitment. The two can be vastly different things.'

Lottie tried not to wince. Her mother had never been one to sugar-coat the truth, and sex had always been an open conversation—mainly, Lottie suspected, because her mother hadn't wanted Lottie making the same mistake she'd made.

And she was glad her mother seemed to be still active in that department, but the fact she was so adamant about being alone somehow made Lottie feel sad.

'Well, this isn't either,' Lottie said.

'What's this professor of yours researching?' her mother asked, and Lottie was glad for the change of subject.

'He's writing about the gold rush era and the Compton gold mine. Did you know that Alexander Compton's wife just vanished off the face of the earth?'

'No, can't say I did.'

'Damian's trying to figure out what happened to her. You should see all the research material he's been going through searching for clues. It's really interesting.'

'Sounds like quite the mystery. How strange that it's not more widely known. I don't think I even know that much about Alexander and his gold mine either. Clearly the Jack McNally legend was far more interesting at the time.'

Lottie made a low sound of agreement. 'How are the new blends going online?' she asked, picking up a label that read *Just Act Natural*, with chamomile to help you unwind when you've become overstimulated. She chuckled before picking up the others to examine. Menopause tea called *Night Sweats and Rage*. *Partied Too Hard*, a pick-me-up tea. *Ain't Got Time for a Cold*, immunity boosting tea. *Morning Woodstock*, for men.

'Selling like hotcakes,' her mother said happily. 'Online and in the cafe orders too.'

'That's really awesome, Mum. I'm so proud of you, making all this such a success.'

'Do what you're put here to do and you can't go wrong,' she said, lifting her gaze from her blending to smile.

Who knew that a once hard-partying, carefree-drinking woman would end up wearing an organic hemp ensemble, creating natural medicines and teas and raking in a fortune? Her mother was a certified, born-again hippie, if that was a term. Complete with her philosophies on natural herbs that she used to make special bespoke teas, using a variety of not-so-legal, organically grown herbs, that her clients swore by for pain relief. Lottie had given up trying to warn her mother of the consequences should her *special* blend ever get brought into the public eye, but her mother stubbornly refused to let something as annoying as the law interfere with what nature had provided. Thankfully, that particular tea wasn't going to make an appearance at the market.

Lottie had just arrived home and taken the samples her mother had given her to the kitchen when there was a knock on her front door. Turning on the outside light, she opened the door and felt a pang of surprise leap in her chest.

'Hi,' Damian said. 'I hope it isn't too late to come around. I didn't get into the shop this afternoon and I wanted to see you.' His words seemed to rush out and he looked uncertain.

'No, it's fine. I just got home from my mum's. Do you want to come in?'

'Thanks. If you're sure I'm not interrupting anything?'

'Nope. I was just about to put the jug on and try out a new tea blend my mother gave me. Would you like to join me?'

'Uh, sure. Tea?' he asked.

'My mum makes herbal teas.'

'Oh. Nice.'

Lottie led him into the kitchen, her gaze stealthily darting around the room, checking it was tidy enough for unexpected company. He took a seat at her kitchen bench and shrugged off his bike jacket. She tried her best not to stare at the way his shoulders and torso moved as he twisted then straightened but swore slightly when the jug overfilled in the sink, splashing her hand.

'What kind of tea are we sampling?'

'Well, there's a sleepy one.' She held the packet up for him to inspect.

He chuckled. '"Sleepy AF?" Really?'

'Yeah, my mother puts her own spin on her marketing.'

'I like it.' He nodded appreciatively.

'Or, if sleep isn't your thing, there's one for studying.'

'"Dude, Focus!"' He grinned. 'I like your mum's style.'

'Yeah, she's hilarious,' Lottie drawled, but smiled. She kind of was.

'Think I'll go with the focus. I have to ride the bike home, so being Sleepy AF might not be a great idea.'

'Good point,' she nodded, selecting the tea and bringing out two one-cup glass teapots. When she finished making their tea—she chose the sleepy one, knowing if she tried the other, she'd be awake for the rest of the night—she placed the cups on a tray. 'Let's go to the comfy chairs,' she suggested, leading the way out to the lounge room, Damian following close behind.

'How's the research going?' she asked, turning slightly to face him once they were seated on the soft sofa.

'Not bad. I took a ride into Armidale, to the university. I've got an old mate who teaches there,' he said, reaching for his cup from the coffee table. 'I've got him looking for any mentions of Catherine in his research material.'

'Nice,' she said, sipping her own tea, relieved to discover it tasted rather lovely, with a soothing mix of lemongrass, lavender and a few other things she couldn't quite name.

'I also met Daphney. She caught me on the way out this afternoon, so I didn't get to talk for long. She's quite the taskmaster.'

'Yes, she's the kingpin,' Lottie said, biting back a smile. 'I didn't think it would take long before she heard you were in town.'

'She seemed a bit put out that I was here early.'

'How dare you arrange something on your own without committee approval,' she said mockingly.

'That's pretty much the impression I got.'

'Well, I expect a summons to an emergency meeting any minute now,' Lottie said seriously. 'Prepare to be wined and dined.'

'This was why I wanted to come early without anyone knowing.'

'She'll be too busy to bother you that much,' Lottie said reassuringly. 'The festival is way too close for her schedule to have many times open for unexpected entertaining.'

'I hope so. I've got too much work to do.'

'Maybe we need to take our research sessions at the shop more seriously. No more make-out sessions,' she said teasingly, casting her eyes down as she sipped her tea.

He didn't reply, and Lottie felt a flash of panic. *Why would you try to be cute?*

She heard him set his cup down on the coffee table and slowly lifted her eyes to find him watching her. Her heart was pounding hard against her chest and she found herself trapped in his heated gaze as he slowly leaned towards her until there was barely a hair's breadth between them.

'I don't think so.' His lips were strong and warm against her own, and his hands felt enormous as they slipped around her waist and pulled her gently closer.

God, he smelled divine—a mix of something sweet, yet smoky, masculine and salty and altogether way too intoxicating. Lottie couldn't believe a kiss could make her head feel so light and her body as though it were on fire. Maybe her mother had snuck some special herbs into the tea?

The kiss deepened, and Lottie found her hands were pulling his head even closer. She couldn't get enough of this man. Even though they were practically glued against each other, it still wasn't close enough—not nearly enough. She needed *more* . . .

This is crazy.

Sixteen

Damian pulled her small frame against his own and almost groaned at the way she melted into him, a perfect fit.

He had just wanted to see her. He swore to himself when he'd pulled up that he hadn't come here tonight to make a move. He'd wanted to take things slowly, enjoy the intellectual stimulation of her incredible mind as well as the physical intimacy of her incredible body. He'd felt a little like he was losing his grip on his sanity, and he hoped that the long ride to Armidale and back that day would help him cool his heels, and other parts.

The notion seemed laughable now. The first chance he'd got, he'd swept her up in his arms . . . although it hadn't been all him. She'd teased him, invited him to respond, and the way she was kissing him back, she clearly wanted this as much as he did.

Her thin, long-sleeved shirt lovingly hugged the outline of her breasts, dipping just slightly to allow him a glimpse of the cleavage that had been driving him insane for the past few days. Now he could feel her softness pressed against his chest and his fingers itched to undress her and taste that delicate skin beneath her earlobe that had driven him to distraction. His heart gave a small lurch as he felt her fingers slip under the hem of his shirt and he held himself still, not wanting to make a wrong move. His patience paid off as he felt her hands slowly, almost hesitantly, glide upwards, and he let out a shaky breath against her mouth.

Removing one hand, she found his and placed it on the bottom of her own shirt. He didn't need any further encouragement. His hands gently traced the soft skin of her torso and up to her rib cage. With a small, frustrated sound, Lottie eased back and removed her top before helping him discard his own, leaning forward to claim his lips once more, the kiss becoming even more fevered.

His hands fumbled and he found himself swearing silently. Why did he suddenly feel like a kid in his first make-out session? He was a reasonably apt lover—or so he thought, he'd never had any complaints—yet right now, he felt about as suave as a bull in a china shop. *Get it together, man.*

She moved, sliding onto his lap, and all previous concerns abruptly ceased as instinct took control. He felt the warmth of her against him and something almost primal replaced his insecurities, leaving nothing but the need to feel her skin against his, her body under his own.

Lottie lay quietly as she listened to their breathing slow back to a normal level and stared at the ceiling, her hand still interlinked with one of his, resting on the pillow above her head.

She opened her mouth but closed it again without saying anything. What was she supposed to say? Everything that came to mind just sounded . . . stupid. How did she express what just happened without making it sound cliché or cheap? Because it was neither. It had been . . .

'Wow,' Damian breathed.

She let out a small breath and felt a smile touch her lips. *Thank goodness.* 'Yeah. That was . . . unexpected.'

'It was. But I'm not sorry.'

'Me either,' she said, biting her lip before forcing herself to turn her head and look at him. Why she was suddenly crippled with shyness, she had no idea. When it had been happening, it felt as natural and right as though they'd been lovers forever, but now, with reality seeping back in, the truth came with it: they were basically strangers. Sure, they'd shared some stories and some kisses, but she didn't really *know* him.

She let her gaze run across his broad cheeks and high forehead, soaking in the features her fingertips had traced only moments earlier. He rolled his head sideways to face her, and her heart skipped at the intense way his eyes probed hers. She remembered that look—the way he'd stared into her as he took her breath away so gently and yet with a powerful, aching longing. She swallowed hard. There had been a connection, something she'd never felt before with anyone else. This had been more than some pleasant way to pass the end of an evening. It had been so much *more*.

There was something, even now, a potent kind of feeling, something she couldn't put into words but that somehow didn't *need* words. It was as though their eyes were simply saying what neither of them seemed able to articulate with words and somewhere inside, she understood everything he was saying. It seemed corny and ridiculous even as she thought it, yet she couldn't dismiss the rightness of the whole, weird, situation.

Her phone dinging broke whatever had been holding them in their little cocoon. Another ding from his phone quickly followed.

'That's weird timing,' he said, seemingly reluctant to release her hand when she made to sit up.

Reaching for her shirt, she quickly pulled it on to cover her nakedness before picking up her phone. 'It's from Daphney,' she said drolly.

'Mine too,' he said slowly. 'Looks like your dinner invitation prediction was spot on.'

'Yep. It's started.' The call-out to a hastily arranged early welcome dinner for their guest of honour had been set for tomorrow night.

'Do we have to go?' he groaned. 'Can't we just stay in bed for the rest of the week?' He wiggled his eyebrows suggestively.

Tempting . . . 'Trust me, you do not want to say no to Daphney. Probably best to get it over and done with.'

'Great,' he said, sounding less than excited at the prospect. 'At least you'll be there. That'll make it tolerable.'

'You'll do fine,' she said, suppressing a grimace. Soon, Damian would no longer just be the handsome stranger who'd arrived in town to do some research; he'd be the festival's main person of interest and everyone would want a piece of him. And Lottie wasn't sure she was ready to share.

The pub was busier than usual. A man in a big black Akubra was sitting on a stool in the corner of the room, playing some upbeat country music on a guitar to a number of very loud country music fans and it was also meat raffle night.

Lottie made her way towards the meeting room that had been decorated as a private dining room for the evening in honour of their guest.

Her gaze fell on the far end of the room, where Damian stood, drink in hand, wearing a pair of jeans and a blazer. Maybe it was just the absence of his usual bike boots and T-shirt, but there was definitely something a little more professorial about him tonight. Not that she was complaining—he wasn't any less attractive in a suit jacket than a leather one. He was listening carefully to whatever Terry and Shorty were discussing—more than likely the weekend's footy results, or quite possibly their racehorse they part-owned and were very proud of.

Damian caught her eye, sending her a smile while appearing to continue to listen avidly to Shorty, who seemed to be imitating a jockey triumphantly riding a horse across the finish line. At least, she hoped that was what they were talking about.

'What do you think of our guest?' Janelle asked, coming to stand beside Lottie where she'd taken up position beside the plate of cheese and biscuits on a small side table.

'He seems . . . nice,' Lottie said awkwardly. It was sowing season, and it seemed the ladies from the farms were a bit behind on the local gossip about her and Damian. *What a relief.*

'He's a bit of all right, if you ask me,' she said appreciatively, reaching across a stunned Lottie to scoop up a large dollop of dip on a round cracker before shoving the whole thing in her mouth. She chewed thoughtfully. 'I was a bit disappointed when Daphney said we could only find a university teacher instead of a celebrity, but she didn't mention he looked like *that*.'

'I think he's a professor, actually,' Lottie said, trying to soften the blunt comment.

'He's yummy is what he is,' Janelle continued unperturbed.

Lottie couldn't disagree but it felt completely wrong for Janelle McTaggert to have noticed too.

'I take it we're talking about our man of the hour?' Christine said, joining them.

Damian seemed to have inspired the women of the committee to forget their earlier disappointment in not finding a celebrity as guest of honour.

'You think he's single?' Janelle asked, seemingly sizing Damian up like a piece of prime sirloin steak.

'You're a happily married woman, Janelle,' Christine pointed out.

'And I have an exceptional eye for a stud,' Janelle shot back bluntly.

'Looking like that?' Carol put in, cutting in front of the small group to load up a biscuit with soft cheese. 'Doesn't matter, I reckon he's most likely gay.'

Lottie coughed into her wine, feeling increasingly trapped in this conversation.

'Well, I think he looks quite distinguished,' Solene said when the others had wandered away from the table. 'Exactly what our festival needs.' She picked out a few nuts from the platter. Draped in a long, loose-fitting dress with flowing bell sleeves, Solene looked as ethereal and graceful as usual. Lottie often envied her style. She was always clothed in something that made her look like a fairy or some other dainty mythical creature. On most people, it would look like they were trying too hard to play dress-ups, but on Solene, it just looked natural.

'I think so too,' Lottie agreed.

Solene offered her a sly smile. 'A little birdie told me the two of you have been spending a lot of time together recently,' she said quietly.

'Oh really?' Lottie replied. 'I didn't think you listened to gossip.'

'I don't *partake* in gossip,' Solene corrected. 'It's just impossible not to listen to it in this town. And Judy from the bakery tends to be right.'

'True,' Lottie conceded with a small smile. 'And this time, the gossip would be correct, I guess. But I'm just helping out with some research.'

'Is that what they're calling it these days?' Solene murmured, selecting a dried apricot from another plate. 'I say good for you.'

Lottie noticed Damian had moved on and was with Corbin, who was talking animatedly, and Elijah. Damian was listening intently, and seemed to be asking incisive questions, if the look of delight from Corbin was anything to go by.

Lottie found his curiosity, and his patient listening, endearing. Maybe it was something to do with his passion for research and desire to learn. Curiosity seemed to be part of his nature. Whatever it was, he clearly had the ability to make people feel special when they spoke, an admirable quality. *His students must love him.*

Finally, he broke away and headed for the table of food.

'You seem to be a big hit,' she said, watching with slight amusement as he made a small noise in his throat, scooped up a square-shaped quiche and ate it in one mouthful.

'I feel like I'm under a microscope or something, with everyone looking at me. It's not my favourite thing.'

'You're the guest of honour.'

'It feels like a lot of attention for a boring old professor,' he said, shooting her a smile.

'There's been a lot of interesting topics covered, though. I've actually seen Elijah's work in a gallery. He's pretty famous, did you know? And—Corbin? I think his name was?' he asked tentatively, before continuing when she nodded. 'Did you know he's won the Chelsea Flower Show? That's huge! And they live here, in Banalla.'

'I know,' she said smiling. 'He's always travelling away for work. His client list is insane. But he wanted a quieter life for his kids, so he's willing to do the travel and commute. Although I suspect, going by the impressive property he owns, he does a lot more overseeing than actual labouring nowadays.'

'Every time I think I can't be more impressed by this town, it surprises me again.'

'It's the location,' she said with a shrug. 'It's central to a lot of bigger regional places and has great access to airports. Heaps of people still work in the bigger cities and come home on weekends.'

'I'm starting to consider the idea of moving here myself.'

'Really?' she asked, startled.

'Well, I mean, potentially . . . It was just something I was tossing about in my head a few days ago.'

Move here? She was so caught off guard that she couldn't quite process her reaction to the news before they heard a cheerful shriek of 'There you are!' as Daphney approached.

'Dinner is ready and as our guest of honour, you need to be at the head of the table,' Daphney said, linking her arm through Damian's and almost frogmarching him to one of the two seats positioned at the end of the long table. Her royal highness took the other for herself.

'Don't let her muscle in on your man,' Cher murmured in Lottie's ear, making her jump.

'Stop it,' she replied with forced calm. 'He's *not* my man.'

'Well, he's *certainly* not *hers*,' Cher added pointedly.

'Let's try to not make a scene and just get through the evening,' Lottie said, selecting a chair further down the table.

She caught Damian's eye, which held not an altogether small amount of fear, and sent him a sympathetic smile. They'd discussed her desire to try to keep whatever this thing was between them as private as was possible in a town this size. She really didn't want to make a big deal about it in front of her business neighbours. When he left town after the festival, the gossip wouldn't necessarily end—there'd always be the questions hanging over her head: *So what's happening with the professor? Are you two still seeing each other?* She could hear them already, and she gritted her teeth tightly.

But he might stay, came the tiny reminder, and she felt the stirring of hope briefly before she shook it away. He was probably letting the idea run wild while he was here. Once he returned to the city and his old life, he'd realise living in a small town like theirs was very different from city life. For so many people, the peace and quiet was nice, but only for a limited time. No, it was best not to hold on to that. This was just a bit of a fling—something unexpected and fun while it lasted. And she most definitely *did not* want the whole town getting any funny ideas about a relationship. *No thank you very much.*

Seventeen

The evening flowed along with the wine and conversation. Damian loved talking about history—it was his life—but he was a little self-conscious when it came to talking about it in a social setting. A girlfriend had once mentioned she didn't like standing around while he gave another dull lecture, and while he'd thought the comment unfair, it had stayed with him. He now often found himself trying to gauge if he might be boring the company around him, and it was no burden to ask about their lives and interests. Everyone in Banalla seemed to have an interesting story.

During the main meal, he'd taken a moment to think back on the comment he'd made to Lottie about moving to Banalla. He'd noted her surprised expression and wasn't sure if she was horrified or delighted. After hearing how so many others had successfully tree changed, he'd started to realise just how feasible moving could be. Maybe some part of him also wanted to test the waters and see what Lottie would say . . . not that he had really got an answer. He couldn't stop looking at her, sitting down the table and patiently listening to the middle-aged woman flashing up pictures of her grandchildren. He was curious to bring the subject up with her again.

'Oh, Terry, I'm sure Damian isn't that interested in horseracing,' Daphney said, breaking into the story the other man had been telling over the remains of the main course. Actually, Damian had been very interested, but the formidable woman turned to him and asked, 'Tell me, how are you finding Banalla?', effectively shutting down the previous conversation.

'It's really surprised me how much there is in such a small town,' he replied. 'I'm enjoying my time here quite a lot.'

'Have you tried the beer up at the top end of town?' Shorty asked. 'I had me doubts about this new-fangled *boo-tique* stuff they were makin' up there but, I tell ya, it's not too bad at all.' He nodded, looking as though he was surprised he was admitting it out loud.

'No, I haven't gotten there yet,' Damian said. He was about to ask more about it when Daphney cut in once more.

'I'll have to get you out to Glenmore Station. We open the gardens up to the public once a year and raise money for the local emergency services. My high tea is *quite* sought after,' she added pretentiously. He caught Shorty and Terry rolling their eyes at each other from across the table. Mr Hindmarsh sat beside Daphney, on his third glass of scotch from what Damian had counted, deaf as a post and seemingly happy to not have to participate.

Damian was a little disappointed that he hadn't managed to spend time with Lottie other than their brief conversation earlier. Daphney inserting herself into every conversation was getting a little irritating, and the constant touching of his arm every few minutes—each time lingering just a little longer—was increasingly annoying. He'd caught Lottie's gaze on her hand earlier and managed to shift in his seat and withdraw his arm, but it had only lasted a few moments before Daphney had somehow managed to orchestrate another excuse to touch him.

He was conscious of the need to be polite and accessible since the committee was hosting him at the festival, and he felt obliged to not rock the proverbial boat, but the woman didn't seem to understand the concept of personal space.

'I think you've hogged our guest of honour long enough, Daphney,' Cher said, appearing beside him. Never before had he been so happy to see a pink-haired woman in a vintage-looking poodle skirt and tight-fitting cardigan.

'Come on, professor, all the cool kids are down this end of the table,' she added with a wink, leaving Daphney gaping like a disgruntled fish.

'I thought you might need rescuing,' Cher said in a low voice as they moved down the table. He didn't have time to reply before she was announcing, 'Right, you lot. Here's your chance to grill the professor over dessert.'

His seat was conveniently located between Lottie and Tori, a cheerful, round-faced young woman who looked to be in her late twenties. The conversation flowed freely and, despite Cher's open invitation to grill him, the topic soon turned to what had drawn everyone to Banalla.

'For us, it was simply getting out into the fresh air and having so much abundance. The produce for the cafe is all sourced locally, we grow a lot of our own ingredients,' Tori said, grinning as she squeezed Skye's hand. 'We went from a two-hour commute to a zero one, living above the shop.'

'What about you ladies?' Damian asked the three older women across the table. He'd been introduced to them earlier—Carol, Janelle and . . . Christie? No, Christ*ine*.

'We're all born and bred right here in Banalla,' Carol replied, glancing at Janelle beside her.

'And you've been here all your lives?' he asked.

'Yep. I married my boyfriend from high school. His family are farmers, so there wasn't really ever a question of moving away.'

'We're all farmers' wives,' Christine put in.

'I moved away for a few years, but I ended up coming back,' Janelle offered. 'There's something nice about having your kids and grandkids going to the same school you went to.'

Damian envied that. Maybe it was the historian in him once more coming out, but that continuity, the tangible connection to your past . . . he liked that idea. As a kid, his family had moved around quite a bit, so he didn't have any kind of link to a particular town, just the odd memory of certain points in his life connected vaguely to places he could sort of remember. Nothing like a local with generational ties would have to a place like Banalla.

'How's the research going?' Cher asked as she scooped a bite of cheesecake into her mouth.

'What are you researching?' Terry asked, drawing up a spare chair to join them.

'My next book is covering the gold rush era. Part of it is about Alexander Compton and his gold mine.'

'I reckon there'd still be some gold left in that mine,' Terry said.

'It caved in, though, a long while back. It'd take a big operation to come in and clear it up,' Janelle put in.

'I've still got to get that family tree stuff to you,' Cher remembered, looking up. 'There's quite a bit about Kate O'Ryan and her life that might interest you.'

'I look forward to seeing it.' Kate O'Ryan, nee McNally, had led a colourful life and he was genuinely interested in looking at anything that might relate to her.

Once dessert was done, Daphney once again took the reins and talk was centred firmly around the festival. Damian was impressed by the list of events the day would be holding, especially the re-enactment they had planned. He raised an eyebrow slightly at the cabaret show based on the life of Kate O'Ryan and he thought he heard Daphney's voice stiffen when she read that bit aloud. If the smirk on Cher's face was anything to go by, there was clearly a story behind that.

Finally, the evening came to an end and he made his goodbyes as everyone left. He was waylaid for ten minutes by Daphney before he managed to escape.

Taking out his phone, he saw a text message from Lottie.

> Lottie: Night cap and debrief?
>
> Damian: Always happy to debrief with you 😉
>
> Lottie: 😳

He grinned as he put his phone back in his pocket and headed up the hill.

'Cher said she was coming around later to drop off that stuff she mentioned last night,' Lottie informed him the next morning as they drank coffee at her breakfast bar.

Damian frowned, trying to recall what stuff Cher might be referring to. A lot of people had told him a lot of information last night, and then he'd been preoccupied by less intellectual pursuits.

'It's probably the research on Kate O'Ryan,' Lottie supplied. 'She's very proud of her heritage. I know it probably has nothing to do with what you're researching, but I think she's looking forward to showing you. I hope you don't mind.'

'No, of course not. I think it's great she's so into her family history—and a pretty cool one at that. I know lots of people who'd like to be able to trace their ancestry back to an infamous bushranger family.' The fact there were so many locals in this town who could do just that still amazed him.

'It *is* pretty cool,' Lottie agreed.

'Do you think she'll work out I stayed here last night? Will that be a problem for you?' He knew she wasn't keen on making this thing public—which didn't bother him one way or the other, but had people known they were an item then maybe he wouldn't have had to fend off Daphney all night.

'I actually sent her a text this morning,' she said looking sheepish. 'She's my best friend, so I felt like I had to tell her anyway. I don't mind if she knows.'

Cher soon arrived in a flurry of chiffon, placing her sparkling, bejewelled hands with the terrifying-looking talons on either side of his face and planting a loud kiss on his cheek. 'Congratulations on baggin' my girl, you sexy stud, you.' She chortled and then leaned back to level a serious stare at him. 'But if you break her heart—they'll never find your body.'

Damian gave a weak laugh, deciding he wasn't entirely sure if the woman was joking or not. Before he could reach a decision, she let his face go and picked up the long cardboard cylinder she'd brought with her, wasting no time unfurling a large piece of paper from inside it onto the kitchen table 'Well, here it is,' she said, shaking her head slowly as she stared down at it. 'I'm not sure if it's anything useful, but two of my aunties dedicated a lot of their time to putting together the family tree, going back to Kate and Jack's time and beyond, all the way to Ireland. Blows my mind every time I see it.'

Sure enough, there were boxes of names neatly branching off from a very long line of names with dates that seemed far too long ago.

Damian surveyed the intricate document with no small degree of awe. 'This took a lot of dedication,' he said.

'Apparently it took them years to complete,' Cher agreed, before pointing to one of the lines. 'That's my great-great-great-etcetera-grandfather, Finnegan O'Ryan, one of Kate's eleven children.'

'Can you imagine having that many kids?' Lottie said, shaking her head.

'God no,' Damian said. 'There were four of us and that was enough bedlam growing up.'

'And apparently, they lived in some cramped one-roomed bark hut. I remember my mum complaining about our house being too small once, and Dad telling her that if Kate could bring up a family living in a hut with a dirt floor, then she should be grateful for the house she had. Funnily enough, Mum ended up leaving him for a bloke who was a millionaire and lived on the Gold Coast in a two-storey mansion on a lagoon,' she said dryly. 'Apparently, size *does* matter in certain areas.'

Damian deliberately kept his eyes on the family tree, he wasn't about to weigh in on that discussion.

'Would it be okay if I take photos of this to keep in my files?' Damian asked.

'Knock yourself out, handsome.'

Damian lined up the shot before he zoomed in and took a series of closer photos. Maybe he'd one day write a book featuring all the families of famous bushrangers. They were often overlooked in the history books—siblings, cousins, aunts and uncles who were accomplices and abettors, as well as active members of the gangs who never managed to attain the celebrity status of their relatives. The notion began to form, and he tucked it away to make notes about later.

'Thank you, I appreciate you taking the time,' Damian said.

'Not a problem. Any opportunity to watch a professional at work,' Cher said, wiggling her eyebrows suggestively. 'So, what did you think of the get-together last night?'

'It was great to meet everyone. It seems like a very dedicated team.'

'Daphney certainly enjoyed herself. She was practically preening for most of the night.'

Damian suppressed a snort. 'She, uh, certainly seems like a bit of a force to be reckoned with,' he said, trying to stay neutral.

'She means well. The committee really has achieved a lot. She was the driving force behind its revival a number of years back,' Lottie argued, clearly looking to be fair. Damian had noticed she did that quite often, trying to see the good in everything and everyone. He liked it a lot.

'Yes, well she doesn't have to be the centre of attention all the time,' Cher said, sounding somewhat disgruntled.

Damian had realised last night there was no great love lost between the two, and he could imagine the conflicts they'd undoubtedly had over the years. He also knew enough from the few times he'd met Cher that she seemed to be a person who also liked the spotlight. Maybe that was the real issue.

'I think the festival's going to be fantastic,' he said diplomatically. 'You've all done a great job pulling it together.'

'Oh, while I think of it,' Cher said, reaching into her large handbag and withdrawing an envelope. 'Two tickets to the cabaret show. The *sold-out* one,' she added in a victorious tone.

There was no way he was asking what that was about. 'Thanks. I'm looking forward to it. Sounds like a lot of fun.'

'It's going to be a blast,' Cher assured him.

He caught Lottie's expression and wondered if he should be worried.

Later, as he headed back to his motel to change, he shook his head and laughed. Who would have thought that a stagecoach robbery would inspire a festival, complete with a cabaret show. He wondered what Jack would have had to say about it.

Eighteen

Lottie closed her eyes and paused in the doorway of her little shop, taking a moment to enjoy the stream of morning sunshine warming the crispness of the approaching winter air. It was still early but outside, the main street was beginning to bustle as people finished school drop-off and tourists woke up to start exploring.

A smile broke out on her lips as she spotted the now familiar figure walking towards her, carrying a paper bag from the bakery. Lottie's mouth watered in anticipation. Every time Damian turned up at her shop or the house, he came bearing sinful treats from the bakery, which was conveniently located along the walk from his motel.

'Judy said to say hi,' he said. He'd already managed to get to know almost as many people as she did.

He kissed her briefly, yet still with enough lazy passion to get her heart rate tripping over itself. 'I found something interesting,' he said as he pulled back, beckoning her to follow him.

Lottie turned away from the view and allowed him to lead the way into the office. It didn't matter that they'd spent every possible moment over the past ten days together, she still couldn't help the little bubble of excitement that tickled about inside her each time she looked at him.

'What is it?' Lottie asked, coming to stand next to the desk, where he put down the paper bag before extracting a yellow envelope folded lengthways from his back pocket.

'The curator from the National Trust, who are the custodians of Asply House in Essex, sent through everything she could find relating to Catherine from their collection of diaries and letters owned by Lady Agatha Asply, who was Catherine's closest childhood friend.'

'Oh, wow,' Lottie said, eager to see.

'There were two letters in particular that had something interesting. I had them printed out,' he said, handing her a page filled with beautifully written cursive.

Lottie concentrated hard on the words before her. It may as well have been in some foreign dialect, the terminology and the elegant, almost flamboyant, penmanship making for slow reading.

A few words did jump out at her, though—enough to make her take a seat and read the letter with more care.

'Look at this line in particular,' Damian said through a mouthful of vanilla slice, seemingly having no trouble deciphering the handwriting.

I shall miss you terribly, and I worry about you travelling such a long way in your delicate condition. I do wish you would have allowed me to go along as your companion.

Lottie looked up with a concerned frown. 'Catherine was pregnant?'

'Seems so.'

'How long did it take to come to Australia by ship in the 1800s?'

'About three or four months, depending on weather and the time of year.'

Lottie shook her head slightly. It never ceased to amaze her how brave women had to be back then. She couldn't imagine sailing off into the unknown, alone and pregnant.

'It's pretty much confirmed by this,' he said rifling through some more photocopies to place an excerpt of what looked like a diary page in front of her. 'This was from Agatha's diary, which is part of a display at the Asply estate.'

'I don't know how you can read their handwriting,' she said, shaking her head with a frown.

'Practice. You learn how to get the hang of it when you're looking for stuff.'

'You read it, I'll be here all day otherwise,' Lottie said, handing the paper back to him.

"'I shall miss my friend, enormously, however each day I am torn as to the promise I allowed Catherine to swear me to before she left and I fear that I may be contributing to her potential danger. Understandably, her family are against her decision to move to the colonies to be with her husband, as am I. I suspect her parents in particular had hoped that distance and time would end the notion.'"

'It seems it didn't,' Lottie said dryly.

"'At the time of embarking on her hideously long journey,'" Damian continued, "'Catherine took me into her confidence and shared the news that she was with child and had been hiding the fact for some four months. She feared telling her family as they would have tried to stop her from travelling, but ever headstrong, she refused to allow anything to stand in her way of reuniting with her husband. Now I wish I had told someone so as to have stopped her undertaking such a dangerous journey. She would never have forgiven me, of course, but should it have stopped a travesty, I would have gladly accepted my fate. Now, it is too late. If anything happens to her, I will hold myself completely to blame.'"

'Is there anything that mentions Catherine going missing? Poor Agatha, she was almost predicting bad news,' Lottie said shaking her head.

'Agatha died of tuberculosis only two months after Catherine left on the ship. But she was a remarkable young woman. She produced a number of beautiful artworks—watercolours and sketches. There's a couple of which I believe to be of Catherine herself.' He took out his phone and brought up a website of Asply House, which showed a long gallery wall full of stunning artwork. He paused on one portrait and handed his phone across to her. A beautiful young woman with blonde hair was shown sitting on a picnic rug beneath a leafy tree, her head tilted back and her eyes closed as though soaking up the sunlight that was so skilfully painted as filtering down through the leaves above her and glinting on a delicate gold chain she wore around her slender throat.

Damian instructed her to continue scrolling to another portrait of the same young woman, this one more formal but with much finer detail. Her blonde hair was scooped up in an elegant chignon that nestled into the curve of her graceful, swan-like neck, and her enormous blue eyes had been painted with such intricate and realistic detail it was as though she were looking into Lottie's very soul. Lottie noted she wore the same gold chain in this painting as well. It seemed an unusual piece of jewellery—in that it was so plain and simple for such an obviously wealthy young woman to be wearing in not one but *two* portraits.

'How old was Agatha when she died?' Lottie asked as she studied the beautiful paintings.

'She was twenty-four.'

Lottie felt a flash of sorrow. 'So young. What a terrible waste of a talent. So what happened to the baby? Did she make it to Australia before she was due?'

'There's no record of Catherine having a child,' he said, slumping down into a chair across from her. 'This is the first and only mention of the *possibility* that she was pregnant.'

'So we don't know for sure that she was?'

'Not officially, but I can't imagine Agatha would have been so concerned about her friend if it hadn't been true. And if we consider that she was four or so months along and the trip had lasted a little longer than four months by a handful of weeks, she would have been eight months, if not slightly more, by the time she arrived.'

'Talk about cutting it close.'

'Of course, there's the possibility that she may have lost the child at some point, although there was no mention of anything happening in the ship's log. It's not impossible that Catherine could have asked the ship's doctor not to make any notes if she were trying to keep the pregnancy a secret, I suppose,' he mused. 'It's all just a lot of guessing without any solid records, though.'

'How do historians ever manage to piece together history if it's so hard to find records for everything?'

'We do *a lot* of digging,' he said dryly.

Lottie gave him a wry smile. 'So Catherine disappears and she may or may not have had a child with her at the time?'

'Correct.'

'And there aren't any hospital records from back then?'

'Not many. But back in the early days, there was what's known as the Benevolent Asylum.'

'As in mental asylum?'

'Not in this case. This was originally set up to take care of the poor as well as the sick, and for women who found themselves pregnant and with nowhere else to go. It was a place of refuge.'

'Makes sense that Catherine might have ended up there if she were close to delivery when she got here. Although you wouldn't think that she'd need that kind of help, with a wealthy husband waiting for her.'

'Depends on the circumstances. We have no idea what happened to her after she arrived on that ship. But there are no records of her being admitted,' Damian said with a sigh. 'Then again, if she'd been in some sort of situation where maybe she wasn't able to tell anyone who she was, no one would have known.'

'Surely that would have been the first place her husband or the police would have checked when they realised she was missing?'

'I'd imagine so. It was a dead-end anyway, with no record of her ever admitted.'

'From Agatha's letters, it doesn't seem like the theory of her returning home would be logical. She was clearly in love, and Alexander was obviously crazy about her if he went to all the trouble to build his fortune and a house like Frolesworthy for her. So whatever happened must have been something against her will. Maybe she was involved in an accident?'

'It would seem there had to be something like that. But again, Alexander was a man of considerable wealth. He would have undoubtedly looked into any incidents of a woman killed or injured without an identity.'

'Maybe he was only looking for a woman who wasn't with child? What if he dismissed any Jane Does who'd been pregnant at the time? I mean, if he didn't know she was pregnant?'

'It's possible,' he agreed. 'There's nothing we have that suggests he knew about the baby, though that doesn't mean he didn't. She could have written to him and we just don't have the record of it.'

'How sad if he didn't know and she did die all alone in some tragic way,' Lottie said. The idea left her feeling completely gutted. Imagine having travelled all that way, so full of excitement for a future with her husband and child, only to die alone in a strange country, and not even be claimed.

Lottie saw Damian's face soften. He stood, tugging her gently to her feet and held her. 'We don't know anything for sure.'

'We know that she travelled all that way on a ship but never got to live in the beautiful home her husband built for her. She wasn't on the coach; she wasn't at his funeral. I think we both know something horrible had to have happened to her.'

'Most likely,' he said gently. 'But it was a very long time ago.'

'I know,' she said, feeling a rush of emotion. 'But it's still incredibly sad.'

He gave a sympathetic chuckle and pulled her tightly against him. 'You don't have to listen to me rambling on if it's too much.'

'You're not rambling on. I want to hear about everything you uncover. I'm invested in Catherine's story now. I need to find out what happened to her.'

He gave her a smile that crinkled the corners of his eyes. 'Then we'd better keep digging.'

Nineteen

'I swear to God, if I hear one more "just checking in" from Daphney, I'm going to Lose. My. Shit,' Cher ground out through tightly clenched teeth.

Lottie had barely seen her friend lately, between Cher overseeing her cabaret show rehearsals and Lottie spending so much time with Damian. They'd been summoned yet again to a meeting, hopefully for the last time, and the committee was currently inching its way through a final pre-festival agenda with agonising slowness.

'They've been pretty full on,' Lottie agreed.

'The woman is unhinged.'

'It'll be over soon and things will go back to normal,' Lottie offered soothingly. 'How are the rehearsals going?'

'Fabulous. I can't wait for you to see the show,' Cher said, instantly brightening. 'I've had some girls up from Melbourne for a full dress rehearsal on stage. It's going to be amazing. I'm thinking we'll maybe add a matinee,' she informed Lottie with the tiniest of malicious smiles, as she fastened her narrowed gaze under heavy, butterfly-like eyelashes on Daphney, who was deep in discussion at the other end of the table.

'Wow. That's great.' Daphney could say what she will about the show, but even she couldn't deny that Cher and her performers had a pull on an audience. The number of people her musical alone would bring in for the weekend was impressive. It was all great for the town and businesses.

However, right now, Lottie just wanted to be at home, in her comfy PJs, snuggling up on the lounge with Damian. It didn't seem to matter how much time they spent together, it was never enough. She missed him whenever they were apart and found herself counting down the hours till they were together again. Even more so when they were filled with these endless, pointless questions dragging out the already painful meeting. Lottie was struggling to keep her frustration under wraps.

'What's wrong with you tonight?' Cher asked as Lottie wriggled in her chair.

'Nothing. It's been a long day and I would rather be at home.'

'Rather be with a certain motorbike-riding history geek, more like it,' Cher murmured.

'I'm sorry, ladies, is there something you needed to share?' Daphney's clipped tone cut through the whispered conversation.

Feeling like a schoolkid caught in class for talking, Lottie resisted the urge to say, 'No, miss.'

'So it's okay with you both if I continue?' Daphney asked pointedly.

'Could we stop you even if we wanted to?' Cher asked under her breath.

It was close to nine o'clock when the meeting finally wrapped up. Lottie barely stopped to say goodnight to Cher as she dashed out the door. As she stepped outside, she felt her whole body light up as she spotted Damian waiting to walk her home.

This really wasn't like her at all, yet none of that mattered once they were together. The man was like a drug, and around him she didn't have or want any self-control.

And then it was Friday, the day before the festival, and Lottie had never seen the town so busy. She spent the day helping to set up at the showground, organising tent spaces and last-minute booking issues. Her mother had come in to look after the shop for her while she ran around doing committee work, then Lottie was going to help her set up her tea stall early the next morning, before the big day began.

Daphney had been on the radio, plugging the festival far and wide, and had even done a live TV appearance on the local news the evening before. There'd been flyers placed in all the surrounding towns and the event had been featured in a number of the area's tourism brochures. There was no excuse for anyone not to have seen *something* about it somewhere, and the early reports about crowd attendance were sounding positive.

All the accommodation in town had been booked out, and the towns within a fifty-kilometre radius had been pretty much booked out as well. Even the weather was playing nice. It was cool, but not freezing, and there was none of the initial rain that had been threatening to make an appearance on early forecasts.

That evening, the festival officially opened with an invite-only cocktail party. The mayor was there, and the entire council board—directors and councillors alike—drank and toasted and mingled with the festival committee, the town's business owners and various influential community members. Flitting about like she was born to host and hobnob was Daphney, who—as expected—outwardly looked like she had everything under control. It was only by the onslaught of last-minute emails, including some bearing time stamps of ungodly early hours, that Lottie knew Daphney must be functioning purely on caffeine and determination.

Lottie couldn't even get close to Damian, who was encircled by the mayor and his wife, Daphney and her husband and a number of other important officials. She would have been terrified, but he seemed to find chatting with the mayor about goodness-knows-what as easy as talking to Terry about horseracing. She had known this was part of his professional life as a lecturer and author but it was still odd to witness. For a moment, she tried to imagine herself in that world—talking to important intelligent people—and a flutter of uncertainty flitted through her. She wasn't a historian; she owned an antiques store in Banalla. What if she embarrassed him somehow, or simply didn't fit in?

You aren't even part of his life yet, a small voice of logic pointed out, which was enough to quash the slight anxiety attack that had been threatening. She took a gulp of wine to steady her nerves, wishing Cher was here.

The crowd quietened as Daphney, acting as MC of course, addressed the audience to introduce their 'very, *very* special guest speaker'.

Lottie tuned out, choosing instead to admire her view of that same speaker. He was dressed in a navy suit, white dress shirt and polished black shoes, looking well dressed and very sexy. And now, as he walked over to the podium to give his speech, Lottie was bursting with pride.

He spoke in such an engaging and entertaining way about his research, his books and, of course, Jack McNally, that the crowd seemed spellbound. Tomorrow, Lottie knew, he would give a speech prior to the re-enactment, but that would be more of an introduction to the event. She tuned back in to what he was saying.

'History, though, is often revisited when new evidence comes to light, and sometimes these details have the power to rewrite what we thought we knew. As historians, we often only have limited eyewitness accounts—if any—and so need to base our conclusions on the knowledge we already have of society at the time, the landscape and any evidence we may have discovered along the way. But we are always striving to ensure the truth comes to light, be that for better or worse. Sometimes, what we discover doesn't always sit well with current social norms, but we have to keep an unbiased view and remember that by uncovering the sometimes darker side of history we're able to give a voice to previously silenced or untold stories and to learn from them.'

Lottie knew he was talking about Catherine and her disappearance. They'd managed to uncover small hints, vague possibilities about what had happened—but nothing solid as yet. She understood his need to find out the truth about what happened to her. Finding out what had happened to Catherine would ultimately give her a voice, and rewrite a story.

Later that evening, Madame Dubois crackled with excitement. The bar was filled to capacity and the chatter vibrated like a loud engine. Banalla and its guests had turned out in spectacular form—everyone dressed to the nines—and everywhere she looked, from her front-row table with Damian, Lottie saw a sea of happy, smiling faces. Some people stood around chatting to old friends they hadn't seen in a long time, while others sat at long tables with friends and family. Everyone was embracing the start of the festival and celebrations.

Notably absent was Daphney, who had sent her apologies to be passed along to Cher. She simply had far too much to finalise before the festival's main day.

A loud chime sounded and the lights dimmed, announcing the commencement of the entertainment, and as people found their seats and conversations hushed an almost blinding spotlight lit up centre stage, exposing a curvaceous woman in a blood-red sequined dress, posing theatrically with one hand in the air and the other on her sumptuous hip.

'Good evening, beautiful people,' she announced in her deep, sexy drawl, 'and welcome to the highlight of the Banalla Festival. Tonight, you will be entertained and dazzled—entranced and seduced,' she cooed, lowering her tone and wiggling her eyebrows suggestively, 'by the talented beauties I've personally selected from the glitz and glamour of Melbourne—in the most stunning costumes ever seen outside a major theatre—to present to you an original production of the life and trials of our very own Kate O'Ryan!'

She glided off the stage and the red velvet curtain behind her lifted slowly.

'That was . . .' Damian paused, seemingly searching for words to describe what he'd just watched.

'Something.' Lottie grinned.

He chuckled. 'Definitely something,' he agreed. 'I'm trying to figure out which part I liked the most—the six-foot four drag queen with rugby player shoulders playing a prostitute called Daphney, or the chorus line performing the cancan as Kate O'Ryan's eff-you to the troopers.'

Lottie giggled. There'd certainly been something for everyone but, those bits aside, Cher had written some poignant monologues that were truly heartfelt and beautiful, depicting the struggles and discrimination suffered by pioneer women.

'I haven't laughed so much in ages,' Hannah said, coming up to the bar where they stood.

'There you are,' Lottie said, leaning in to kiss her mother's cheek. 'I was looking for you when we first came in.'

'I was running late, as usual,' her mother said flippantly, but her eyes had fixed upon the man at her daughter's side. 'You must be the guest of honour,' she said extending her hand gracefully. 'I'm Hannah, Lottie's mother.'

'It's nice to finally put a face to the name,' Damian said, taking her hand. 'I've heard a lot about you.'

'I hope it's all scandalous,' she said with a smile, glancing at her daughter briefly.

'Not at all. I've even sampled some of your tea. I'm a big fan.'

'Really?' Hannah replied, tilting her head like a small sparrow. 'Then I'll have to get you some of my special reserve stock to sample.'

'That sounds great.'

'Damian! There you are, great show, wasn't it?' Terry said, slapping Damian on the shoulder heartily. 'I'd like to introduce you to some people.' In Daphney's absence, Terry had apparently taken over as committee leader. 'You don't mind, ladies, do you?' Terry asked, already half turning away, his prize in tow.

'Not at all,' Lottie said, sending Damian a regretful look. But he was here as the guest of the festival, and Lottie knew she couldn't just keep him to herself, no matter how much she wanted to.

'You look happy,' Hannah said, sipping her water, having given alcohol away when she'd started on her health jaunt.

'I am. He's really nice.' Lottie watched Damian shake hands with people across the room and accept a beer handed to him.

'Hmm.'

Lottie sighed. 'Don't start, Mum.'

'I didn't say a word.'

'You don't have to.' She never did. The woman had a way of delivering a lecture with only a few well-placed sighs.

Her mother kissed her on the cheek and said goodbye, heading home to rest before the early start.

It was getting late and Lottie was tired, with no sign of Damian returning as Terry continued to introduce him to the crowd. There was no chatting to Cher either. She was busy with her Melbourne friends and the rest of the performers, although Lottie did get to kiss her cheek and briefly congratulate her.

Between the noise and the crush of the crowd, Lottie finally decided she'd had enough. She sent a text to Damian telling him she was going home and would see him later before leaving the din of competing conversations and loud music behind and heading up the hill to the blessed silence of home.

Lottie pulled on her warmest jumper and slid her feet into woollen socks and gumboots before shoving her arms into her favourite lined jacket and heading out to her car. She had some of the boxes for her mother's stall in the boot, as well as extra signage. Her headlights lit up the carpark at the showground, and she saw there were already many people bustling to and fro in the eerie shadows of the lights through a thick early-morning mist.

'Oh God, how cold is it,' Cher said in lieu of a greeting. 'This is insanely early.' She was dressed this morning in a grey jumpsuit, leather jacket and blonde hair tied back with a red bandana. She was the very image of the pin-up girl in the original WWII poster Lottie had on the wall of her shop.

Lottie shook her head in amazement. Even at this early hour of the morning, Cher's outfit and make-up were immaculate.

'At least, with all this fog about, it'll be a nice sunny day.' If not cold, she added silently.

Inside the large tent that had been erected as festival headquarters the day before, there was thankfully hot tea and coffee available, and Lottie gratefully held the takeaway cup between her freezing hands and blew on the hot contents.

As they worked on the final stages of setting up, the sun began to rise and the sound of birds high up in the tall trees surrounding the grounds began to welcome in the new morning, adding a backdrop to the noise of pegs being hammered in for stall tents and the murmuring of voices as they worked to unpack stock and displays. The tantalising smell of cooking bacon and sausages began to fill the air.

Needle in a Haystack

'Will all committee members please report to the festival headquarters tent immediately,' Daphney's voice screeched.

Beside her, Cher jumped. 'I swear, I'm going to stick that megaphone up Daphney's—'

'Here, have a lolly,' Lottie said, shoving an opened bag of sweets under her friend's nose. 'Keep your blood sugar levels up.'

'She's doing my head in, Lotts,' Cher snapped, taking a snake confection from the bag and biting its head off savagely. 'Marchin' around with that thing issuing orders like she's the Queen of bloody Sheba.'

'I know,' Lottie soothed. Boy, did she know. The woman should be running a dictatorship somewhere. It was going to be a miracle if a coup didn't end the festival before it even started.

Later in the morning, with clear skies overhead, Lottie straightened from unpacking the last of her mother's box of teas. She accepted a mug of hot coffee from her mother gratefully and took a long sip.

Across from them in the centre ring, the large draught horses for the show later in the morning were being led out from their stables and given some time to walk around and graze. Lottie had stopped by the previous day, the aroma of fresh straw on the ground and the pungent smell of horse, leather and feed hitting her full force. She'd been allowed to pat and feed the massive creatures some carrots. She'd always loved horses, but had never owned one of her own. She couldn't wait to see them in the re-enactment.

'It's looking great, Mum,' Lottie said as Hannah arranged the teas in their gorgeous packaging along the table. The rustic boho look set off the 'Made with Love' theme of her mother's teas to perfection. Alongside the tea sat a range of pottery mugs and teapots she'd sourced from local artists.

Around them, as far as Lottie could see, was an ocean of tents and people busy unpacking station wagons and small trucks. She could feel the atmosphere of good cheer and camaraderie—after all, this was a chance for local producers, crafters and artists to showcase themselves and their region. There was a great deal of pride among the different stallholders to stand in front of the products they'd poured their hearts and souls into, not to mention blood, sweat and tears in the case of the primary producers, who'd had a number of terrible seasons.

There was a happy excitement all around as the first early-bird arrivals started to filter in. This was it—this was what the last two years of planning had all been about.

It was Banalla's time to shine.

Twenty

It was Terry Fuller's job as announcer to man the loudspeaker, since he was also the president of the show committee and had years of experience on the microphone. Lottie was sure he'd missed his calling in life as a radio voice-over actor as he read out upcoming events and where they were being held across the various locations. The day had a show feel about it—music filled the air, crowds mingled and stopped to talk to neighbours they hadn't seen in a while. The amusement rides drew screams of delight as they moved with stomach-dropping motion overhead, and the jumping castle was a madhouse of ear-splitting excitement and chaos as children tired themselves out while under-caffeinated parents waited patiently.

Lottie was on a break and had stopped by her mother's stall to see how she was going when she spotted Damian standing nearby with another man. She hadn't known what time it had been when he'd finally gotten home the night before, and she'd left before he'd woken up this morning. It really did seem pointless that he should be keeping the motel room when he spent practically every spare minute at her house. She'd thought about bringing up the conversation of moving into her house, but somehow it had just never been the right time or something had interrupted the moment when she'd been about to.

Damian gave her a wide smile as they approached. 'There you are. I missed you this morning,' he said, kissing her briefly before turning back to the man beside him. 'This is Gordon Becker. He's come across from Armidale.' Lottie wasn't sure why she'd assumed he'd be around the same age as Damian, but this man looked a little older. Maybe it was his salt-and-pepper hair, cut short on top with shorter shaved edges around his ears, and his well-trimmed silver goatee.

'It's nice to meet you, Gordon,' Lottie said, smiling and reaching to take his outstretched hand.

'Same here, Lottie. I've heard a lot about you.'

Lottie's gaze swung across to Damian's in surprise.

'All good things,' he assured her.

'Oh, well, that's good. Are you enjoying the festival?' she asked.

'I am. It's a great turnout.'

Her mother finished serving a customer and Lottie turned and introduced her. 'This is my mother, Hannah, and this is her stall. Mum, this is Gordon Becker, a colleague of Damian's.'

'Yes, I've been waiting to say hello,' Gordon said smoothly. 'Damian's talked up your products and I came to see what all the hype was about.'

'Is that so?' Hannah asked, lifting an eyebrow. 'It's nice to meet you, Gordon,' she added.

'The pleasure's all mine,' he said, his smile stretching slowly as he held her mother's curious gaze.

'Are you a tea man, Mr Becker?'

'If I wasn't before, I'm seriously considering becoming one now.' He picked up one of the boxes and his lips quirked in amusement. 'I don't think I've tried anything like these though.'

'Maybe it's time to try something a little bit different?'

Lottie stared at her mother. Was that a note of flirtation she detected in her mother's tone? Surely not. She glanced quickly across at Gordon.

'Maybe it is.'

She sent a look over at Damian and he seemed to be just as bemused by the whole exchange as she was.

They watched as the two moved to the other end of the stall and Lottie stepped closer to Damian. 'What was *that* all about?'

'I believe we just witnessed the initial courtship dance of an older male attracting a female,' he said in an impressive David Attenborough imitation.

Lottie giggled. 'That's what I thought,' she said. 'Poor bloke,' she added shaking her head.

'Why? Your mum seems pretty into it.'

'He doesn't stand a chance.'

'Aww, come on, for an old guy, Gordon's in pretty good shape. I'd even go as far as saying he'd be a pretty good catch.'

Lottie gave a sympathetic smile. 'I know he's your friend, but my mother is not the courtship kind,' she said with a shrug.

'Don't rule Gordon out so fast. The guy's got game—look at him,' Damian said, nodding towards the pair.

If body language was anything to go by, he was right. They were both smiling rather coyly and leaning slightly in, even across the tables that separated them. There was definite chemistry going on there, but Lottie knew her mother's rule about men. They were okay to have fun with, as long as they remembered when it was time to go.

'Hmm, well, don't get your hopes up,' Lottie warned. 'Anyway, what have you been doing?'

'Mainly avoiding Daphney,' he said, glancing around quickly. 'She keeps roping me in to do stuff. Later on, I'm apparently the guest judge of the CWA bake-off. Not that I'm complaining about that one,' he admitted, 'but earlier, she had me weigh in on the advantages of artificial insemination in sheep while we were greeting all the stallholders in the livestock pavilion. What the hell would I know about getting sheep pregnant? I probably sounded like an idiot.'

Lottie gave a sympathetic chuckle and hugged his arm. 'I'm sure you didn't. Besides, most people around here know what Daphney's like. They'd understand your predicament.'

'Hey, I'm sorry about last night. I couldn't get away from Terry.'

'It's okay. He was taking his duties very seriously. Did you have fun?'

'It was a blur of faces and beer—way too much beer,' he added with a small wince. 'My head's a bit foggy this morning. I missed you.'

'I missed you too,' she said. 'But I thought you might need a sleep-in, so I didn't want to wake you before I left.'

'I've caught glimpses of you running around. They're keeping you pretty busy.'

'In the infamous words of Shorty Norton, I'm busier than a blue-arsed blowfly.' She grinned. 'Maybe we should just sneak off and hide somewhere for a while.'

'I like your way of thinking,' he said, snaking an arm around her waist and leaning down to kiss her. For the briefest of moments, she stiffened, remembering they were out in public, but then she allowed herself to ignore the uptight warnings in her head. So what if people saw her kissing the guest speaker? This was just the local antiques dealer making out with the non-famous back-up guest they'd found to fill the festival position. *Nothing to see here.*

A screech came over the loudspeakers, causing them to pull away and cringe as a raspy voice declared with a slight slur, 'Welcome to Banalla. I'm Dougie Walters and I'm going to be your announcer for the day.'

Dougie Walters? Lottie frowned. What was *he* doing on there?

'Let's kick things off with a little limerick I wrote called "Mary McTrunt",' he continued.

Oh no.

'Sorry, I have to go,' she said, planting a kiss on his lips before turning to rush towards the announcer's box, where she found Daphney pounding on the door and making a series of unladylike, rather violent threats against the man inside.

'He's ruining everything!' Daphney yelled, turning to face the small circle of volunteers now gathered. 'Someone get that lunatic out of there!'

Through the glass windows at the front of the announcement box, they could see Dougie sitting, proud as punch, enjoying his moment of glory.

'He's locked himself in there and no one can find the spare set of keys.'

Cher came forward and pushed Daphney aside with a flick of her hip. 'Step aside, Daph. Let me handle it,' she said before knocking on the door and softening her tone. 'Dougie, it's me. Open the door, honey.'

The man's eyes lit up. 'Look who's here. My next guest has arrived. The lovely Cher.' The speakers echoed across the showground. 'Just in time, too. I wrote a poem for you.'

'Oh wow, I can't wait to hear it. Open the door and I'll come in and listen to it,' Cher cooed in a coaxing tone.

'No, I want to share it with the folks who've come along today.' He cleared his throat. 'There once was a girl named Cher, who's voice was as gentle as a purr. Her legs went forever, she was terribly clever and had a set of tits as big as your head.'

'There are children listening!' Daphney screamed. 'Get him out!'

'It doesn't even rhyme,' Shorty muttered to the other bystanders nearby, sounding disappointed.

'Stand back,' Damian said to Cher, as he moved from Lottie's side and rammed the door with his shoulder. It gave way with a splintering jolt. Cher gingerly stepped over the timber fragments on the ground as she went inside.

'Hey, Cher!' Dougie slurred, as though surprised to see her. 'I just read a poem about you, you wanna hear it?'

'Why don't you tell me over another drink, down at my bar?'

'I like your bar,' Dougie said, smiling. 'You're the prettiest girl I know,' he added with a sigh.

'You're a sweetie. Come on, let's get you out of here.' But Dougie wasn't giving up the microphone so easy. 'What do you reckon folks? Isn't she beautiful?'

'Oh, for the love of God,' Daphney muttered.

'Thank you, pet.' Cher plucked the microphone from his hands. 'I'm sure we all enjoyed that little deviation from the program. Let's hear it for Dougie, everyone, and don't forget the matinee cabaret show starts at midday at Madame Dubois with a tribute to Kate O'Ryan,' Cher said before Daphney switched off the microphone with a glare.

'Get him out of here.'

'Don't get your knickers in a knot, sweetheart,' Cher said. 'Come on, Dougie, let's go and discuss finding you a part in one of my shows. I think you've got some natural talent hidden away there.' She sent Lottie a wink as she escorted the tipsy man away from all the commotion, and order was once again restored.

'Are you okay?' Lottie asked, turning to Damian, and running her hand over the arm he was carefully shrugging.

'Yeah, it's a bit tender, but nothing major.'

'Thank goodness you were here, Damian,' Daphney gushed, batting her eyelashes at him briefly, before turning to face the gathered sprinkling of committee members and bystanders still lingering. 'And what were you lot doing while all this was going on? Did no one notice that horrible little man getting into the announcer's box?'

'He's harmless, Daphney,' Lottie said, realising no one else seemed to be about to speak up in the tense silence that followed her chastising.

'Harmless?' Daphney's lethal gaze zeroed in on Lottie's face.

'Everything's under control again.'

'No thanks to anyone around here,' Daphney snapped.

'Here Daphney,' Hannah's calm voice cut in smoothly from behind Lottie and she turned to find her mother approaching. 'Let's sit down for a few minutes and I'll make you a nice cup of tea,' she said, sliding a hand around the other woman's waist and guiding her across to the festival tent without bothering to listen to Daphney's spluttering denials about not having time.

Lottie bit back a giggle as she spotted the bag of tea labelled Chill the Eff Out that her mother clutched behind the woman's back as they walked away.

'Your mum might just be on to something,' Damian murmured.

'If I know Mum, she'll probably add a dash of her special tea blend to it and *really* chill Daphney out.'

'We can only hope,' he sighed.

'I'll see you at the bake-off later, Mr Judge,' she said, kissing him once more before regretfully heading back into the fray.

Lottie was kept busy, manning stalls for the committee and keeping stall owners happy, ensuring events stayed on track and running a gazillion errands that Daphney kept coming up with and ordering her to complete over the radio. She'd lost track of Damian again but caught up with him prior to the main event—the re-enactment of the coach hold-up.

Terry stood in the centre of the ring and introduced Damian, who took the microphone and opened the re-enactment with an emphatic reading of a poem written in the late 1800s about Jack McNally and his gang, and the many hold-ups they'd undertaken over the years.

Lottie beamed with pride as he waved a hand at the round of applause that followed and jogged from the centre of the ground as the jingle of metal and the clip-clop of hooves filled the arena.

'That was awesome,' Lottie whispered as he came to stand beside her.

'You're awesome,' he whispered back, placing a kiss on her lips before they settled in to watch the show.

The big coach—a timber and glass replica of an original coach from the era of the robbery—looked magnificent as it did a lap of the show ring, the heavy Clydesdale horses' manes floating in the breeze and their big hooves pounding the dirt beneath them. The coach creaked and groaned its way past, complete with a driver, two men dressed as police and another man inside, presumably representing Alexander Compton.

As the coach prepared to do another lap, five men on horseback came galloping into the ring, shooting fake guns and circling the coach until it came to a stop.

The riders surrounded the coach and dismounted and a shootout followed, until the policemen, driver and Alexander all lay dead. The horsemen remounted and rode away with bags of money unloaded from the coach.

The crowd applauded loudly as the coach moved out of the ring, and a short time later riders once again burst into the arena, this time a lone man on horseback, wildly firing shots over his shoulder as a group of mounted police officers followed in pursuit. After a heart-racing few rounds of the ring, the bushranger dismounted and the final shootout between an injured Jack and the police took place, until Jack crumpled to the ground and went still.

Despite the fact Lottie knew it was a staged act, she couldn't help the clench of her heart as Jack's final moments played out in front of her. The crowd cheered again, the applause continuing as the riders and the coach returned to the centre ring for a final lap of honour.

'Wow. That was amazing,' Lottie said as the last horse went past and the crowd began to disperse.

'Pretty powerful stuff,' Damian agreed. 'Even if a few details were left out.'

'Well, we couldn't get everything completely accurate, Mr Historian,' she said in a mock-haughty tone. 'We had to work with what we could get.'

'That's *Professor* Historian to you,' he replied with a laugh.

The afternoon became a little less busy as it wore on. Yet all the way through to pack-down, the markets attracted a lot of people, and the stallholders she spoke to as the shadows lengthened were happy with the way the day had gone. Equally, the shops in town had attracted a lot of business from the visitors strolling through the streets as they took in everything the town had on display for the festival. All in all, it had been an extremely successful day.

The next morning, Lottie woke to find the bed beside her empty and the sun well and truly up. She could hear Damian in the kitchen and smelled the delicious scent of toast, bacon and coffee.

Then the man himself appeared in the doorway. 'Hello. I was just about to come and see if you were awake,' he said kissing her gently.

'Why didn't you wake me earlier?' she asked.

'You needed your sleep. You were dead to the world when I got up.'

'I was supposed to go back to the showground and help finish up this morning,' she said with a quick look at the kitchen clock. It had been almost midnight by the time they'd got home after helping with the pack-up, and they'd immediately dropped into bed, exhausted.

'I'm sure they have it all sorted,' he said as she walked across to her handbag and pulled out her phone. There was a text from Cher saying that there was no need to come down, that the council had supplied a clean-up team and there was nothing left for the committee to do.

It was rainy and cold outside so they lit the fire in the lounge room. Damian was taking notes as he read through papers, completely absorbed in what he was doing, which should have been frustrating for Lottie. Yet it wasn't, because she was free to type away on her laptop without feeling bad that she was neglecting him. She loved the way they could both do their own thing separately but together. Every now and then, he'd reach for her leg and give it an absent squeeze or rub, and Lottie smiled, knowing this was a connection she'd never felt before.

She could get used to this. 'So, I was thinking,' she said, finally voicing the idea that she had been nervous about bringing up, 'why don't you just check out of the motel and stay here for the rest of your visit?'

His hand stilled where he'd been rubbing her leg moments before.

Oh crap. Maybe she was being too pushy. 'It was just a thought. No big deal,' she blurted.

'I think it's a great idea. But I don't want to intrude on your space or make it tricky for you if people work out that I'm staying with you.'

'I'm pretty sure the cat's out of the bag well and truly by now,' she said with a shrug. 'And seriously, I don't care. I'm a grown adult. I can invite anyone I want to come and stay in my house. Let 'em talk.'

'I guess I'm pretty much staying here already,' he conceded. 'I'll go and pack the rest of my stuff in the morning.'

It was true that they'd been spending a lot of time together. They'd practically been joined at the hip except when she was working, but even then, he'd work from her back office for part of the day, so their time together wouldn't really change. But somehow, it made everything feel a lot more . . . *real*.

She settled back down against him and smiled. Yep, she could get very used to this.

Twenty-one

Damian finished stacking the kindling he'd just chopped for the fireplace and looked around the cosy room. This was so much better than a bland motel room.

In all honesty, he hadn't been expecting to still be here once the festival was finished. His original plan had been to head back to the city and continue writing and teaching, or possibly take a sabbatical from teaching in order to focus exclusively on his writing. But that was before he'd met Lottie. Now, it seemed impossible to leave. It wasn't as though he had to, which was the beauty of writing—he could do it anywhere. And the last few days had been amazing.

Through the day, he wrote, did a few zoom sessions with some of his post-grad students, then cooked dinner and tried to earn his keep by helping out with chores around the house while Lottie worked at the shop. They spent the afternoons and evenings learning every single little thing about each other. He loved her playful sex kitten persona in bed, which was such a contrast to the quiet, reliable, community-minded Lottie most people knew. Waking up through the night and finding her tucked up against his side filled him with an unexpected protectiveness and contentment. They just fit.

He'd fallen hard for this woman he'd only just met. Damian gave a small grunt of affection when he remembered how upset she'd become over what may have happened to Catherine. Her compassion tugged at his heartstrings. He understood her sadness—he felt it too, although he tended not to allow his emotions to run away from him the way Lottie sometimes did. She was unapologetically emotional and made no excuses if she let whatever she was feeling show. He'd witnessed the glisten of tears as she'd thought about Catherine, the beam of happiness when he'd taken her on the bike, the unbridled passion crossing her face when they made love. She hid nothing, and the experience floored him every time. The only thing he hadn't seen from her yet was anger, and he was fairly sure she wouldn't hold back with that either.

He still couldn't explain what she'd done to make him fall so hard and fast. She was on his mind all the time and whenever she wasn't with him, he could smell her. He wasn't sure if she was somehow imprinted in his senses or if he was imagining it, but he could be alone in a room and suddenly catch the faintest hint of the perfume she wore just wafting past, almost as though on a breeze. He'd never considered himself a hopeless romantic—he was far too practical for that—yet here he was, listening to the words of sappy love songs and impatiently waiting for the next time he could talk to her or see her, like some love-sick idiot.

He found it difficult to concentrate whenever he was away from her. Which was crazy. He'd never been easily distracted from his research before. It had actually been one of the biggest complaints from women he'd dated previously, that he was *too* absorbed in his work and would forget about everything else. Not anymore. Now, he found himself having to force his attention away from thinking about Lottie.

With the fire started, he forced himself to sit down with his laptop and open the document Lottie had sent him earlier: her manuscript. He knew how hard it was to allow someone to read through a work in progress—he rarely allowed it. There was always something incredibly vulnerable about baring your writing to another person, especially when it was still in its early stages, and he felt privileged that Lottie trusted him enough to let him read it.

Initially, he was hoping there might be something in the earlier part of her book that was set locally and in the same era as his own research. Unlikely, but he was experienced enough to know that sometimes it was the smallest detail that could suddenly unlock a mystery and send things on a whole new trajectory.

He was impressed with the amount of research she'd done so far. The file she sent contained all her online resources, including old newspaper articles from different eras and anything that potentially might relate to the years around the subject she was writing about. He opened the information she had filed under Emeline and found himself engrossed in the unfolding saga of the young woman who was abducted by the murderous bushranger Jack McNally.

There was a wealth of articles and poems, as well as stories published in subsequent years, on Jack and his bushranging career. These had been meticulously gathered and placed in the file, and he read through them with interest. Nothing really jumped out at him for his own research; still, it was interesting reading.

He opened another file and discovered the photos that Lottie mentioned she was including in her book and began scrolling through them. The women in her family almost all bore a startling resemblance to Lottie herself, particularly in the earlier photos, varying from the 1920s to the early sixties and a scattering from the 1940s and 1970s. They all appeared to have the same heart-shaped face and pouty lips . . . the kind that he often found himself thinking about far too often. The coppery hair also seemed to be a family trait.

He paused at the next image and studied it curiously. It was a close-up of the hand from one of the black-and-white portraits he'd just looked at, and a large oval-shaped ring caught his attention. He moved on to the next photo, another cropped image of a woman's hand and a ring. This photo was in colour, and he realised now that the ring was a large opal, no doubt more stunning in real life, but even in an old photograph he could tell the stone was something special.

Something started to gnaw in the back of his mind...

After a moment, he got up from his seat and walked across the room to remove a manila folder from his box of research. He wasn't sure exactly what he was looking for, but he couldn't shake a feeling of familiarity. As he shuffled through the pages, he pulled out a photocopied article from an online history page he'd come across one day. He rocked back on his heels—he'd found what he was looking for.

Lottie hung her handbag on the hook inside the front door after work and smiled as she saw Damian pacing the room. 'Hey.' She'd texted him to say she was on her way home a few minutes earlier, but her smile slipped a notch as she noticed his strangely intense expression.

'Is everything okay?'

'Yeah, I was reading your manuscript,' he said, kissing her briefly and taking her hand to almost drag her from the door to the kitchen. *Oh God*, she thought, feeling her stomach drop. *He hated it.* The negative thoughts started raining down on her in quick succession.

'Tell me about this ring,' he said, pulling out his phone and showing her a photo from her book.

Lottie blinked uncertainly. That wasn't what she'd been expecting. 'It's my mother's and before that my gran's. It's been passed down from mother to daughter for generations.'

He eyed her for a few moments before taking the phone from her and flicking through screens quickly to show her an internet page. *British Royal Designs Throughout History*, the article headline read.

'What's this?'

'Scroll down a bit,' he said.

Lottie gently ran her finger up the screen, wondering what she was supposed to be looking for, when an illustration came up, a design sketch for a ring . . . a ring that looked almost identical to the one her mother refused to wear. The text beneath said:

> The giant opal was sent to Philip Borndoff, who was master jeweller and designer to Her Majesty Queen Victoria, to be designed as an engagement ring for a wealthy family. The opal's size and magnificent colour was unusual at the time and long stood out in Borndoff's memory. It has since disappeared, feared lost by the family who no longer have ownership of the valuable piece. If it were valued in today's market, it would be worth a fortune. The curator of the Borndoff jewellery collection at the London Museum said, 'Anything designed by Philip Borndoff is as priceless and sought after as a Da Vinci or a Van Gogh in the art world.'

Lottie snapped her head up and stared at Damian. 'You're not thinking that our ring is . . . *this* ring?' she asked, doubtfully.

'I don't know what to think, only that it has an uncanny resemblance.'

'It was probably a copy. Maybe after this ring, it became the fashion or something? Besides, what would my family be doing with a ring designed by a royal jeweller?'

'I did a search and found out who the family that commissioned it was. Lottie, it was the Comptons. As in Alexander Compton.'

Lottie felt her eyes widen.

'It's too much of a coincidence.'

'But how . . . *why* would it be here?'

'Alexander had the ring made. He went back to England for his wedding to Catherine, where presumably he gave it to her.'

'Then why would it not still be in her family?'

'Who knows? Maybe she sold it to buy passage home some other way and that's why we can't trace her through passenger records.'

'She came from a wealthy family, why would she need to sell off her engagement ring to buy a ticket home?' Lottie argued.

'Maybe she didn't sell it. Maybe it was removed from her,' Damian emphasised pointedly.

'As in . . . stolen?'

'Who do we know out here who made a living from stealing from the rich?'

Jack. She nodded thoughtfully. 'That means she at least arrived here. But how would Jack have had the opportunity to steal it?'

'The only way we can legitimately place Jack and that ring together would be through the coach robbery somehow,' Damian said, shaking his head. 'It doesn't prove Catherine was here.'

'Maybe Compton had it with him?'

'Maybe,' Damian said. 'Tell me about your family connection to the ring.'

'We're fairly sure it traces back to Emeline,' Lottie said. Suddenly, it made sense. She'd never actually considered the ring had been a gift from Jack—he wasn't a rich man and he never had the chance to spend what he stole in the coach robbery. Then there was the letter to Adelaide and the mention of passing on the one special thing given to her by Hattie's father . . .

'Her daughter, Hattie, was left the ring.' Lottie paused, then explained about the letter to Emeline's cousin and the possibility she may have been referring to Jack being the father of her child. 'I just didn't connect the ring to him because Henry Oldsfield, the man she went on to marry, had come from a wealthy family. It just made sense he'd have bought her beautiful jewellery.'

'A husband would probably be suspicious of his wife having such an expensive piece of jewellery if he hadn't been the one to give it to her.'

'Henry passed away while Hattie was still in her early teens. It's entirely possible he never knew about it . . . or anyone else for that matter. She would have been able to wear it later, and no one would have questioned where it had come from.'

'Are we sure the ring hadn't been passed down to Emeline from *her* mother?'

'I could only find reference to it from as far back as Emeline. Before then, there's no mention of any other female in the family having passed it down.'

Damian raised an eyebrow thoughtfully. 'The evidence seems to be leaning more and more in favour of Jack as the link.'

'What if Catherine *was* in the coach?' Lottie asked. 'You couldn't find her listed on any return ships to England, so could it be that Alexander went to Sydney to bring her home?'

Damian shook his head. 'There's no mention of her having been there, not in any of the newspaper or police reports. They would have made mention that the wife of a murdered man was present.'

Lottie mentally flicked through her research of the stagecoach robbery. 'But there were no witnesses.'

'No. The gang had killed the coach driver and the two guards, as well as three policemen.'

'What if Catherine *had* been there but there was no one left alive to confirm it?'

'There was no body recovered,' Damian said. 'I mean, Jack was a murderer, no doubt about it, he'd shot and killed before, but he'd never harmed any women or children in any of the robberies he and his men had done. Even during the homestead robberies across the country, he never harmed any women. They all mention how much of a gentleman he was, even while robbing them.'

'Maybe Jack let her go. After taking the ring,' she added as an afterthought. 'The bush would have been easy to get lost in. Maybe she was out there and no one even knew she was missing?'

'I'm not dismissing the idea, but surely at some point someone would have stumbled across a body out there?' Damian replied.

Lottie shrugged. 'I just can't help but think that if Catherine had gone missing before the robbery, wouldn't her husband have taken out ads in the paper and hired detectives? Wouldn't there have been some kind of search for her? Surely he wouldn't have given up so easily and returned home without her that fast? The fact that there isn't any evidence of that happening kind of makes me think that maybe she *wasn't* missing before the stagecoach was robbed.' She saw him nod a little at her words, so pressed on. 'There was no listing for her on any ships that left after. It's unlikely she simply turned around and got back on another ship to head back to England after enduring almost four months at sea, possibly heavily pregnant.'

'That scenario has never really felt likely to me either,' Damian said with a shake of his head. 'But linking this ring to Catherine . . . that definitely sheds new light on a few things.'

'*If* it's the same ring,' Lottie stressed.

'There's only one way to find out. We need to get it appraised.'

Lottie snorted. 'Mum's never going to agree to that.'

Damian shot her a puzzled look. 'Why not?'

'She genuinely fears it.' Damian still looked confused, so she added, 'I'm telling you, she won't even look at it.'

'Why not?' he asked again.

'Because . . .' Lottie began, faltering as she realised she was talking to a man who dealt in facts and accurate information. Not someone likely to believe in cursed rings. 'She's just got this thing about it,' she finished lamely.

'Would it help if I spoke to her? Asked her for permission?' Damian asked. 'I can take all our evidence along.'

'I guess you could try,' Lottie said slowly. There was no way her mother was going to have anything to do with it.

Twenty-two

'Of course!' Hannah said, clasping her hands around the knee she'd just crossed over her other long leg.

'What?' Lottie gaped at her mother. They'd just sat down over morning tea and Damian had launched into his theory about Jack McNally and the family ring and how they hoped to get it appraised.

'Why wouldn't I want to help?' she asked her daughter, looking bewildered.

'I asked to get the ring out so I could photograph it when I started writing my book and you freaked out.'

'This is different. It's *scientific*—it's nothing to do with the heart,' Hannah explained, giving her daughter a forthright look.

'The heart?' Damian repeated, glancing across at Lottie for clarification.

'The curse. Surely you told him about that?' her mother said, sounding surprised.

'Only vaguely,' Lottie murmured. Great. Just when she'd hoped maybe a guy she really liked wouldn't think she came from a family of Froot Loops.

'The family curse you mentioned when we first met—that you were writing about?' Damian asked, curiously.

'It's the ring. I can't believe you didn't tell him the story, Charlotte,' her mother admonished.

I can't believe he's about to hear it. Lottie groaned inwardly.

'This opal has been handed down from mother to daughter of every generation of women in our family for as long as anyone can remember. And every, single, time, it leaves death and heartache in its wake.'

'I see,' Damian said slowly. 'How exactly does it do that?'

'True love. That's the curse. Once you find true love, the ring takes it away. Every woman who has worn the ring loses the love of their life. Tell him,' she said, turning her attention back to Lottie.

'Mum, it's got nothing to do with the ring,' Lottie said wearily.

'Name one woman who hasn't been widowed within a year of marrying?' she challenged.

'It doesn't mean—'

'You can't,' she cut in. 'You can't put six generations of women widowed almost as soon as they married as a simple coincidence. What are the scientific chances of that, Damian?'

'Well . . .' Damian looked like a deer caught in the headlights.

'There's no scientific explanation needed. It's just bad luck,' Lottie argued, shaking her head.

'Bad luck, cursed, call it whatever you want. But I'm telling you, it's all linked to that ring. I'm happy to have it appraised, but it won't change my mind. It's getting buried with me so it can't do any further harm. I should have just got rid of it years ago, somehow—thrown it into the ocean or had it melted down.'

'Mum?' Lottie frowned at her mother uncertainly.

'What? I told you, there's no way I'm risking your happiness by passing it down to you. To be honest, I haven't thought about it in a while, but maybe it's time to consider getting rid of it once and for all. Now your grandmother is gone, there are no real ties to it.'

'Except it reminds me of her,' Lottie snapped. 'You can't tell me that you don't think of her wearing it and how much she loved it? She was proud of the heritage it had. How can you consider destroying it when it's been part of this family for a century and a half?'

'Because I know what I know. That ring brings nothing but sadness.'

She can't be reasoned with. Lottie sat back in her chair and bit her tongue. Her mother was stubborn in her beliefs and there was no changing her mind once it was made up.

'Maybe getting it appraised will give us some information about where it came from. Maybe we'll find some answers?' Damian suggested.

'Like I said, I'm happy for you to get it appraised if there's a possibility it can bring you the answers you're after. It's never been about the value of the thing.'

'It is about the family history, though.'

'And look where that's gotten us,' Hannah said sadly.

There was a lingering silence, and Damian was suddenly very interested in drinking his tea. But thankfully her mother, being the gracious host that she usually was, changed the topic of conversation.

'You should have a brownie. It might help you relax,' Hannah said with a smile.

'No, thank you,' Lottie said, sending her a silent message to behave.

'They're extra chocolatey,' Hannah continued sweetly.

'I like chocolate,' Damian piped up eagerly.

'No,' Lottie cut in quickly, straightening in her chair. 'Thank you, Mother,' she added firmly. She noticed Damian seemed to slump slightly. 'We should probably get going.'

'I'll be going into town tomorrow, so I'll drop the ring in at the shop for you to pick up, Damian,' Hannah said, smiling graciously.

Clearly the man had worked his magic on her mother too—there was no way Hannah would have agreed to handing over the ring had she asked for it.

They farewelled her mother and got back into Lottie's car.

'Why didn't you mention the family curse thing?'

'Because it's not a thing,' she said briskly. 'Surely you of all people don't believe in curses?'

'I'm not saying I do. I just think, considering you're researching the women of your family, the topic of a curse would have come up in your book.'

'I'm writing the book to prove to my mother that there's no such thing. My family are a living example of how history changed people's lives. Men went away to war and didn't come home. Happened to thousands. Disease swept through places and people died. Mining accidents happened all the time.' She shook her head, frustrated. 'It's just my mother and all her woo-woo tarot reading, meditation and getting-in-touch-with-your-spirituality stuff that makes her believe there's something inexplicable going on.'

'Maybe making this ring the villain is the way your mum copes with the idea of the fickleness of life and the injustice of it all. For someone with a very optimistic view of the world that unexplainable randomness can be really difficult to accept. You are two very different personalities,' he commented, taking in the scenery out his window.

'My mother's always been a free spirit. Earlier, it was simply having a good time and being around other people. She was always out, and she loved dancing and blowing off steam, but later she kind of mellowed a bit with the whole drinking and partying thing, before she got into all this spirituality stuff.' Lottie shrugged. 'She's never cared about what anyone thought of her, never worried about being judged by other people's norms.'

'People change as they get older. They figure out what's important to them. She seems happy with her life.'

'She is. And don't get me wrong, I love that she's happy. Only, she hides behind all this new age stuff. She'll tell you she doesn't need a partner or someone to grow old with, that she's happy on her own, but I don't think that's necessarily true.'

'Maybe she is?' Damian replied. 'Some people are happy on their own.'

'Maybe,' Lottie shrugged. 'But I know how fiercely my mother loves me and I can't help but wonder how a person just turns that off to other people. I hate the thought of her turning away a chance at happiness with someone because she chooses to believe a stupid story about a family curse.'

'And has she? Turned someone important away?'

'They never become important. She has men *friends* now and again, but as soon as they begin to hint at wanting anything more, they're gone.'

'It could just be her personality?'

'Maybe.' But she doubted it.

'I really would have liked to try your mum's brownies,' he added after a moment of silence fell between them.

Lottie gave a small chuckle. 'Trust me, you really wouldn't.'

'Is she a bad cook?' he asked curiously, turning his head to face her.

'They aren't the *usual* type of brownies. My mother tends to incorporate . . . herbs into her cooking. You wouldn't be getting much work done today after you had one.'

'Oh,' he said, drawing the word out as comprehension dawned on him. 'I really like your mum.'

'She clearly likes you,' Lottie said.

The merry jingle of bells sounded as Damian pushed open the door to the bakery. Instantly, a waft of pastry, hot pies and freshly baked bread hit his senses. Judy bustled out from the back of the store.

'Damian! I haven't seen you in here for a few days. I thought you'd got sick of my vanilla slice!' she said with mock horror.

'Never,' Damian promised, then gave a sheepish grin. 'I just had to use some restraint when I realised my clothes were beginning to get a bit tight.'

'Oh, you don't have anything to worry about there,' she dismissed with a wave of her hand. 'You could use a bit more meat on your bones. My boys were raised on this stuff, all grew up to be strapping young men.'

Lottie had introduced him to one of Judy's boys at the festival—strapping he was indeed, all six foot, five inches and at least one hundred and thirty kilos.

They chatted about the festival for a few minutes and Damian gave her his order for the usual vanilla slice, coffee and meat pie.

'We're all very excited that you and our Lottie seem to be getting serious. Have we managed to get you to swap city for country life yet?' she asked coyly as she selected his items with long tongs and placed them in white paper bags.

'I'm considering it,' he said somewhat awkwardly, still unused to this direct kind of questioning and trying not to offend. He'd never exchanged more than a hello and a thank you with a baker before coming here. Discussing his private life and future plans with practical strangers was still a tad confronting.

'Well, we hope you do. It's always lovely to have new faces settling in around town. It's nice you didn't have to rush off after the festival.'

'Yeah. I've got a bit of time off and it's peaceful enough here to get some writing done on my new book. It's worked out great.' He paid for his purchases and breathed a sigh of relief. That was going to take some getting used to.

Now he understood Lottie's hesitation in making their relationship public—not that it was enough to make him regret doing so. He didn't care if the whole world knew they were a couple, but there was still a lot to work out between them and that was hard enough to do in private without the whole town watching on and adding in their two cents' worth.

Country life was not for the faint of heart.

Twenty-three

'I need you to understand this is not me passing down this ring,' her mother said, raising her voice and tipping her head back, as though to address the heavens.

Damian shot Lottie a quizzical look, and she suppressed a sigh.

'Here, you need to wear this,' she said to Lottie, talking normally once more as she reached up to clasp a necklace around her daughter's neck 'and, whatever you do, *do not* put that ring on your finger. Do you understand?'

'What's this?' Lottie asked, lifting the dangling black stone that had been fashioned into a cylindrical shape with a small, pointed end.

'Black tourmaline. For protection,' Hannah added.

Of course. 'Thanks Mum,' she said, knowing there was no point in dismissing her mother's belief in all things mystical.

'Damian, I'm trusting you to keep my girl safe. That means keeping *this* somewhere safe,' Hannah said, looking pointedly at the bag containing the ring.

'You have my word.'

'All right then. I have to get back. I've got clients this afternoon,' she said, hugging Lottie tightly before leaving the shop.

'I really want to open it,' Damian said, looking down at the package.

'So open it.'

'But your mum's kind of freaked me out about it, now,' he admitted.

Lottie rolled her eyes. 'Oh please, not you too.'

'Well, I'm more worried about the pressure of being responsible for something that's been in your family for so long.'

'I'm sure you've had much older, and far more precious artefacts in your hands before.'

'True . . .'

'Just open it. Here, let me,' she said reaching towards the package.

He lifted it high above his head. 'I'll do it. I don't think your mum wants you too close to it.'

'Oh, for goodness' sake, I wore it once when I was a child. It's all just a load of crap.'

'Does your mum know you wore it? She specifically said you weren't allowed to,' he pointed out.

'Oh, yeah, she knows about it . . . and naturally, there was a reason why nothing happened: "It wasn't your time; the ring had to go through me first." I mean, seriously,' Lottie threw up her hands. 'It's a rock. It doesn't have any superpowers. It's not cursed. It's just a pretty mineral formed in the cracks of rocks.'

'Still, *she* believes it,' he emphasised, 'and I gave her my word I'd look after it. And you. I'll open it.'

He took the small package out of the bag. It was a timber box with a brass latch that he undid before carefully lifting the lid. Inside, the box was lined with a rich, purple satin and nestled in the centre was a burgundy leather ring box that looked well worn and was covered in scuff marks. One edge of the oval box was worn slightly and had clearly had a hard life.

'The case looks vintage, maybe 1900s?' Damian murmured. 'Not early enough for Catherine's time, I don't think, but I'm not an expert in this department. We should get a better idea once the assessor has a look.'

Lottie held her breath as she watched him slowly ease open the case, then suddenly, there it was, just like she remembered, only somehow more vibrant. The deep blues and greens seemed to twinkle beneath the shop lights. It was beautiful. An image of her gran gently running a finger across the smooth surface popped into her mind and for a moment, she saw the gentle face of her grandmother and could smell the faint perfume of the talcum powder she used to use.

'Wow.'

Damian's words dragged her away from her memories.

'I've never really seen an opal up close before—and never one this big. They're pretty awesome.'

'This one certainly is,' she agreed. 'I need to get some photos for the book while we have it,' she said decisively.

For the next few minutes, she concentrated on the best angles and snapped off a ridiculous number of images, knowing that it was better to have too many to choose from.

'Are you sure you're okay to shut the shop?' he asked as she put her camera away.

'Yeah, it'll be fine.' She felt the tiniest twinge of guilt that she had barely hesitated before agreeing to go along on the road trip with him when he'd arranged an appointment with the jeweller. Closing the shop for two days was a big deal, but this was huge. This appraisal could change what they knew about the origins of the ring and everything her family had been led to believe for generations.

The other bonus was getting to spend two whole days and an overnight stay in Sydney, away from prying eyes and gossip. It was a win-win situation.

'Do you have a safe or something we can put this in?'

Lottie smiled at how seriously he took the guardianship of the ring. 'I'm sure we don't need to go to extremes. It has managed to survive the last hundred and fifty or so years and multiple generations of women who I'm fairly sure did not have a safe installed in their house.'

'I'm not taking any chances,' he said adamantly.

A customer came into the store and Lottie went to see if they were looking for something in particular. When it was clear that she was going to be taking some time, he waved goodbye from the doorway. She couldn't help the little thrill of excitement she felt race through her at the thought of two whole days together.

The dawn sky was painted in delicate strokes of faint pinks and blues when they started driving the next morning, and fog lingered across the dams and rivers they passed by. Eventually, the sun rose and turned the sky into a beautiful periwinkle blue. Slowly, the morning chill disappeared and the sun streaming in through the front windscreen warmed them comfortably.

After stopping for breakfast at a small service station, Damian took over driving so she could have a rest. It had been an early start to ensure they made their appointment with the jeweller. Lottie looked down at their joined hands and smiled at how natural it felt. Their first few weeks had been a whirlwind of excitement, but ever since the festival they'd settled into something a lot deeper. She shied away from examining what it was—it was so fragile and new, she didn't want to risk ruining it—so she turned her head to the window and enjoyed the warmth of Damian holding her hand.

'Were you really worried about people knowing about us?' Damian asked, breaking the silence that had followed getting back on the road.

Lottie enjoyed a road trip conversation, the ones where you discussed all the things you probably wouldn't normally, simply to fill in time. The downside, of course, was that there was really nowhere to go if those conversations became uncomfortable. Like now.

'I wouldn't say I was worried,' she hedged. 'It's more like . . . I don't know. I just hate people knowing my business, I guess,' she said shifting in her seat to face him a little. 'It doesn't help that, once you have to go home, I'll have everyone wondering about what happened. It's just . . . awkward.'

He stared at the road, seeming to digest her words. Finally, he said, 'I'd like to think we're exploring the potential of something . . . more.' She felt a flutter of awareness run through her at his words as he continued. 'I'm at a stage of my life where I'm not interested in casual dating for the sake of dating. I'd like to find the person I want to be with.'

She was processing this quietly, but he must also have been feeling a little anxious. 'What about you?' he prompted.

He was right. This thing between them didn't feel like anything she'd ever had before with anyone else. The thought of him leaving and simply going back to her life before he'd entered it had been weighing on her mind. The closer they'd been getting, the harder it was to think about saying goodbye. Although they'd known each other such a short amount of time, it felt like they'd known each other for years. She wasn't interested in the whole online dating thing—asking the same questions each time you met someone new, laying all the polite groundwork only for either the conversation to dry up or to be ghosted and have to start again. She hadn't connected with anyone the way she had with Damian in a long time, and she was happy that he seemed to be feeling the same way.

'It's just that your life is back in Sydney . . .' She gave a small shrug as the sentence petered out.

'The logistics are not ideal, granted,' he agreed. 'But I guess that's what this time now is about, if it's something we both want. Then we move on to finding a way to make it work for both of us. There's always going to be a solution. We just have to find out if this is something we both feel is important enough to invest ourselves in.' The music from the stereo floated between them for a few moments before he took his eyes from the road briefly to glance at her. 'Personally, I think it's obvious that this is something pretty special.'

His words filled her chest with a warm sensation that swirled to the bottom of her stomach and back again. She smiled, squeezing his hand. 'Me too,' she said.

He returned her squeeze, holding her hand for the rest of the drive.

The city traffic was something Lottie had not missed. She'd grown used to the slower pace of life in Banalla and surrounds, and it was always a shock to find herself stuck in gridlock each time she came back to Sydney.

After navigating the worst of it, Damian parked the car and they located the office of the expert he'd found to inspect the ring.

'It's a real Borndoff,' the jeweller said, looking up at the stunned faces before him with a half-chuckle. 'You've got something pretty special there.'

Lottie felt a lurch of shock at the words.

'So you're saying this is the same ring?' Damian asked slowly.

'Yep.' The jeweller put the ring back under the magnifier. 'It's got the maker's mark. No doubt about it, it's a Borndoff original that perfectly matches the design in your article.'

'So this ring belonged to Catherine Compton?' Damian asked faintly.

'If she was the owner of the Philip Borndoff original design listed in that newspaper article, then yes.'

'Oh my God,' Lottie whispered. *It was true?* 'So it came from Jack?'

'It would appear so,' Damian said with a nod.

'Hope it's insured. It's worth a small fortune,' the jeweller informed them. 'Borndoff's designs have sold for millions in the past.'

'Holy crap.' Lottie gaped at the older man. She'd always imagined a moment like this—finding that one, unicorn antique item that would set records—but she'd never imagined it would be a piece that had been passed down through her family, or worn to the odd Banalla View Club luncheon.

Another thought suddenly occurred to her. She'd played with this ring as a child . . . a child had been allowed to play dress-ups with a ring designed by a royal jeweller!

Damian discussed obtaining a valuation certificate, ever the details man, and they left the little store shortly after.

Needle in a Haystack

Still in shock and processing the turn of events, at first Lottie paid no attention to where they were going, but curiosity nudged her back into the present when she noticed that Damian was driving into a basement carpark beneath an unobtrusive but well-maintained looking apartment building. He parked neatly and led her towards a set of stairs.

She waited as he unlocked his front door on the third level and stepped inside. *This is where he lives.*

'Well, here we are,' he said, holding the heavy door open for her with one hand and throwing wide his other as she stepped over the threshold and took in her surroundings.

The apartment wasn't quite what she was expecting—somehow she had pictured him living in an old terrace house or some other heritage-listed place with plenty of history oozing from its walls. This place was rather modern, with sleek lines, galley kitchen and open-plan lounge and dining area. However, what the structure lacked in character, his decorating definitely made up for. The walls displayed a variety of old, framed posters, ranging from a WWI recruitment poster to photos of old cars and motorbikes. His coffee table was an old steamer trunk with its original brass locks and leather strapping. She gestured towards it. 'Is this an original nineteenth century?'

'Yep. Belonged to a ship's surgeon who came to Australia in the early eighteen-hundreds. It's got his name on the brass plaque on the side. I bought it at an auction a few years ago.'

'It's gorgeous,' Lottie breathed, running her hands across the beautifully preserved timber.

Bookcases lined the opposite wall, stacked and overflowing with hundreds of books, and on a long hall table a collection of old telephones and antique clocks was displayed. This was a man after her own heart.

'It doesn't have the charm of your little cottage, but it does the job, I guess,' Damian said, dropping their bags inside a doorway framed by the bookshelves.

'It's lovely,' she said, moving across to a set of sliding glass doors opening onto a small balcony that looked out through the crowns of leafy trees to a busy street below.

'Have a seat while I open a few windows and let in some air,' he said, and she settled herself on a brown, overstuffed sofa. Beside her on a side table were a set of three photo frames and she carefully examined them one at a time. The first was of an elderly couple, standing on an empty beach of white sand with a turquoise ocean behind them, arm in arm and smiling at the camera—obviously his parents. The man had grey hair but could have been Damian's much older twin. She put the frame down and reached for the photo of four people—Damian and his three sisters, she assumed. She smiled back at the laughing faces staring up at her. All of them had the same warm, brown eyes and dark lashes.

'My sisters,' he said, sitting down beside her. 'And that's my mum and dad, and those are my nieces and nephews,' he said pointing to the last photo, where four gorgeous-looking children ranging from baby to early school age were captured in a candid moment together.

'You have a beautiful family.'

'Yeah—they're okay, I suppose,' he said with a grin.

'Am I going to get to meet them while we're here?'

'Absolutely not,' he said decisively.

'Why not?' she asked, trying hard not to feel hurt by his response.

'Trust me—we're not ready for that level of interrogation and outright intrusion just yet,' he said, shaking his head. 'They know absolutely no boundaries, and there's no way I'm risking them scaring you off so fast. I just found you,' he added, leaning over to kiss her gently.

His answer alleviated her initial fears, somewhat. He was right, this was all still new, and meeting the family—especially one as big as his—was a pretty big step.

'Let's get out of here and grab a drink,' Damian said. 'I know a place close by. We can walk,' he added, standing up and holding his hand out to help her to her feet.

We certainly aren't in Kansas anymore, Toto, she thought wryly, five minutes later. They dodged another jogger, vying for footpath space as they walked past boutique shops, restaurants and a grocery store. She noticed that no one stopped to chat to anyone or smiled as they hurried by on their way to wherever they all seemed to be in such great haste to get to. Buses roared past and car horns blared every so often, and she found herself missing the laid-back main street of Banalla. Damian stopped outside a pretty stone building. A set of topiary pine trees in large pots stood on either side of the doorway, and she realised that through the door was a bar.

Inside, they found themselves a cosy nook and ordered drinks. Lottie settled on a cocktail, feeling like she needed something to match the extravagant revelation earlier in the day. As they waited in companionable silence, she finally felt like she was beginning to get her head around it all.

'So Jack acquired the ring at some point during the stagecoach robbery. But we still don't know if it was from Alexander, and why he'd have his wife's engagement ring,' she mused.

'We still can't prove that Catherine was there, so for now, we have to assume Alexander had it on him. Maybe he found out what happened to her. Maybe she and the baby died in childbirth not long after she arrived and he was able to collect her belongings and take them home.'

'But surely if that was the case, he would have sent word back to her parents before he left Sydney, and there would be hospital records and an obituary in the newspapers.'

'Which there isn't,' he nodded, then shrugged. 'The only thing we *do* know is that Jack obtained the ring during that robbery and gave it to Emeline.'

Their drinks arrived and Lottie smiled her thanks to the dark-haired young woman who placed the tall, royal blue cocktail on the table before her. 'It's all so frustrating. I don't understand how you manage to stay so unfazed by the *not knowing*.'

Damian took a sip of his beer. 'I'm fazed on the inside,' he said with a grin. 'But I guess it's sort of like working on a giant jigsaw. You have to sort through the pieces and find out where they belong until something fits. It takes patience—something I've had to learn over the years.'

'I still can't believe our little old ring is so . . . important. I mean, it was designed by someone who designed royal jewellery,' she said faintly. Not only was the bloody thing supposedly cursed, but it was also, apparently, stolen. There was absolutely no way she could wear it now, and especially knowing how much it was worth, even if her mother decided to give it to her one day. Which was never going to happen.

Twenty-four

12 April 1863

Jack lightly brushed a lock of hair away from Emeline's face as she lay beside him sleeping.

A pair of small wallabies grazed near the camp; their outlines just decipherable in the pre-dawn light, and he could hear the horses shifting their weight where they'd been tied nearby overnight. Soon the sky would pale and the first slivers of daylight would begin to pierce the shadows. He wished he could freeze this moment and savour it at leisure, but he knew that was impossible. It was only a matter of time before the police caught up with him if they continued to travel at the pace they'd been going. The only way to lose them would be to cut through the mountain range, into the bush where there were no roads. No tracks, even. But it was dangerous, with steep descents and almost impassable terrain, and Emeline, as good a horsewoman as she was, was not cut out for that kind of hard riding. Her mount even less so. Also, he was supposed to have met up with his brothers and the rest of the gang at one of their hideouts deep in the bushland hills two days ago. They would be worried about what had happened to him, and he was worried they might do something rash.

His dream of starting a life with Emeline was becoming just that—a dream. His heart was heavy as he faced the reality of their situation. I have to send her away.

He watched as her eyes fluttered before opening slowly. His breath caught in his lungs. God, she was beautiful. Her full red lips softly parted as she smiled a sleepy smile up at him and his heart momentarily stopped before lurching into a gallop. 'What are you doing?' she asked softly.

'Just watching you.'

'Is it time to go?' she asked, the lazy slumber quickly vanishing from her eyes.

'Soon. But not just yet. I just want a moment longer to savour you, just as you are right now.'

He loved the way she blushed when he spoke his heart to her, open and unafraid of how ridiculously romantic it sounded. He'd often used words to sweet-talk women into pretty much anything he wanted, but it wasn't till Emeline came into his life that he realised the true meaning of love. The way just a smile from her could render him speechless—one look and he was putty in her small, delicate hands. She owned him, heart and soul.

He lowered his head to kiss her lips. They felt soft and warm underneath his, and although he hadn't planned on anything more than just a gentle kiss, the passion between them reignited almost immediately. Her soft moan sent his senses reeling and she opened her mouth, deepening their kiss until desire became a raging inferno and they began to hurriedly discard their clothing.

In the aftermath, just as the sunrise flushed the sky, they lay spent and breathing heavily on the coarse blanket beneath them. He would love this woman until the last breath left his body, and then he would continue to love her throughout eternity beyond.

'I'll get ready to leave,' she said eventually, after they'd caught their breath and their bodies had cooled.

'No. Wait,' he said, and the urgency he'd wanted to hide clearly caught her attention.

'What is it, my love?' she asked.

'I have to get you back.'

For a moment, confusion crossed her beautiful face. 'Back?'

'Home. To your family.'

'I'm not going back,' she stammered. 'I can't go back.'

'You must. It's too dangerous to stay.' Jack shook his head. 'I can't take you where I need to go. It's too remote, too rough. And there's no other way to escape them.'

'I go where you go. That's what we agreed to,' she said stubbornly.

'That was when I thought we could outrun them,' Jack argued. 'We can no longer do that and I will not risk you being caught in the crossfire if they manage to ambush us. This is my fault, Emeline. I allowed my selfish desire to be with you outweigh my common sense. I should have waited until I was in California and then sent for you, not put you in harm's way like this. I was a fool,' he added bitterly.

'No, you weren't,' Emeline said, gathering his hands in hers and cradling them against her chest. 'I wanted to be with you too. Besides, my father would have had me married off before you could have sent for me. I cannot go back. They will disown me after running away.'

'You didn't run away. I abducted you and sent a ransom note.'

'You did what?' She stared at him incredulously. 'When? Why?'

'For this very reason. If anything were to happen to me, I wanted you to be able to return to your family, to be protected.'

'Jack . . .' She seemed lost for words.

Jack reached into the pocket of his coat and took out the ring. He'd imagined giving her the ring on their wedding day as they'd stood in front of a priest and made their vows, but there was no time for that now. 'This is for you.'

'Oh, Jack,' Emeline breathed, her eyes widening as she stared down at the magnificent opal he slipped onto her finger.

'Take care of it until we are together again. My darling, I promise I will send for you. I will organise passage to California and we will go together the moment it's safe to do so.' He tilted her face towards him and searched her sad eyes. 'I would never suggest leaving you if I thought there were any other way. But I will come back for you. I promise.' He kissed her deeply. 'We have to get moving.'

They made short work of dressing and had just finished saddling the horses when a shout of warning came. Barely moments later, the first shot hit a tree nearby. Jack reached for his gun and fired back before he even saw who he was shooting. He grabbed Emeline and pushed her down behind the rocks where they'd set up camp as he continued to return fire.

He swore as Emeline's thoroughbred reared and broke free, galloping into the surrounding bush. His own mount, set off by its high-spirited companion, pranced sideways but remained reasonably calm, despite the noise and confusion around it.

There was no time to second-guess his next move. He grabbed Emeline, one arm around her throat and held the gun to her temple, dragging her to her feet and shouting, 'I will kill her.' He knew the terror in Emeline's struggling was real but could do nothing to reassure her. 'I swear to God I will.'

There was a moment of silence as the shooting stopped and he heard low murmuring. 'Let the girl go,' *a toffy-sounding voice demanded from the tree line.*

'I'm not stupid. She's my hostage and I'm keeping her until I have safe passage.'

'You will never leave, McNally. Not alive, anyway. We have you surrounded.'

Jack calmly scanned the area and detected slight movement on at least three sides of the camp. He knew the way behind him was a ridge and the slope down too steep for anyone to have snuck up from that direction. 'Then you'll have to explain to Judge Oldsfield how you stood by and watched as his intended daughter-in-law was killed.'

'Let her go and it will be taken into leniency.'

'And you are a man of your word,' *Jack scoffed.*

'I am,' *the trooper assured him, sounding affronted at the challenge to his honour.*

'All right,' *Jack called back.* 'I'll send her out.'

'No, Jack,' Emeline sobbed. 'Please.'

'I love you,' Jack whispered roughly against her ear. 'I'll come back for you,' he vowed, pushing her out in front of him. He waited until they passed the safety of the rocks, then pushed her to one side, leaping away and making a dash for his horse. The shots peppered the ground at his feet as he sprinted, darting and weaving between the trees. Within moments, he was on his horse and heading along the edge of the ridge. The sound of general confusion was followed by the jingle of metal and the pounding of hooves but they faded into the distance as Jack leaped over the edge of the ridge and down the steep incline to the gully below.

Twenty-five

'Are you serious?' Hannah exclaimed, eyes widening.

'Yep. The ring was given to Emeline by Jack McNally. Stolen from Alexander Compton in the big coach robbery. And there's more. It was designed by a famous jeweller whose pieces are worth . . . well, a lot. I'm not sure exactly how much but, yeah . . . *a lot.*'

'That would explain the curse,' Hannah murmured.

'Mum,' Lottie started.

'I don't care what you say, I believe what I believe and I'm telling you, crystals and gems are more than expensive jewellery. They have their own frequencies and energy, opals even more so.'

'Well, anyway,' Lottie said shaking her head slightly, 'I just wanted to let you know. Damian's asked the jeweller to send you out the valuation certificate, and you should probably get that back into the safe as soon as possible,' she added, nodding down at the ring box.

'Okay.' Her mother smiled, but she still seemed a little distracted.

'Are you going to see Gordon again anytime soon?' Lottie asked casually.

'As a matter of fact, I am. Tonight,' Hannah added, and a smile tugged at her lips, causing Lottie to lift an eyebrow curiously. 'Yes, I know,' her mum said. 'It's taken me kind of by surprise too.'

'I think it's great,' Lottie said.

'It's . . . fun,' Hannah said, dropping her gaze to the placemat she was fiddling with. 'He makes me laugh and he challenges me—in a good way. He thinks I'm intellectual,' she chuckled with a small note of self-deprecation.

'Why wouldn't he?' Lottie asked, not liking to hear anyone put her mum down—not even herself. 'You're a savvy businesswoman and you've always been good at financial stuff.'

'I'm not book smart like he is—as you know I worked as a barmaid and a cleaner for most of my life before taking over Gran's shop. He's smart—but he doesn't use it to make himself sound important—you know? We have these deep discussions about all kinds of things—spirituality, religion, philosophy and he doesn't belittle my beliefs. He doesn't exactly share a lot of them, but he respects them, and that's so refreshing to find. We can talk without arguing or trying to change each other.'

Lottie found herself smiling at the sparkle in her mother's eyes as she spoke.

'And he's one hell of a sexy man—he's got the whole George Clooney, silver fox thing going on and it's—' her mother paused to close her eyes and give a little moan of appreciation.

'Okay. That's all I want to hear, thank you very much,' Lottie said, covering her ears with her hands and standing up.

A meditation class was due to arrive any moment anyway, so she hugged her mum and headed back into town to meet Cher at Madame Dubois.

'So, tell me. What happened in Sydney?' Cher asked.

'It's the same ring that went missing. It originally belonged to Alexander's wife, Catherine.'

For a moment Cher just stared at her. 'You mean, it's really worth a fortune?'

'Apparently.'

Cher let out a low whistle, and then another thought appeared to occur to her. 'Which means, if Emeline ended up with it, the rumours about her and Jack must be true,' Cher surmised. 'He must have given it to her for a reason.'

'I guess. But that means that it doesn't belong to my family.'

'It's been in your family now for more than a hundred and fifty years,' Cher reasoned. 'You've had it longer than the original owners.'

'I'm not sure that matters,' Lottie replied. 'What does matter is that this puts a whole new spin on the ring's history.'

'Awesome content for your book, though.'

This was true. She'd already been writing in the new twist—it had its own chapter.

'How's the sexy professor?'

Lottie smiled, still finding it strange to talk about their relationship. 'He's great.'

'I don't think I've ever seen such a smitten look on your face before. Dare I ask how serious this thing is?'

Lottie tried not to squirm under the watchful gaze of her friend. 'We're playing it by ear for now,' she said, doing her best to look unperturbed by the question.

'So *it is* serious,' Cher said, leaning closer.

'Maybe,' Lottie said, giving up her attempt at the whole blasé thing.

'I'm so excited for you.'

'We seriously haven't worked anything out long term yet,' she hastily added.

'Details,' Cher dismissed lightly, 'The main thing is you've finally broken the drought.'

Not a very dignified image, Lottie thought, slightly miffed until she noticed her friend's attention shift to the man who'd just walked through the door.

'Ohhh,' Lottie said quietly. 'Isn't that the rude gourmet-pie guy from up the road?' She watched as he glanced around the bar with that same unimpressed, too-cool-for-school look he'd had last time Lottie had seen him. 'Maybe he's here to check out the competition.'

'Uh, yeah . . . maybe,' Cher said, clearing her throat. Lottie's attention immediately switched to her friend's face and she noticed a more than slightly cagey expression.

'Is there something going on?' Lottie asked slowly.

Cher sent her a brief glance and a frown. 'He wants to take a look at the freezer I have for sale out the back.'

'Oh, does he now?' Cher was acting far too strange for this not to be *something*.

'If you'll excuse me,' Cher said almost haughtily.

Lottie gave a small chuckle. *Well, well, well . . . how the mighty have fallen.* Could this be another budding romance in the air? The two seemed so unlikely that it actually made complete sense. There had been a definite chemistry between them the first time they'd met, and clearly there'd been some kind of further conversation that Cher hadn't told her about.

Lottie watched them head into the kitchen and disappear from sight. She'd be keeping an eye on this developing situation, for sure.

'So, I've been thinking,' Damian suddenly said, making her glance up from her keyboard. 'Now that we know there's some kind of link between Jack and the ring, I've been trying to rethink this whole thing.'

'As in?' Lottie prompted. Damian seemed to be even more energised in his search for Catherine since their return from Sydney two days before.

Needle in a Haystack

'Widening the search, so to speak. Before, I was focusing on looking for Catherine in Sydney, but since this new development with the ring, I can't rule out the possibility that Catherine may have been on that coach. I mean, there's still no proof, but we've run out of options looking at everything else.'

'I know you need proof,' Lottie said slowly, 'but my gut is telling me she was there.' She closed up her laptop and set it aside.

'In my line of work, I've found that following your gut can go either way. It either leads you to the truth or it sends you on a wild goose chase.'

'If Alexander didn't find her in Sydney, I don't believe he would have returned on that coach.'

'Alexander had to get back to pay his miners and his builders.'

'The man crossed the world to build a fortune and a mansion for her. He paid a royal jeweller to design her engagement ring. That's a devoted man, not someone who would simply return home if his wife wasn't where he expected her to be.'

Damian listened, nodding slowly. 'You're right.'

'So, working on this theory,' Lottie asked, 'what's your next step?'

'As I was watching the re-enactment at the festival, I was thinking . . . what if Catherine *was* on the coach? The shootout with Alexander and the escorts and then the police . . . was

Catherine killed in the crossfire? It makes no sense that Jack would kill a woman now, when he'd never hurt women in the past. So what would have happened here to change that? What if Catherine *had* been caught up in the fight and had maybe been injured? Would Jack have left a wounded woman alone?'

Lottie frowned, thinking. 'You don't think he would have?'

'Everything I've ever read about the man suggests that, despite the fact he was a criminal and had no hesitation in robbing anyone he came across, he was first and foremost a gentleman towards women,' he said. 'He went out of his way to ensure the women were never harmed—to the point of finding one woman a chair in a bank robbery because she looked faint.'

'So where do we look now?'

'We have to work from the stagecoach location outwards. Something Cher mentioned at the dinner the other night got me thinking. She was talking about how remote these farms were at the time. There's a historical marker where the house Jack once lived in was, and we saw the ruins of Frolesworthy Hall. I'd like to track down some of the other places that Jack and his gang might have gone to. They were on the run for two days before the authorities even found the coach and the massacre. None of the stolen cash was ever retrieved, which makes me think they had to have had hideouts for stashing their loot along the way. Maybe that's where they took Catherine, to one of these places?'

Lottie knew there were various caves around the district that had been lookouts for Jack and his gang. It was possible

Catherine could have been taken away from the ambush location, accounting for the fact that no one had found her.

'That would kind of make sense,' she agreed. 'But how do we figure out where these places were? There's the caves on the tourist routes, but if there was anything to be found in those, it would have been found by now.'

'But they had to have safe places,' he said, 'otherwise the authorities would have turned up the stolen money.'

Neither of them had any answers, so Lottie tried to go back to her writing.

Damian picked up the book he'd been reading again but then put it aside. 'I, uh, did something today,' he said, sounding nervous.

Lottie wasn't sure what to expect the something to be, but his unusual lack of confidence had her on high alert. 'Oh?'

'I applied for a casual teaching job at Armidale,' he said in somewhat of a rush.

'Really?'

'Gordon says they've been looking for staff.' He shrugged. 'I'm not sure if there's actually a position available, but I thought I'd give it a go.'

'If there is, how long before you think you'd start the job?'

'Hopefully within a few weeks.'

Lottie's eyes widened.

'I thought I might stick around a bit longer, so I've taken some extra time off until I hear about this job.'

A smile broke out over Lottie's face and relief spread through her chest. She'd been so sure he would be leaving within the next few days, and she really hadn't been ready to say goodbye. Now, thanks to his leave, they wouldn't have to just yet. They settled back and he returned to his book.

'Gordon seems like a nice man,' she said cautiously.

'Yeah, he's a good bloke.' Damian nodded. 'Your mum seemed kind of keen on him too,' he added, clearly seeing where Lottie was going with her comment. 'You'd have to be blind not to see the sparks that were flying off them.'

'Mum's never shown an interest in anyone like that before. I tried calling her earlier and her phone went to message bank. She never doesn't answer my calls—or, at the very least, she always calls me back. Something very strange is going on with her.'

'I've known Gordon for years. She could do worse.'

'She won't let it go that far,' Lottie said with a sigh. 'She doesn't believe in love or relationships.'

'Maybe she's just never met the right person.'

'That's what worries me,' Lottie admitted. 'She's never allowed herself to fall for anyone, but if she meets someone she has no control over her feelings with . . . I'm just not sure how she'll handle it. She might end up hurting him.'

'They're both grown-ups. I'm sure they'll work it out.'

Lottie knew how stubborn her mother could be, especially about men and the cursed ring. But Damian's optimism was maybe rubbing off on her, as she considered the possibility that her mother might actually finally enjoy a relationship.

Twenty-six

'This is a disaster!' Hannah declared as Lottie walked into her mother's kitchen. She glanced around and noticed dishes in the sink and empty wineglasses on the bench.

When did she start drinking wine again? 'What is, Mum?' Lottie asked as she watched Hannah cross to the sink and begin to run some water.

'Everything,' she snapped. 'What have I always said about men and relationships?'

'That you shouldn't mix the two,' Lottie said automatically, taking a seat at the bench.

'Exactly. And I have *always* stuck by that rule.'

'Until you met Gordon,' Lottie said, suddenly working out the issue and feeling her heart begin to sink.

Her mother glanced up from the sink and sent her daughter a serious look. 'It's completely ridiculous,' she said, shaking her head irritably.

'What is?'

'I only just met the man,' Hannah said.

'And?' Lottie prodded.

'And,' her mother let out a loud huff of annoyance, 'everything I've ever told myself somehow just . . . doesn't make sense anymore,' she finished, sounding less annoyed and more helpless. 'I just don't understand what's happening! Everything's been fine and now suddenly I can't seem to function when he's not here . . . it's like a piece of me is missing. I've become some codependent, ridiculous . . . idiot!'

'Oh, Mum,' Lottie breathed, a mixture of surprise and happiness colouring her tone.

'It's completely insane!' her mother snapped.

'Where is he now?' Lottie asked, nervously glancing at the doorway, half expecting to see him appear at any moment, and really hoping it wasn't out of the shower.

'I sent him away.'

'You *what*?'

'I'm not doing it! I refuse to fall in love.'

'Mum!'

'What?'

'You ended it because you felt like you were *falling for him*?' Lottie demanded.

'I mean, *clearly* I wasn't,' she scoffed, 'I don't *do* love.' She said it like she was reminding herself rather than Lottie.

'You mean you haven't *allowed* yourself to do love before,' Lottie pointed out.

'Well, of course not. Why would I want someone I love to up and die on me?'

'Mum.' Lottie sighed wearily.

'Don't *Mum* me,' her mother said, narrowing her eyes. 'If anything, you should *now* believe in the curse. You found out where the ring came from. It's obvious.'

'The ring is *not* cursed,' Lottie said tightly.

'Oh really? A stolen opal? You think that doesn't come with a whole heap of bad juju? We're not talking any old gemstone here, we're talking about an *opal*.'

'So let me get this straight,' Lottie said, rubbing her temples lightly. 'You met an amazing man who you instantly felt a connection with—the first connection you've *ever* felt with someone—and you sent him away? Because you're *still* convinced a lump of rock has some kind of power to curse true love?'

'I refuse to be the reason someone dies,' she said stubbornly.

'Everyone dies at some point, Mum,' Lottie snapped. 'It's not you. Or a ring. Or a stupid curse. It's just *life*. And now you've sent away a man who could have been your one chance at finding love. And now you won't find out if it was love or not. All you'll have to keep you company is the stupid fear of a curse that doesn't exist.'

'It's a chance I'm not willing to take,' her mother said adamantly.

Lottie got up from the bench, unwilling to listen to any more of this nonsense. 'Then I genuinely feel sad for you,' she said. And she meant it.

'How was your mum?' Damian asked as she walked inside and kicked off her boots. 'Did you get to the bottom of the mystery?'

'Yep. She and Gordon have been together practically every day since the festival . . . and then she kicked him out and ended it.'

He frowned. 'Why? What happened?'

'My mother happened!' Lottie burst out. 'She suddenly remembered she's cursed.'

'Because of the ring?' Damian asked, lifting his eyebrows.

'Yep. Apparently, she and Gordon hit it off, but she got cold feet and ended it.'

'That's . . .' He let the sentence trail off awkwardly.

'Crazy?' she supplied helpfully. 'Insane? Yes, it is. That's my mother.'

'I guess I should give Gordon a call later.'

'Just reassure him it was nothing personal. My mother just didn't want to be responsible for him carking it.'

'Uh . . . maybe I'll just play dumb and let him tell me what happened.'

'So, what did you get up to while I was gone?' she asked, changing the subject. She was still too angry to talk about it anymore.

'I've located the original deeds from the O'Ryan homestead, where Kate and her husband lived,' Damian said, showing her a page with a map printed out on it.

'Kate's house? Why?'

'I'm glad you asked,' he said, flashing her a grin. 'Because *this* is where the hut was,' he said, pointing to a small square marked with a number before dragging his finger along the page to another part of the map. 'And this,' he said, glancing up at her with an undeniable spark of excitement in his eye, 'is where the stagecoach was attacked.'

Lottie looked back down at the map. 'You think that Kate was involved in the robbery?'

'Not necessarily, though, who knows? The whole family had prior run-ins with the law over the years leading up to Jack forming the gang. My point is that Jack would have been able to make it to his sister's place within hours of the robbery. If Catherine was on the coach and injured during the shootout, then my guess is she'd been taken from the scene.'

'To Kate's?'

He shrugged one shoulder slightly. 'It's just a theory, but it would explain why Catherine hadn't been found if she *had* been on the coach.'

'But . . . why would they take her?'

'Maybe they panicked and took her with them before they thought it through. Or maybe Jack had an attack of conscience and couldn't bring himself to leave a helpless—potentially wounded—woman out in the bush, alone.'

'A woman who might have had a baby with her . . . or was even in labour,' Lottie added gravely. 'We haven't ruled out the possibility she might still have been pregnant.'

Damian nodded thoughtfully.

'Okay, so just say he *does* play the noble hero and takes her to his sister . . . would they have killed her?' Lottie asked.

Damian shook his head. 'It doesn't follow his usual modus operandi. Let's go with the woman in labour theory,' he continued, beginning to pace. 'We suspect she'd have been close to her due date, and after everything she'd been through—a rough carriage ride, witnessing her husband's murder, men being killed around her, possibly being injured as well—it wouldn't be unreasonable to think she *could* have gone into labour. Kate was an experienced mother, and she'd likely have assisted other women in childbirth. It would make sense for Jack to take Catherine to Kate for help. But that would be a horrendous trek for a woman in her condition to make, added to the fact she may have also been caught in the crossfire and wounded.' He shook his head as he thought about it. 'Catherine's chances of surviving childbirth would already be quite slim, even without other factors playing a part. I suspect she and the child died in childbirth.'

Lottie felt her heart drop. She'd grown attached to Catherine over the last few weeks—uncovering her story from letters and listening to Damian talk about her. To think of her suffering in that way was too horrible to imagine.

'It would also explain why she was never found. Had she survived, she would have eventually turned up somewhere.'

'But if she died . . . what would they have done with her?'

'My guess is they would have buried her in an unmarked grave somewhere in the bush,' he said simply. 'Which is why I need to go up there.'

'You're going to look for a grave?' Lottie asked uncertainly. 'After all this time, you still think you'll be able to find something?'

'I won't hold my breath, but I still need to go. If for nothing else, then to get some photos for the book. But it won't hurt to look around.'

'Okay. When do we leave?'

He shot her a look of surprise, followed by a grin. 'It's pretty rugged up there. You sure you want to come?'

'I've come this far,' she said with a small smile that quickly faded. 'I'd like to go up there with you. For Catherine.'

Twenty-seven

Lottie rested a hand against the trunk of a nearby tree as she caught her breath. They'd been steadily climbing all morning, making their way through overgrown bush and across open paddocks. Part of the track was on private land and the other was now national park. They'd worked out with a local farmer, Tony, who owned the land bordering on the national park, which would be the best way to get to the homestead location and they'd come up with the route they were now on. There'd been a lot of climbing through rusty barbed-wire fencing and crossing narrow creeks, but they were getting closer.

'Just up this next ridge,' Damian said, turning to wait for her. 'Then we'll be there. You want to stop for a while and sit?'

Lottie shook her head. 'If I sit, I might not get back up. I'm okay,' she said, dragging a tired smile to her face. Maybe she'd been a tad hasty agreeing to come along. She really wasn't in the best shape . . . But every time she'd felt like giving up, she'd remember Catherine. This was, quite literally, a walk in the park, compared to what she likely went through.

As they reached the bottom of the ridge, Damian stopped. 'This should be it,' he said, looking around to get his bearings.

'How can you tell?' she asked, seeing only denser bush, although there was a small clearing with less undergrowth across from them.

'This is the GPS location.'

Lottie followed gingerly behind Damian as he brushed aside saplings and lifted low-lying branches, coming to a stop with a small sigh.

'There,' he said, pointing at a tall column of bricks and stone, sitting like a monument in a small clearing, the only remaining parts of what would have once been a small hut.

'The chimney,' Damian said needlessly. It was quite obvious, even to a novice like herself.

'I haven't been up here for years,' Tony said, looking around in a slow circle. 'It was always pretty overgrown, but it's a lot thicker than I remember.'

'Do you remember if there were any other landmarks? Foundations for outbuildings or anything?' Damian asked.

'Not really. It was only the chimney and fireplace left behind. We've had some pretty big fires go through over the years, and I remember my granddad sayin' his dad had told him the hut was built out of timber and had been starting to fall down back then. A hundred and fifty-odd years would be a long time for anything to survive out here.'

Damian took some photos of the chimney and the area surrounding it before wandering further away to look around. Lottie could hear the faint sound of a creek and decided to see if she could find it, suddenly longing to splash her face with something cool. She found it not far from the homestead site and tried to picture how it would have looked back then. Quite similar to how it was now, she imagined—secluded and rather isolated. It would have been a long and tiring trek to simply go into town, despite the location being only fifteen or so kilometres away. Roads would have been mere tracks, and the terrain would have made riding a horse quite challenging.

Her hands tingled in the cold water as she scooped it up and took a long sip. She closed her eyes and listened to the calming sounds of water trickling and birds singing, feeling it soothe everything away until she felt the most incredible feeling of peace and solitude.

She opened her eyes and blinked as she found a small tan and black wallaby watching her from the other side of the creek. She hadn't heard it approach, but with its colouring, it could have easily blended into the bushland surrounds. Which reminded her—if a cute little marsupial could camouflage itself, so could *not so* cute things, like snakes. She quickly glanced down around her feet, scanning the sticks and leaf matter, grimacing at the thought. Movement from the corner of her eye brought her attention back to the wallaby and she saw that it had inched a little closer to its side of the water.

Lottie smiled and lifted her phone, clicking off a few photos. 'You are so cute,' she cooed as one of its little ears twitched at the sound of her voice. It seemed quieter than other wallabies she'd seen in the wild, which had always been rather skittish. The only time she'd ever been this close to one before had been in tourist parks, where they were used to people and got fed. It didn't seem likely that this particular one would have had much contact with people. 'Are you lost or something little guy?' she asked, holding its gaze as it seemed to study her.

The crunch of a stick nearby sounded loud, fracturing the peaceful bubble she'd been enjoying. Lottie jumped and glanced over her shoulder, straightening from the edge of the water and tucking her phone back inside her pocket as she waited for Damian to reach her. She glanced over to find her new little friend was no longer there.

'Any luck?' she asked.

'Unfortunately, no giant, labelled headstones,' he said with a half-smile.

'Well, that would have been too easy,' she said, turning to walk across to a row of tall straight trees. 'I wonder how old these are? They're huge.' She tilted her head back to try to see the tops and stumbled as her foot slid on some small rocks, making her give a small gasp.

'Careful,' Damian said, crossing to her side. 'I'd really rather not have to carry you back to the car with a broken ankle.'

'So, you'd just leave me up here?' she asked, rolling her eyes.

'I'd send someone back to get you . . . eventually,' he said, slapping her backside playfully, but then stopped to stare at the ground at her feet.

'What?' Lottie asked curiously as she watched him crouch down and run his hands across the pebbles and gravel she'd almost slipped on.

'I don't know . . . but this doesn't look quite right.' He glanced over his shoulder at the small creek.

'What do you mean?'

'All these pebbles and rocks,' he said, looking up at her. 'They're probably from the creek . . . but it looks like they've been put here, just in this clearing. See?' He walked further away, kicking the leaf matter with his boot. 'There aren't any rocks here, or on the other side. Just in this area.'

'What does that mean?' she asked, confused.

'I'm not sure exactly,' he said frowning. 'Might be nothing. But it's strange.'

The three of them sat down and had something to eat before retracing their steps back to Tony's place. By the time they reached the car, it was almost dark. When Lottie got home she realised she'd never been so glad to see her bathtub and promptly decided to soak for at least an hour.

The days following the hike up to Kate's hut signalled a change in Damian. The playfulness and almost indulgence of their time together so far seemed to shift as Damian's historian mode kicked in, and he became more focused and determined. He spent a lot of time on his computer, emailing back and forth to various people, and on the phone, discussing what his next step should be.

Lottie was careful not to get in the way. She realised this was a big break for him, and something important was unfolding before them, yet, part of her was a little annoyed that it was interfering in their personal life. There were no more lazy nights on the lounge, holding hands and talking till all hours of the morning. No getting out of town on the bike, just to enjoy a ride together; now, it was all work—*his* work.

This version of Damian was not one that she'd seen before. However, there was something that had been weighing on her mind over the last few days, and after work one day she decided to finally bring it up—the job at Armidale.

'So, about the job,' Lottie said, placing a coffee beside Damian as he studied the map on the table.

'Hmm?' he murmured, without looking up. 'Job?'

'The Armidale job. Have you heard anything back yet?' she prompted.

He glanced up briefly. 'Oh, yeah. I turned it down.'

For a moment, she wasn't sure she'd heard him right. 'You turned the job down. And you didn't tell me?'

'I meant to, but it kind of slipped my mind, you know, with all this going on. Besides, I'm not sure it's the best time to accept a new job, not with all this suddenly looking so promising.'

She was still trying to wrap her head around the fact he'd turned down the job. 'What do you mean?'

'I called Mike the other day.'

'Who?' She frowned.

'Michael Gearsley.'

'The TV presenter?' she asked, surprised.

'Yeah, I've known him for years. Anyway, I wanted to get his advice and gave him a run-down of what I had, and he agrees that the next move should be investigating if those rocks were part of an old family cemetery. We can work out who was likely to have been buried there, using the church records to account for family buried in the town cemetery and anyone earlier who would have been buried at the homestead.' He stopped to slurp his coffee. 'It's just not the right time to start a new job.'

'I see.' Her stomach dropped as disappointment flooded her. Not the right time? Suddenly, after all the plans they'd talked about and all the hopes she'd gotten up, he had just unilaterally decided it wasn't the right time?

Don't get ahead of yourself, a little voice cautioned.

His phone rang and he reached out to pick it up. 'Speak of the devil,' he said, looking up. 'Sorry, I have to take this,' he added, leaning across to kiss her briefly before standing up and walking out of the room.

He hadn't said he wasn't taking the job at all, she tried to reassure herself. It made sense, with all this going on that it wasn't the right time. She sipped her own coffee, trying not to feel dejected.

'Great news!' Damian announced with great excitement as he walked back into the kitchen. 'Mike's got some keen interest in the story. He reckons we can get an archaeological dig organised, if we can turn up enough supporting evidence for our theory. I have to head back to Sydney to brief his backers.'

'What?' *Back to Sydney.* 'How long will you be away for?'

'It shouldn't be more than a day or two. I'm going to throw a bag together and have a shower. If I get on the road now, it'll save time travelling tomorrow.'

'Now?' she almost yelped.

'Sorry, I know it's all a bit sudden, but if we want to find answers, the only real way is to find evidence,' he said in a rush. 'We need a body to prove our theory, and I need Mike and his connections to make that happen. I'll be back before you know it.'

It was all happening so fast. Lottie had barely gotten her head around the fact he was no longer intending to take the job that would keep him here in town, and now he was leaving for a few days?

She sat on the end of the bed and listened as he hurriedly threw in clothes and went over a list of things he'd need to do once he reached Sydney. All the while, Lottie found herself desperately trying not to cry.

'Okay, that's everything, I think,' he said glancing around to check he hadn't forgotten anything. 'I'll call you when I get settled.' He tugged her to her feet and circled his arms around her waist, kissing her deeply. For a moment, Lottie felt her concern ease. Nothing had changed, it was the same as always . . . but then it stopped abruptly as his phone rang. Damian stepped back, picking up the phone and mouthing only a 'Sorry, gotta go' before he answered and was once more invested in whoever was on the other end of the call.

Suddenly, everything she'd been so certain about was feeling a lot more unsure.

Twenty-eight

Lottie greeted Cher as she sat down across from her at Skye and Tori's cafe. She'd been sulking around the house ever since Damian had left, and Cher's invitation for a coffee seemed like a good idea to get out of her own head for a while.

After giving her order to the waitress, she noticed Cher seemed unusually subdued. 'Is everything okay?'

'Just dandy,' she said briskly.

'Doesn't sound like it.'

Cher gave a small huff, before rolling her eyes. 'Well, you're aware that Clive and I had been . . . seeing each other.'

Lottie frowned. *Who's Clive?* Then it clicked. 'Oh, Mr Broody from the old cafe, now pie shop?'

'Yes . . . well, I should have realised there were a few red flags, but you know me. I'm like a bull, attracted to the damn things,' Cher muttered. 'Turns out, he's got a wife and family back in Woy Woy. He's decided to go back there.'

'So the gourmet pie shop's closing?' Lottie asked, shocked.

Cher sent her a sidelong glare. 'That is not exactly the point of what I'm saying right now.'

'Oh. Sorry,' Lottie said, wincing. 'That really sucks, Cher. I'm sorry.'

'It wasn't like we were a *thing*. I'm more annoyed that I didn't pick up on the signals. I must be losing my touch.'

'If it's any consolation, I would never have picked him for someone who had a wife and kids back home either,' Lottie said.

'Thanks, pet,' Cher said, patting Lottie's hand on the table, 'but you don't exactly see anything bad in anyone. I, on the other hand, should have known better.'

Lottie blinked, unsure if being called naïve was insulting or not. 'Well, I'm sorry he turned out to be a dirtbag.'

'Anyway, that's my excuse for looking down in the dumps. What's yours?'

Lottie sat back in her seat and smiled her thanks as her coffee was brought to the table, grateful to have the extra time to school her face into the epitome of calm, cool and collected. 'I'm just missing Damian. He's still in Sydney tied up with meetings about the dig.'

'Oh? Any more news? When do they plan to start?'

'He didn't have any solid dates. They're still talking to investors and lodging forms to whoever they have to notify about their intentions. Apparently, it's pretty involved.'

'I'd imagine.' Cher nodded thoughtfully. 'Has he heard back about the interview for the job in Armidale?'

'That's not happening now. Well, at least for the moment,' she amended.

'Why not?'

'He wants to concentrate on the dig at Kate's.' She shrugged, like it was no big deal.

'And you don't want him to?'

'I do,' Lottie corrected quickly, 'I mean, of course, it's super exciting,' she said, then sighed. 'It's just that he made all these huge decisions without even talking them over with me—turning down the job, taking off back to Sydney—I feel like suddenly everything fell into place and he didn't need me anymore. Like now there are more important things he's invested in. I say it out loud and I know I sound like a pouty girlfriend. I guess I was looking forward to him starting this new job and seeing where it went with us, and now it just feels like it's at a standstill.'

'You don't sound like a pouty girlfriend. He *should* have included you in those conversations. But maybe it was just a case of everything happening at once and he wasn't thinking straight? You should talk to him about it.'

'I don't want to rain on his parade—he's got so much going on at the moment.'

Cher nodded. 'But honey, I've seen the way that man looks at you. He might be distracted with all this Catherine business right now, but there's no way he's not planning on coming back to you and picking up where you left off. Just give it some time.'

'You're right, I know. It's all happened so fast, I lose track of how long it's actually been since we met. I've just got to be patient.'

'When the heart knows, it knows.' Cher squeezed her hand. 'But I can't wait to see what they uncover once they start digging,' she said, looking far more animated than when Lottie had first arrived. Lottie found her previous disappointment also begin to fade as she thought about what they might find. 'But I'm still so excited that you found Kate's hut. I wish I'd been with you.' Lottie had sent through some photos as soon as they'd regained reception on the way back from the hike, knowing Cher was waiting for news.

'Which reminds me, I only sent you Damian's photos. I think I still have some on my phone.' Lottie scrolled back to the hut hike and handed the phone across to her friend, moving her chair closer to explain what each one was.

'What a shame. There's nothing really left,' Cher said sadly. 'It looks so beautiful up there, but can you imagine having all those kids, washing and cooking and trying to keep them all warm?'

'But imagine the life those kids would have had with a creek at their doorstep and all that bush around them,' Lottie said with a smile. She continued to scroll through the photos of the site, then frowned as she realised the ones near the creek weren't there. 'I thought I had some photos of the creek to show you, but the stupid camera mustn't have clicked. Oh well, hopefully you can get up there and see it for yourself.'

'Maybe once they put in some kind of road. Madame Dubois doesn't hike.'

'A road would definitely make it easier,' Lottie agreed. She felt better after talking it through with her best friend. Cher was right—as she usually was when it came to practical advice. Damian hadn't given her any reason to believe he'd changed his mind about their relationship. She just needed to stop worrying about it. And that was fine for someone who likes to live in the moment, but a tad more difficult when you were a person who liked to have a plan.

Damian's return three days later brought a small measure of relief. He hugged her tightly, barely making it into the house before he was kissing her.

'God, I missed you,' he said, bowing his head to look down into her face.

'I missed you too.'

'Yeah, but I *really* missed you,' he said back, smiling that familiar, sexy half-smile.

She led him inside and down the hall to her bedroom and spent a long time arguing over who, in fact, missed whom the most.

Later, over a hastily made dinner of scrambled eggs and toast, Lottie caught up on all the news he had to share. Mike would be bringing a team of producers and archaeologists to inspect the homestead site and begin a survey of the area. It was going to take time to find the answers they were after, but this story was clearly just as fascinating to others as it was to Damian and Lottie, and people wanted answers.

Around town, word had spread about the interest in the old homestead site and talk of treasure hunters searching for the missing bushranger loot soon began circulating. It hadn't mattered how many times Lottie had personally corrected anyone retelling her the gossip, everyone was convinced the dig was about locating the valuables that folklore told Jack McNally and his gang had hidden over the years and which had never been recovered.

Lottie couldn't understand how anyone would consider that more interesting than locating the body of a woman who'd been missing for over a century and a half, but it seemed yet again that bushranger legends held a lot more appeal, and missing loot was more exciting than a woman no one remembered.

Life found a new routine. It was now a waiting game for the dig to get organised, which could take months. It wasn't exactly how she'd thought life after the festival would be. With everything that had been going on around them, she'd never really managed to think about what that might look like, but at least he was still here. Yet, she didn't feel settled. There was an unpredictability to it, as though at any minute, it could all change. They spent the same, if not more, time together since he'd moved into her house . . . but he *hadn't* moved in, not really. He'd unpacked a duffle bag.

She decided to raise the subject that had been on her mind one evening after dinner. 'Have you thought about what you might do once all this finishes?'

'To be honest, I haven't been thinking about anything that far ahead at the moment. Why?' he asked, glancing up from the plate he was drying.

'I just wondered,' she said with a shrug. 'I mean, what if the Armidale job isn't available later? Then there's what to do about your apartment. You might need to sort some stuff out soon.'

'There's plenty of time for that.'

'I just thought—'

'You,' he said, leaning in close and kissing her lips, 'think too much,' he finished, taking the glass she was washing out of her hands and placing them around his neck.

'I'm dripping all over you,' she tried to protest as water soaked his shirt.

'Just the way I like it,' he whispered into her ear, swallowing her emerging smile, steering her from the kitchen into the bedroom and effectively ending the discussion.

She understood things weren't quite as straightforward as they'd hoped them to be when they'd discussed him taking a job in Armidale, but he hadn't really committed to this new job up here, and he hadn't made any move to end his lease on his apartment or to find anything up this way. Every time she tried to bring it up, he told her not to worry. But she did worry. She was sure it was nothing and yet, in the back of her mind, it felt as though he was holding out on committing to the plan he'd seemed so keen on.

Everything was still the same as it had been before, kind of. She went to the shop and he stayed home and wrote. He'd sometimes bring his computer to the shop and work in the back room while she continued to plug away at her book. In the evenings, they'd read in bed or talk about their research, and they still couldn't keep their hands off each other most of the time . . . but there was just *something*. Everything seemed to hinge on this dig. *Once* he found Catherine . . . *Once* he found the missing piece of the jigsaw that continued to elude him . . . *Once* he had the answers for his book . . . *Then* they could concentrate on the future and make their plans.

The question that nagged at Lottie was: what if he *didn't* find Catherine? What if he *never* got his answers about what happened to her? Would he be able to let go of all that? Finish his book with no fact-based resolution and move on? She worried about the answer to that question more than she cared to admit.

Winter had well and truly settled in. The days were sunny, but the air was cold.

Cher had received an invite to go on tour with her old company and would be away for a few weeks, leaving the bar to be run by the capable Lenny, and Lottie missed being able to drop by to catch up with her friend at random. Her mother had decided to deal with her near-love situation by completely wiping it from her mind and preparing for back-to-back, week-long retreats at her spa. For someone who embraced her inner wellbeing, she could conveniently ignore her own advice.

'Let's take a break,' Lottie announced one lazy Sunday morning as she and Damian sat at the kitchen table, drinking coffee over their usual reading material.

'A break?' Damian lifted his eyebrows.

'Yeah. We haven't been for a ride in a while. We never got out to Gostwyck Chapel, and I've been wanting to take some photos for ages.'

While Damian got the bike ready, Lottie threw together some food for a picnic, albeit a picnic that would fit into the rather limited space in the gear bag on the back of the bike. She wasn't sure if she would ever be able to do a long trip on a bike like Damian often talked about doing. Packing light to Lottie meant using one suitcase instead of two; on a bike, it meant packing maybe only *two sets* of clothing. What kind of psychopath did that?

'It's going to be cold,' Damian warned her as they pulled on helmets.

'It'll be fine,' she told him blithely. How bad could it be?

Turned out, it could be pretty bad.

The wind seemed to pass right through the long-sleeved shirt she wore underneath the jacket and into her bones. Lottie was pretty sure she'd never been this cold in her entire life, but she was determined not to let Damian know. Her fingers felt like ice chips. *Gloves*, she mentally added to her list of things to buy.

However, the scenery helped to take her mind off the fact she might end up with hypothermia. She'd been out to the little chapel a number of times, and it always took her breath away. It constantly changed its appearance, depending on which season you visited. In summer and spring, the old stone building was covered in a deep green vine, but in autumn, it turned a brilliant deep crimson and was absolutely breathtaking. The avenue of two hundred golden-coloured elms surrounding the chapel looked like something out of a medieval story book. It was hard to believe it had only been built in 1921.

'Wow,' Damian said, taking in the view after he parked the bike and they had removed their helmets.

'Isn't it beautiful?' She never tired of looking at it, and even though she must have taken a hundred photos over the years, she could never resist taking more each time she visited.

'How are your hands?' he asked, stepping closer and taking them in his.

'I don't know yet, I stopped being able to feel them about half an hour ago,' she said lightly, although she was only half joking.

'I'll warm them up,' he said, unzipping his jacket and tugging her closer so her hands could wrap around his warm torso. She loved him right at that very moment because she was positive, if the roles were reversed, there was no way on

God's green earth she would let Damian put his freezing cold hands anywhere near her warm body.

She could have stood there all day, snuggled close and wrapped in his arms, soaking in the beauty of the old chapel, and she probably would have if another car hadn't driven up and parked nearby.

Tourists, she thought with a touch of irritation at having her idyllic moment interrupted, before remembering she was basically a tourist too. *But still . . .*

They moved apart and strolled around the grounds of the small church. Lottie snapped a heap of photos and swore these were even more breathtaking than the last lot she took. She managed to take a few sneaky ones of Damian as he studied the building and was no doubt tucking away something history-related in his brain to pull out and examine at a later date. She loved the angles of his face—his jawline and the column of his throat as he tipped his head back to look up at the roof. She snapped the photos and experimented with the settings, blurring the church in the background and focusing on the man in the forefront. She looked down at the screen and scrolled through the images she just took. She loved everything about him.

'How are they?' he asked, startling her as he came up beside her.

'Yeah. Great,' she said quickly, closing the camera app and looking up at him, catching her breath as she lost herself in his beautiful eyes. She'd never understood the phrase she sometimes read in books about drowning in someone's eyes until this very moment. That was exactly what it felt like. His slow smile melted her heart and she felt herself being drawn towards him. As their lips touched, she felt him pause before his smile widened and his mouth took hers gently. She would never get tired of that sexy smile.

I love him.

The thought felt so intense that, for a moment, she thought she'd said it out loud. She should tell him. *Just say it*, a little voice urged her, and she took a breath in. At that moment a high-pitched laugh sliced through the air from a woman rounding the corner with two friends and the spell was broken, the moment lost.

'Come on, I'm starving,' Damian whispered, and—even though she was disappointed that a perfect, romance-movie-worthy moment had been ruined—being tucked in tightly by his side as he smiled tenderly at her was all she really needed.

'These sandwiches are amazing,' Damian said, after devouring two halves and reaching for another. 'What do you do to them?'

'Nothing, really. It's just chicken and mayo,' Lottie answered with a shrug, munching happily as the sun finally warmed through the last of her frozen extremities.

'Well, they're the best I've ever had.'

'Play your cards right and I might make them for you again one day,' she told him with a playful wiggle of her eyebrows.

Needle in a Haystack

His phone interrupted and he sent her a lopsided grin of apology before pulling it from his pocket and looking at the screen. She saw his look of surprise before he answered and listened intently. 'That's brilliant news, mate,' he said finally. 'Yeah, absolutely. No worries. See you then.' He gave a small, pleased huff as he put his phone back in his pocket and looked up at her. 'That was Mike. We just got the go-ahead. We're starting the dig as soon as he gets up here. As early as the day after tomorrow.'

'That's great,' she enthused, and it was. The sooner they got this dig over with, the sooner the uncertainty she was feeling about their future could be put to rest. Then she felt a twinge of guilt. This was a big deal to him—well, to everyone, if she was being honest. Actually finding out what really happened to Catherine and bringing her story to light, well, that would be huge. This was bigger than those niggling doubts. She just needed to let things unfold and see what happened.

If only it was that easy to switch it off.

Twenty-nine

'Any news from Area Fifty-one?' Cher asked over the phone a week later.

Lottie gave a dry chuckle. The dig had a film crew following along to document the entire thing for a future TV documentary, which put a shroud of secrecy around the project. 'Nope. Apparently, things move very slowly.' First, there was all the red tape, heritage and council approvals to go through. Then it was marking grids and evaluating the area, checking maps and records and research, which was where Damian's expertise came in. Once they actually started to dig, it was more uncovering than actual digging, so the process was clearly not going to be completed in a matter of days.

'Have you been up there yet?'

'Not since the day we located it. I'll probably wait until something exciting happens. It's one hell of a hike just to go and watch them do nothing much,' she said.

'How's Damian going?'

'Fine. He's been camping up at the site. There's a lot to oversee and it really doesn't make sense to come all the way back here every day.'

'Why does that sound like you're trying to convince *yourself* that it's fine?' Cher asked, sounding sceptical.

'I mean, sure, it's not great that I don't see him as much, but it's to be expected. He's working.'

'Are you okay?'

'Of course,' she said, forcing some enthusiasm into her tone.

'Really?'

Oh, for goodness' sake, Cher was like a damn dog with a bone sometimes. 'It's not exactly how I thought things would be going,' Lottie conceded. 'I guess we've been inseparable for the most part and now, suddenly, he's never here. I just need to get over it.'

'This excavation stuff will be over soon, right? And then life will go back to the way it was.'

'Absolutely. Anyway, enough of that. How's the tour going?' Cher predictably, warmed to her favourite topic, and Lottie was glad to have the subject changed. She was being a big sook when she needed to be a mature, supportive girlfriend. She decided then and there: no more complaining.

Damian hunkered down beside the campfire near the dig site and breathed on his cold fingers as the sun crept its way slowly into the sky. It was freezing, thanks to the fact the camp was in the middle of the bush with tall trees forming a dense canopy above them and blocking out much of the sunlight.

Mike emerged from his tent nearby and wandered over to join him by the fire.

'How are you coping?' Mike asked, reaching his hands out towards the heat of the fire.

'Bit disappointed in the accommodation—I expected a superstar like you to have motel rooms and room service,' Damian joked.

'Not on the budget we have for this one, mate,' Mike said, shaking his head with a chuckle.

As excited as Damian was for this whole thing, he missed waking up beside Lottie every morning. He missed her more than he'd ever missed anyone before—and it wasn't *just* because she would have warmed him if she had been sharing his sleeping bag. He just missed . . . *her*.

'You've been a bit quiet lately—what's going on?'

Damian dropped teabags into two tin mugs as he considered his answer. Usually, once he was on a site, he was completely focused and barely thought about anything other than the job at hand. But this time it was different. Sure, he was focused when he had to be, but slowly it had been dawning on him that this *wasn't* the most important thing to him. The thought had shocked him. Up until now, his work had been everything.

He was also feeling slightly unsettled because this dig wasn't like any he had previously been part of. This one was being filmed—and not just for posterity. There was a producer and a camera crew, and others with roles that were a mystery to him, yet here they were, hanging about, waiting for a big break. Mike was a good bloke, but he was also a businessman and a celebrity. His projects were backed by TV companies and investors and there had to be a worthwhile outcome. There was extra pressure driving the project forward, and he was beginning to notice how everyone was looking to him for results. It was unpleasant, and he knew he had risked 'selling his soul' by going to Mike with this idea, but it had been the only way he could get the project moving. By himself, the timeframe would have stretched out who knew how long. He knew Mike's work, and trusted him to be true to the project, but there were different agendas, and—despite the fact he had equal control with Mike over the dig and anything they uncovered—he was finding it difficult to relinquish control of the research. It had been his baby for so long.

He gave Mike a half-smile and a shrug. 'It's all happened so fast—it's taking a bit to get my head around it. It's been a lot to juggle.'

Damian lifted the kettle off the coals and poured the teas, his mind jumping back to a conversation with his eldest sister a few days earlier.

'How's Lottie taking it all?'

'She's great about it—she understands.'

'Really? Weren't you making plans to move in together?'

'Well, yeah. But then this all happened. She gets it.'

He grimaced to himself. The conversation had kept replaying in his head ever since, and he was beginning to suspect that maybe Lottie wasn't as okay with it as he'd first thought. He realised he hadn't seen her light up in a long time, and it occurred to him that he'd never really gone over everything with her—Mike had needed answers on the spot and there'd been a tight schedule. Maybe he should have talked things over with her first—but this was his career. He had to admit, between the Armidale job or doing this with Mike, it really hadn't been a tough decision. This was possibly a once-in-a-lifetime opportunity and he hadn't hesitated.

'You're married,' he said to Mike as he passed across the hot brew. 'How do you handle doing all this stuff? Being away all the time?'

'Lucy's also in the industry and she's away just as much as I am most of the time. This lifestyle suits us, but it's not for everyone. You got problems at home?'

'A new relationship . . . it's been bad timing.'

'Ah,' Mike said. 'Yeah, that would be tricky. I don't know what to tell you, except that it takes a strong relationship and good communication to work a job like this. It could be the turning point in your career—we've all taken a gamble on this thing—but you always have to figure out what things in life you're gambling with and if the potential gain is worth the risk. It's never easy.' Mike stood up and clapped him on the shoulder then headed off.

Damian shook off the reservations that were crowding him. The only thing that mattered was uncovering something that would help piece together his theory about Catherine—at least, he hoped they uncovered something. Otherwise, it was back to the drawing board again, and his book wouldn't have any of the answers he'd been hoping to find.

They'd brought up a Ground Penetrating Radar machine to help detect areas where the ground had been disturbed at some point in a non-natural way, like if it had been dug up and something had been buried beneath. GPR equipment was used in a number of fields, but he hoped it would help them to locate the gravesites he was looking for. Already it had helped them map out the hut, and a few other areas where structures would have once stood, giving them a clearer idea of how the small holding would have been laid out.

He wondered what Lottie was doing.

He listened to the phone ringing, and felt a small trickle of warmth as her voice filled his ear.

'I was just thinking about you,' Lottie said. He wished she were standing up here on this ridge beside him instead of on the other end of the phone. 'How's it going?'

'Not great,' he admitted, and his earlier disappointment flooded back.

'But you found graves?' she prodded.

They had, which had been exciting a week ago, but since then, his excitement had slowly started to ebb away. 'Unfortunately, not the one we were looking for. All the graves seem to line up with the records from the church register. There's nothing here. The chimney is the only part of the original homestead. There's nothing of any archaeological value left to find. It's been a complete waste of time.'

'So is that it? They're pulling the plug?'

'We've got another two days before they shut it down. We were at least hoping to find something remaining from the era, stables or more of the original homestead building. Something connected to bushranger history in the area. But we don't even have that. If there's no economic value in continuing the dig, there's no point in continuing.' It took a lot of funding to enter a project like this, and ruins had to be able to justify their worth. Maybe if they'd been able to uncover a solid foundation that would have laid out a floor plan of the house or given them something they could have potentially restored for a tourist interest and been able to manage for heritage value, it would have been different. But this was a primitive set-up. The house would have been built of bark and timber, with a dirt floor. Kate and her family had not been wealthy, and with a large family of mouths to feed, they would have been struggling for much of the time they had lived here. Eventually, long after losing her husband, Kate sold the land and moved out of the area, and the little hut was abandoned.

'I'm so sorry it hasn't turned out the way you were hoping,' Lottie said sadly, bringing him back to the conversation.

'It happens. Unfortunately, we tend to run into dead ends and disappointments a lot in this field.'

'Well, you still have two days,' Lottie said. He smiled at the optimistic little lilt in her words.

'Yeah, who knows? We might get a miracle.'

'I miss you,' she said softly.

'I miss you too.'

They said goodbye and Damian slid the phone back into his pocket. He took a moment to look around his surroundings. From up here, he could see far into the distance across gullies and tree-topped ridges. He breathed in deeply and the smell of the bush around him filled his senses. Eucalypt and warm earth, moss and damp leaf matter and the lingering smell of campfire smoke melted together in a heady, invigorating scent that filled him with solace.

He knew he shouldn't have got his expectations up. He'd gone through plenty of setbacks in the past while working on different projects, but this one, he supposed, had become a lot more important to him. He'd lost his professional detachment and let it become personal.

The cool air touched his face and he realised the afternoon sunlight was beginning to fade. Time to make a move back to camp. He gave the view one final glance and turned away.

Thirty

As he followed the track winding its way downwards to the camp, a movement in the bush caught his eye. A small wallaby, startled by his presence, had jumped from its feeding spot and was now watching him curiously. He'd seen a number of kangaroos and wallabies in the time that they'd been up here, as well as other wildlife, birds and insects. The team frequently heard the rustle of smaller creatures like echidnas and native marsupials digging around on the bush floor in search of food. He wondered what they made of the humans digging about in the dirt.

The little wallaby remained nearby, still watching him, its brown eyes holding his in an almost calm way that was unusual. The way it watched him so intently began to strangely unnerve him. He started walking again, and the animal hopped along beside the track, as though following him.

Needle in a Haystack

'What's your problem, little guy?' he finally asked.

The wallaby just looked at him.

Maybe it was injured? He studied it carefully, not seeing any obvious signs. There was no blood, nothing looking abnormal. He made to step towards it and it jumped out of reach. *Okay, that's more normal behaviour.* He turned to walk away and again the wallaby hopped along beside him, then jumped sideways into the bush as he turned to watch it.

'What is it, Skip?' he asked with a grin, mimicking the old *Skippy* reruns he'd watched as a kid.

Oddly, the animal hopped slightly sideways again, looking back over its shoulder, almost expectantly, as though waiting for him to follow.

Right, he found himself thinking sarcastically, *the wallaby wants you to follow it into the bush. Because that's a completely normal thing for a wallaby to do.* But each time it took a small hop forward, it would continue to look back over its shoulder at him. 'I have to be losing my mind,' he muttered before giving a fatalistic sigh and moving off the track towards the animal. It began hopping slowly, getting a few paces ahead then stopping to wait for him. It crossed his mind that this would make a great horror movie—a lone camper in the Australian bushland gets lured from the track by a cute wallaby to be attacked by a pack of wild dogs . . .

As far-fetched as the idea was, he was definitely having second thoughts about following the damn thing when he glanced over his shoulder and realised how far off the track they'd ventured. He really wasn't looking forward to the possibility that Mike and the camera crew would have to come and find him if he got lost. But just as he was convinced this was the craziest idea ever, the wallaby stopped and allowed him to get closer, until they were almost side by side. Then it turned its head from him to look straight ahead. Damian was not feeling overly confident that he hadn't somehow fallen asleep and was dreaming this entire weird situation, but as he followed the direction of the wallaby's gaze, he found himself frowning.

Across a small creek was a rock face covered in overgrown vines and bushes. He noticed that there was an odd crevice, a shadowy area behind the overgrowth that looked out of place. Carefully, he made his way across the ankle-deep water of the narrow creek to the wall of rock. He carefully moved aside some of the overgrown vines and leaves, and to his surprise discovered it was an opening to a narrow cave.

He turned the torch of his phone on and held it up to shine around the inside, realising it opened into a large space before breaking off into two separate tunnels. Damian had always found caves fascinating and he was glad he'd stumbled upon this one, but he reluctantly realised it was getting late. He didn't want to be fumbling his way back to camp in the dark. Maybe he'd mark the GPS setting in his phone so he could come back later to explore it a bit more.

He'd just finished loading the coordinates when he glanced up and spotted something on the wall of the cave. At first, he thought it was just some graffiti that kids might have left behind, but as he held the torch up closer, he reconsidered his first reaction. It *was* graffiti of sorts . . . but it was a poem.

And it was signed: JACK McNALLY.

It seemed to be written in charcoal and measured about half a metre or so across one wall:

> *In the heart of the Australian bush, Where the tall trees whisper and kangaroos bound, two souls met, in a dance of fate.*
>
> *She, with hair like bronze fire, so young and so slight, he, a master of the bush, a ghost of the night.*
>
> *Through the dust and the heat, their love did grow, beneath the Southern Cross, a secret only they would know. He stole her heart with a bandit's charm, she tamed his wildness with her gentle calm.*
>
> *Moments stolen from the world's harsh glare. Amidst the camps and hideaways they'd share, In the quiet of night, 'neath starlit skies, They'd whisper vows, of a future bright.*
>
> *Though fate may part them, trials would bind, their love burned bright, no man could divide. For in the tales of bushrangers bold, their love story would be forever told.*

Damian stared in disbelief at the writing before him. He began snapping photos, still unsure if this was real or just a dream.

He left the cave and retraced his steps, marking the spot on the pathway where he left the trail so he could bring Mike up and show him what he'd found. Maybe they hadn't discovered what they'd been looking for, but perhaps not all was lost. If this turned out to be an unknown cave used by Jack McNally and his gang, maybe this was something even bigger.

He glanced around, but there was no sign of the wallaby.

Lottie pulled up outside her mother's house and spotted Hannah kneeling beside a bed of herbs, pulling weeds.

'Hello,' Hannah said, looking up from under a wide-brimmed hat. 'This is a nice surprise.'

'I brought dinner,' Lottie said, holding up a bag with two containers of soup she'd picked up on a sudden whim from Skye and Tori's cafe.

'What's the occasion?'

'No occasion. I just wanted to have dinner with my mum.'

Hannah smiled and stood up, dusting off her pants and wrapping an arm around Lottie's shoulders. 'Checking up on me, you mean?'

'Well, that too,' Lottie shrugged as they walked inside and Hannah washed her hands. 'You've been quiet lately.'

'The same could be said of you. How's the big dig going?'

'It's not going as well as they'd hoped it would,' she admitted. 'How have you been?'

'Busy,' her mother said, taking down two bowls as Lottie found spoons. 'Too busy, really,' she said with a long sigh. 'All I seem to do is pack orders and drive into the post office.'

'So they've still been rolling in since the festival?' Lottie asked.

'They haven't stopped. I've picked up two more stockists and they're keen to take on more, but I'm struggling to keep up with demand.'

'Is it time to maybe think about expanding and hiring staff?'

'I'm not sure that's the direction I want to go, to be honest. When I started this, I wasn't trying to grow a company. I just wanted to make my tea for people who enjoyed it. My first love is the retreat and the spirituality side of this place, but the online stuff . . . it's like a demanding child I'm constantly having to feed and give all my attention to. It's draining.'

'Is that the only thing going on? You really don't seem like yourself lately,' Lottie said, taking a sip of her soup

'I'm starting to realise that I may have overreacted slightly where Gordon was concerned. I'm finding myself . . . thinking about him . . . a lot.'

'Have you told him?'

Hannah shot her a startled glance before shaking her head. 'No.'

'Why not?'

'Because after the way I acted, he probably thinks I'm some sort of psycho.'

'I think if you explained to him and told him why you acted like that, he might surprise you.'

'No, I can't. It's probably for the best anyway. I've never wanted a relationship. It's probably too late for me to change now.'

'Don't be ridiculous, Mum,' Lottie said gently. 'It's never too late. You should think about it.'

'I don't think so,' she said after a slight pause, then changed the subject. 'How's the book going?'

'Damian's?'

'Yours,' her mother corrected, tilting her spoon into the creamy broth. 'I haven't heard you talking about it for a while.'

'It's going,' she said slowly.

'That didn't sound too convincing. What's going on?'

'I'm not really sure my heart's in it at the moment. This whole thing with Catherine and the dig ... there's kind of been a lot going on.'

'Maybe this time apart from Damian will reignite your spark again. You have been a little consumed by him and his project since he arrived in town.'

'That's not true,' Lottie protested. 'I've been working on my book and at the shop. But this Catherine thing is huge.'

'Yes, it is, but it's no more important than your project is to you. You've spent years researching and writing. You've come too far to give up on it now.'

Her mother's words stung a little bit, possibly because of the truth in them. She had been neglecting her book. Living with a real author had shown her just how much of a novice she really was. 'I just haven't had the same drive that I had at first.'

'You just need to spend some time getting back into it. You'll find your mojo again,' her mother said confidently.

Driving home later, Lottie thought about her mother's words. She *had* been ignoring her book. The research had taken so much time and now that she was doing the actual writing, she really wasn't sure what she was doing. When it was just a hobby—something to do for her mum—it hadn't seemed like such a big deal, but now that they'd discovered the truth about the ring, and what had happened with Catherine, that changed everything. Her whole family history. It was a lot of responsibility and suddenly, it was no longer just a fun little project she was working on. It was, in fact, quite daunting and she wasn't sure what do with it.

The previously quiet bushland was no more. With the discovery of the cave came a renewed energy. Everyone was busy. The hidden cave entrance was now where the team was focusing its attention. Care had been taken to ensure no damage was being done to the area and to keep track marks to a minimum as they assessed the site for further artefacts and historical relevance, but Damian was sure this place had never before had this many people coming and going at one time.

The date on the poem was just after the stagecoach robbery and prior to Jack taking Emeline hostage, though the poem seemed to well and truly put doubt over the 'hostage' version. Damian knew this would be of great interest to Lottie and her family research and he couldn't wait to show her. Despite the whole area being hush-hush due to the filming and the documentary, Damian knew they wouldn't be able to keep any of the discoveries under wraps for too long.

Within three days, the team had uncovered a number of interesting pieces. There was a stash of personal items—an old tobacco pipe, the rusted remains of what may have been a tin cup and plate, empty bottles—and a tin box that had been buried, which contained a few banknotes and some nuggets of gold and other small gems.

The question now was how did this new piece fit into the puzzle of what they already knew? If Jack wrote the poem the day after the robbery, the banknotes they'd found were likely to have been part of their plunder. They were waiting on the partial numbers they could read on the money to match the serial numbers they had on record of the stolen cash. So how, if at all, did Catherine fit into this now?

Damian still firmly believed she had been on that coach, and quite likely taken from the scene. In the likely event she and the baby had passed away, he'd assumed the family plot at Kate's was where they would have buried her. But then, why? If word got out about Catherine being on the coach—if someone in Sydney had come forward and told the authorities they'd seen her leave with Alexander—the police would come looking, and likely have noticed a newly dug grave. They wouldn't have risked it. So therefore, Catherine could still be out here somewhere, her remains forever lost in the bush.

He'd been half hoping that maybe they'd uncover some human remains inside the cave, but deep down he knew that wasn't how Jack or his brothers would have treated the remains of a lady. She would have had a burial—that much he knew for certain. They may have been hardened bushmen and criminals, but they weren't animals.

He sat down back at the new camp, where they'd relocated to be closer to the cave, and opened the esky to take out a beer. He wasn't sure what he was feeling at the moment. He was excited, of course, by the discovery of the cave, and the vital pieces of evidence they'd managed to find, but he was still frustrated and deeply disappointed that his own research had come to a halt.

He tipped his head back and drank deeply. The cold brew felt good running down the back of his parched throat. As he lowered his hand and looked straight ahead, he paused. Two brown eyes stared at him a few feet away—a small wallaby watching him intently. *It couldn't be.* He held himself still. He hadn't mentioned his weird encounter with the wallaby to the others when he'd returned to camp after finding the cave. After all, when he'd replayed it over in his head later, even *he* thought he was crazy, so there was no way it was going to sound any less crazy out loud.

He reached slowly towards a small camping table and picked up a dry cracker, then tossed it across to the wallaby. It didn't take its gaze from him. 'What do you want?' he asked it quietly. Almost immediately, it turned, took a jump and looked back at him. 'You've got to be kidding me,' he muttered. Surely this couldn't be happening again?

Reluctantly Damian got to his feet and gave a small chuckle of disbelief at what he was about to do. What was the worst that could happen—ending up on a wild goose chase? At least he could finally put the first encounter down to some kind of fluke.

This time, the wallaby moved a lot faster, to the point that he lost sight of it now and again and found himself swearing and cursing as he trudged across uneven ground, snagging his boots on large sticks and branches, avoiding rocks poking through the surface and loose ones on the top. It was on one such loose rock that Damian lost his footing and fell, landing hard on his side and momentarily winding himself. Pain shot through his side and arm as he tried to ease himself upright. He dropped his head, breathing heavily as he caught his breath.

He closed his eyes and took in another deep breath. The familiar smells of the bush helped focus him. Eucalyptus, wattle, the freshly disturbed earth beneath him and the heady scent of roses . . .

He opened his eyes and frowned. Maybe he had a concussion . . . *roses*? Wincing, he heaved himself off the ground and looked around. A few feet away, much to his disbelief, was a blossoming rose bush.

What the hell was a rose bush doing in the middle of nowhere? Limping slightly, Damian made his way across to where the pale cream-flowered bush grew. He didn't know a lot about gardening or plants, but this definitely smelled like a rose, even if the flowers were smaller than he would expect, maybe only about five centimetres across. There was an abundance of them clustered on the small bush.

In the quiet surrounding him, he unexpectedly detected a murmur of voices and turned his head to locate the direction the sound was coming from. Although his ankle still ached, it wasn't as painful as it had first been, and he managed to hobble his way up a gradual incline, using small saplings and trees to pull himself up until he reached the top and looked down on the rest of the team outside the cave entrance. From his position, he turned and looked back the other way and could work out where their camp was, as well as where the previous camp was located, not far from the homestead ruins. A stirring inside his chest began to flutter. The location of the rose bush suddenly didn't seem so random.

Damian stumbled his way down towards the cave, causing Mike to look up at him and frown as he saw him limping.

'What happened? You okay?'

'I need the GPR up here,' Damian said without preamble.

'What? Why?'

Damian ignored the throb in his ankle. 'I think I've found her.'

Thirty-one

The days following were a blur of elation and painstaking excavation.

On closer inspection, the rose was found to be an older variety, one lesser known and rare to be found in gardens nowadays, called a Scots Rose. It had been brought to Australia from Scotland and the UK in the early 1800s to beautify colonial gardens, and it could not have ended up here accidentally. The reason for its position soon became obvious once the GPR machine uncovered a grave-shaped area beside it.

There had probably never been a headstone or marker, but either someone had planted the rose bush by the grave or it had somehow grown from a flower left on it—Damian wasn't sure. But, despite the fact they had no solid evidence that this was even Catherine's grave, he knew in his heart that it was.

Needle in a Haystack

Lottie had been cooking dinner when her phone rang, and she was surprised to see it was Damian. He never called this late. Her heart picked up speed as she answered, worried. 'Damian? Are you okay?'

'I think we found her.'

At first, she didn't know what he was talking about, still sure he was calling to tell her something was wrong, but it only lasted a split-second. 'Catherine? You found Catherine?'

'It's got to be her,' he said, and she could hear the grin in his voice, finding a matching one spreading across her own face.

He went on to tell her how he literally stumbled upon it, and although she'd continued listening to his story, her mind had latched on to the bit he'd glossed over.

'Did you hurt yourself?'

'Not really. I've got a bit of a sore ankle, nothing serious.'

'Did you get it looked at?'

'It's just a sprain,' he brushed it off lightly.

'I'm coming up,' she said, suddenly deciding now was as good a time as any.

'You're more than welcome to come up, but if it's because you're worried about my ankle, I mean it, I'm fine.'

'Well, it'd be pretty cool to see what you've found too,' she admitted. 'And I've missed you.'

'I miss you too.' His tone lowered, making her stomach do a little flip-flop. 'I really want you up here with me, but maybe give it a couple of days. I probably should be resting it for a bit and I want to be able to walk on it to show you the dig site.'

She *knew* it. He wasn't telling her the whole truth about his fall. She was ready to hike that damn mountain immediately except common sense reminded her that all sorts of creepy crawlies came out at night, not to mention that it was cold.

'Okay,' she agreed, reluctantly, after he promised to organise to meet her in a few days' time.

Now that the day was here, Lottie was experiencing a range of feelings. She was eager to see Damian after three weeks, and she was also excited by the prospect of watching an actual, real-life archaeological dig. And she was very, very cold.

She pulled her coat around her more firmly and braced herself against the chill as she waited for the four-wheel drive that was coming to pick her up from where she'd parked the car. At least this time she wouldn't have to trek, since a track had been made in order to transport equipment to the campsite for the film and excavation crew. Damian had warned her that the track was narrow, steep and definitely not suited for the likes of her little car.

Finally, a vehicle came into view, crawling over the steep inclines and around treacherous bends.

When it pulled to a stop, Damian opened the passenger door and slowly got out of the car to greet her.

'Are you okay?' she asked, worried by the tightness of his face.

'I'm fine.'

'Yeah, well, your idea of fine and mine seem to be two different things,' she replied. 'I wanted to make sure you were *really* okay.'

'It's just a sprain,' he assured her before introducing her to the tall, skinny man who climbed from the driver's seat. 'This is Ben.'

'Hi Ben,' Lottie said.

'Apparently you've got some supplies for the camp?' Ben asked after they had exchanged some brief small talk.

'Oh, yes, in the boot.' Lottie went to the back of her car and helped unload a number of grocery bags and a parcel she'd been asked to collect from the post office. Once they were loaded, she locked her car and left it in the same clearing they'd parked in the first time they'd hiked up here.

It was a white-knuckle drive back to the campsite, and Lottie almost preferred walking. As far as tracks went, it was crude and barely passable in places, but they eventually made it and Lottie was just glad it was over.

There were a few people around the camp, some sifting through buckets of dirt, others recording information and photographing unrecognisable items, and a few carrying supplies to a large tent that had tables and cooktops set up inside, presumably for preparing meals for the workers. The rest of the crew, so Damian informed her, were out working at the gravesite. The tedious preparation work was still being done to get ready for unearthing the actual grave, so progress had been slow.

Everyone seemed young and fun and energetic. Damian had told her that since the discovery of the cave the mood around the camp had been rejuvenated, and now, with the discovery of the grave, excitement was building.

Damian showed her to his tent and she dropped her duffle bag to the floor, realising how small the accommodation was going to be. As she turned back to face him, Damian pulled her close and she melted into his kiss, feeling the familiar slow burn of need unfolding low in her stomach. She'd never tire of being loved by this man, she thought blissfully, as they dispensed unnecessary clothing and sank to the surprisingly comfortable mattress and sleeping bag beneath.

'I missed you,' he said later as she lay in the crook of his shoulder, breathing in the scent she'd missed so much.

'I could tell,' she murmured lazily.

'Does that mean you missed me too?'

'Terribly,' she said, leaning up on her elbow to kiss him.

'I'm sorry everything's taking so long. That's just the way it goes, unfortunately. Stuff like this can't be rushed.'

'I know,' she said, holding back a sigh. She *did* know and she hated that she sounded like a whining girlfriend. But now they'd found what they'd been looking for, everything would finally get back on track. The end was in sight and that was enough to make the last few lonely weeks worth it.

'I can't wait to see what you've found,' she admitted.

'Then let's go take a look,' he said.

'Are you sure your ankle is up to it?' she asked, realising she hadn't given it much thought a few moments earlier.

'Yeah, I've been managing to hobble about on it, and as much as I'd rather stay in here with you for the rest of the day, I think my absence would eventually be noticed and people would come looking for me.'

That possibility alone was enough to get her up and dressing.

When they were both respectable once more, Damian took her by the hand and they headed slowly along the track.

They found Mike, shooting a piece to the camera, at the site. He seemed just as charismatic in person as he was on television. When he'd finished, he came over and greeted her warmly. 'How about our man here?' he asked, slapping Damian on the shoulder like a proud dad. 'He's our lucky charm.'

She saw Damian wince, but didn't think this was from his ankle, which made her a little curious.

'No idea how he managed to find not one but *two* of the biggest finds of the project. And just in the nick of time too.'

'Deadlines are a big motivator,' Damian said, smiling quickly.

'Well, we're close to the big reveal. Guess we'll find out what's in there soon enough. I better get back. Good to see you up here, Lottie. This bloke needs someone to keep him out of trouble.'

'He's something, isn't he,' Lottie said after Mike walked away. He was probably the closest thing to a celebrity Lottie had ever met.

'Yeah,' Damian said, and she looked at him, seeing he looked a little distracted.

'Is everything okay?'

'Yeah, why?'

'You just seem a little, I don't know . . . off? Are you worried that it won't be Catherine?'

'No. Well, I mean . . . it's possible, I suppose, but it seems to fit entirely with our theory . . . so much so that it doesn't make sense that it *wouldn't* be her.'

'How *did* you come to find the cave? It seems a little bit out of the way?'

'Just a fluke. I wandered off the track and just . . . found it.'

When she didn't comment further, he looked over at her and shook his head. 'You wouldn't believe it if I told you,' he said, sounding uncomfortable.

It wasn't that she wouldn't believe it; it was more that he sounded as though *he* didn't believe it.

'Believe what?'

'Nothing.' He shook his head and smiled. 'It's just been a series of very strange coincidences.'

'Well, however it happened, I guess we should just be grateful.'

'We've got something,' Mike shouted.

Thirty-two

Lottie watched as Mike and Damian filmed a piece to camera for the documentary. They'd been filming ever since they started digging and had caught the moment they'd unearthed the first item from the grave.

At first, Lottie couldn't tell what it was, despite the fact the others were clearly all excited. There was some painstakingly slow brushing away of dirt and delicate digging to be done, but eventually, the team uncovered the first fragments of bone and small pieces of fibre from the remains of clothing.

'This is pretty exciting,' Damian said calmly during one of the first interviews for the documentary. 'We'd hoped to find *something*. We couldn't even be sure it *was* a grave but now that we've glimpsed bone and other matter, we can move from *what* was in this hole to *who* is in there.'

'Do you think we'll be able to identify anyone?' Mike asked.

'We have bone that we can test for age, and it's looking like we may have fabric of clothing. If we're lucky, we may have enough to get it identified as well.'

Lottie watched on with pride swelling her heart. Damian was a natural. He spoke with an easy, unpretentious air that allowed the subject matter to sound interesting and alive.

'Do we believe we know who this person is?'

'That's the exciting part. So far, everything we're finding seems to be following the trajectory of a theory we have about Catherine Compton, the missing wife of Alexander Compton. And if this turns out to be true, then we're dealing with a very different version of history than what we know at the moment. That's always exciting as a historian, to find evidence that tells a different story.'

The team worked around the clock under massive spotlights and in cold temperatures. Lottie pitched in and helped out wherever she could, mainly delivering food and drinks from the campsite to the archaeologists and crew and doing her best to stay out of the way.

She could see Damian's frustration with his injured ankle, making it difficult for him to move as he normally would, but he seemed to push through, albeit with a bit of a limp, to be in the thick of it anyway. They took small breaks to sleep and eat, but there was an underlying excitement that kept everyone focused and eager to get the grave excavated. The process was slow and meticulous, but, piece by piece, a body was being uncovered.

While Lottie was back in camp, helping to prepare dinner, she heard her name over the radio.

'Lottie, you need to get up to the site,' Claire, one of the film crew, announced. 'Damian needs you.'

She dried her hands and grabbed her coat, her mind racing. Had he hurt himself again? Had his ankle gotten worse? Surely someone would have brought him back down to the camp if that was the case. By the time she'd reached the dig, she'd come up with a number of scenarios . . . none of which involved him greeting her with a beaming smile.

'Check this out.' He took her hand and led her closer. The earth had been removed all around the original gravesite, creating a terraced-type access point to where the bones had been uncovered. She nervously followed Damian down. This was the first time she'd been this close. The significance of the moment almost overwhelmed her.

'Look,' Damian said, squatting down and pointing to where one of the archaeologists worked, dusting away dirt from something in the earth.

Thanks to painstaking clearing away of debris, they'd uncovered a necklace, and while it wasn't shiny—being still partially covered in dirt—it was definitely gold.

An image of the portraits Agatha had painted of Catherine flashed through her mind. Lottie tore her surprised gaze from the delicate line of gold in the ground and looked over at

Damian. 'It's her,' she said quietly. She saw his eyes crinkle in the corners as a gentle smile grew across his face.

'It's her,' he said. 'Although, technically, I'm not supposed to form any solid conclusions until we have all the facts in front of us.'

Lottie gave a small scoff. She didn't need any more proof. Deep down, as soon as Damian had found the grave hidden up here in this isolated place, she'd known just as he had that this was Catherine.

Late one afternoon a few days later, Lottie found herself contemplating the isolated gravesite as she stared out at the rugged bushland surrounding the spot. She shivered as she took in the solemn work going on around her.

'You look cold,' Damian said, coming to stand behind her and wrapping her up tightly in his arms. 'You don't have to stay up here, you know. You should go home, where its warm and civilised.'

She didn't have to turn her head to see the smile she knew he'd be wearing; she could hear it in his voice. 'Are you kidding? And miss out on all of this?'

'Are you okay?' he asked after a few moments of enjoying the closeness and warmth of each other.

'Yeah. I was just thinking about Catherine, and how lonely this place is.'

'They certainly picked the right place to bury a body so no one would find it.'

'Will she be able to be buried in the cemetery? Where Alexander is?'

'There's a long process to go through before we can think about all that. They'll need to do some forensic work and figure out what really happened to her. It'll be months before we have a whole work-up on her completed.'

Poor Catherine, Lottie thought sadly. When would she have some peace?

Damian stood by the excavated site and looked down into the hollow area where the grave had once been, now a widened pit to make excavation easier. The bones that lay there were similar to ones he'd seen in the past, yet these were different. This time, it was like looking down on someone he knew. Or what remained of that someone. He knew with every fibre of his being that this was Catherine, and the scientist in him couldn't even bring itself to caution him; it knew it too.

The bones had fragments of woollen material draped across it, indicating someone had taken the time to wrap the body before placing it in the grave. He steeled himself against the clicking of a camera as the other archaeologists and the coroner photographed the site before the bones were removed. Even though they'd already been able to determine the bones were old and this was not a recent death, it had been decided that the coroner would take over possession of the remains in order to provide an inquest, which, although slightly frustrating in that they had to step back from the investigation, was also a good thing. The coroner would be able to provide a thorough examination but was happy to continue to work alongside the team as they had done the initial preparation and groundwork.

Damian watched as the forensic team carefully removed the bones, grateful that he and his team were still allowed to observe. Had this been a different type of investigation, a more recent death, there was no way the police would allow anyone else to be on site, but this was different.

When the process had finally finished, he watched them pack up and leave. He felt . . . empty. So much had happened and although he'd had plenty of time to process it in the days that had passed, it still hadn't really hit him how momentous this whole thing really was. He'd come here to try to find a few more clues to figure out what happened to Catherine, and here he was, months later, watching her being taken away in boxes—carefully packed boxes, but still, boxes.

He didn't have all the answers yet; they had a lot more work to do. He still didn't feel like Catherine was at peace and, more than anything, he wanted to give her that.

Thirty-three

Banalla had a brief moment of notoriety with the news that a body had been discovered and forensics were on the scene. For the first few days, there was wild innuendo about who they'd discovered and what had happened, until eventually information trickled out that it was an old grave and no one had been brutally murdered in their sleep. There were a few journalists in town after the initial discovery, but they had soon packed up and left after they realised there was nothing interesting to report, and the town went back to its usual pace once more.

Damian had come back to town after the bones were removed and Lottie couldn't help but notice the change in him. She understood that it would be quite a let-down that the coroner had decided to step in and exercise their right to take over an investigation, but they were doing it with good intentions. A proper police investigation made her feel as though, finally, people were seeing Catherine, after she had been wiped from the face of the earth for so long. Now there was a chance that the mystery surrounding her disappearance would be solved and history could be rectified to include her at last.

Lottie loved having Damian back home. She knew it was only for a few days, and there was still work to be done on the documentary and finishing up with the cave, so she made the most of it.

While for the first two nights, they stayed at home and just enjoyed time alone, on the third night, her mother invited them out to dinner. Upon arriving at the pub, where the table had been booked, Lottie was surprised to discover there was someone else joining them.

'Gordon?' Damian said, sounding confused but smiling at his friend, who stood to greet them.

'Here's the man of the hour,' Gordon said heartily. 'You're the talk of the industry right now, you know? Everyone wants a piece of the action.'

'Interesting, isn't it? Used to be I could hardly get anyone to do anything all those years when I was begging for funding projects,' Damian said wryly.

'I reckon you could get pretty much anything you want out of them now,' Gordon said. 'The missing treasure of Jack McNally is pretty impressive.'

'Technically, there hasn't been a lot of treasure,' Damian said. 'But who knows? They're going to continue up there for a bit longer and see what else turns up.'

So far, they'd only found a few pieces—great pieces that tied the robbery to Jack and his gang, but not the enormous amount of loot that historians had been searching for over the past century and a half. It remained a mystery as to where it had been hidden.

Lottie caught her mother's eye during the exchange and raised an eyebrow, conveying an unspoken 'What is Gordon doing here?' question. Her mother sent her an infinitesimal shrug and a small smile. Lottie vowed she would get some answers later.

Over the meal, the four of them chatted about how much of a success the festival had been and the flow-on effect for the town months later, as well as her mother's new business opportunities. She was excited to hear Hannah was considering hiring an extra person to help handle the online side of the business instead of shutting it down like she'd been hinting at last time they'd spoken about it. Now she'd have the chance to concentrate more of her time and energy on her workshops and meditation retreats.

There'd been lots of positive feedback from businesses who had used the market day to promote their products and since gained new customers. It made all the headaches the committee had gone through worthwhile . . . well, most of them.

But mostly, the conversation returned to Damian and his team's discovery.

'It truly is fascinating, Damian,' Hannah said, shaking her head after listening to the story. 'After all that searching, you've finally found her.'

'Well, officially, we haven't got any confirmation yet.'

'Did you get a chance to make any assessments yourself?' Gordon asked, sipping his beer.

'The forensic expert did mention a few things. He believes the skeleton is female. He believes the age of the bones would be about right for how long Catherine would have been missing, and that there was evidence to suggest she'd died of an injury which he was fairly confident had been inflicted by a bullet. Which follows one of the theories we came up with,' Damian said, glancing over at Lottie, 'that Jack would likely not leave an injured woman alone in the bush. It simply didn't fit with his known profile.'

'So he takes Catherine up to the O'Ryan homestead, but she dies of her wounds?' Gordon asked.

'There was also the possibility that maybe she'd died in childbirth, but there was no evidence of any infant buried either with her, or still inside her in the grave.'

'She was pregnant?' Hannah asked, sounding troubled by the idea.

'From what we've discovered in correspondence, it seems she was when she left for Australia. However, we have absolutely nothing on record to suggest she either still was once she arrived, or that she ever gave birth. Had she not lost the baby at any point on the arduous journey, it was entirely possible she would have almost been at full term by the time of the robbery.'

'I can't believe a woman would risk coming to a place like this to birth her child. Surely staying in Sydney would have been preferable to the bush?'

'You would think so,' Damian agreed. 'But from letters and the evidence we've found about Catherine and Alexander, they were completely devoted to each other. Maybe she was just eager to start their new life. Who knows? But not finding any evidence of a child with her,' Damian spread his hands out wide, 'seems to dispute that theory.'

'That's the thing about theories,' Gordon chuckled, 'they don't always pan out the way we want them too. Which is a shame.'

'There's a long way to go yet,' Lottie said reaching for Damian's hand. 'The coroner's report might still turn up something.'

After all, this case had the assistance of not only the coroner but also a forensic anthropologist as well as a forensic archaeologist *and* a historian, and a whole bunch of other disciplines the network used to put together one of Mike's investigative documentaries.

When they eventually decided to call it a night, the two men went off to argue about who was paying the bill and Lottie finally got her chance to question her mother.

'So . . . you decided to call Gordon after all?'

'I was going to, but then he showed up at my door with a potted mugwort. The rare one I've been looking for to make my new tea,' her mother said mildly. 'How could I resist a man with mugwort?'

'So you're going to give it a go?'

'We'll see,' Hannah said calmly, but Lottie caught the hint of a smile on her mother's lips as the men came towards them, and she had a feeling Hannah Fairchild had maybe met her match at last.

'I'm glad Mum's decided to give Gordon another chance,' she said later that night, once they were home.

'They seem happy,' Damian said, bending down to kiss her nose as he handed her a tea.

'It's funny, though. He's not the kind of man I ever expected her to end up with.'

'Why?'

'They're so . . . different. I mean, my mother believes in curses and tarot reading and Gordon's an academic,' she pointed out, feeling somewhat mystified.

'Sometimes people complete each other in different ways. Gordon's never been the type of guy who plays the field or anything, not that I know of anyway. I think if he's decided he wants to get to know your mum, then he must be pretty certain she's special.'

Lottie considered his words thoughtfully. 'It's so weird seeing Mum so . . . optimistic,' she said, looking up at him confused by the whole thing. 'She's been terrified of relationships for so long. I've never seen her like she is around Gordon before. And she certainly never gets worked up over a man the way she has been over him. This is all new territory.'

'Maybe she just hadn't met the right man to show her there was nothing to be scared about,' he said, sipping from his own mug.

'True,' she sighed, resting her head back against the lounge. 'There's been a lot of strange things happening lately; you finding Catherine and the hideout, and now my mother . . .' Her words trailed off. She still wasn't sure what was going on there. When Damian was quiet, she turned her head slightly and frowned at the troubled expression on his face. 'What is it?'

'It *has* all been strange. A little *too* strange.'

Lottie watched him quietly. 'Sometimes that's how things go. They just fall into place.'

'Only finding the cave and then the grave . . . I think it was something more than just luck.'

'What do you mean?'

He gave a small groan and shut his eyes briefly. 'It sounds so stupid whenever I try and put it into words.'

'Tell me,' she said, gently sliding one of her hands into his larger one.

'The day I found the cave . . . I was heading back to camp after talking to you and I was feeling so frustrated. We had nothing from the homestead and there was all this pressure to find something before we had to throw in the towel . . .

And then there was this—' He stopped abruptly and cleared his throat. 'There was a wallaby.'

'Okay,' Lottie said encouragingly.

'That's it . . . a wallaby. I followed a wallaby into the bush and there was the cave.'

'Well, that's . . .' *Not too bad*, she thought, wondering why he was looking so distressed. 'It was just lucky.'

'I was willing to put it down to stupid dumb luck, until it turned up later when I was sitting in the camp alone. I followed it again, and I found the gravesite. I can't write off two different occasions where it was just down to luck that this wallaby would happen to lead me to two significant sites.'

Oh.

'How do you know it was the same wallaby?' she finally asked, then winced a little when he sent her a doubtful look.

'You think maybe there's a whole mob of wallabies out there who all know the locations of lost historical sites?' he asked sarcastically.

Okay, put like that . . . 'I don't know. What explanation do *you* have?'

'I've got nothing,' he said with a frustrated sigh. 'At least, nothing that doesn't sound like I've lost my mind.'

Lottie paused as a thought struck her. 'It's kind of strange, but the day we found Kate's hut, there was a wallaby there too. Maybe it's some kind of sign.'

'Catherine reincarnated as a wallaby?' he scoffed.

'Well, no. I mean that's a bit . . . I'm sure there's a logical explanation. Or maybe there's no explanation. Maybe it's just—'

She was about to say, 'the universe working in mysterious ways' but that sounded awfully like something her—

Oh, good grief. The day had finally come: she was turning into her mother.

'Maybe you're not supposed to think too hard about it. If something led you to those places for a reason, then I think you should probably just accept it and stop worrying about the hows and whys.'

'Yeah, denial is the one I decided to go with too,' he agreed dryly.

'Mike must be over the moon. His documentary will be a winner.'

Damian nodded. 'He's like a kid at Christmas.'

'It is pretty cool, though. I can't wait to see it. You will be by far the star of the show.'

'I doubt it. Most of the to-camera stuff is Mike. It's his show.'

'Yeah, but you're the one who's done all the work.'

'He's the one with the fan base and the money,' Damian reasoned. 'And I don't care about that. I'm just glad I have the answers, and the book will be able to tell the *whole* story.'

'As long as he remembers he wouldn't even have a documentary without you. He better not cut any of your scenes from the final edit.'

Damian chuckled and pulled her close. 'I hope you'll be okay living with a mere author and not a famous filmmaker. Do you know he even puts on make-up before a shoot?'

Lottie giggled at his incredulous expression and cupped his lower face in her hands. She felt the rough hair of his trimmed beard under her fingers and her amusement soon turned into something else. His eyes looked into hers steadily, and something inside her shifted. She loved this man so much. In such a short time, he'd become one of the most important things in her life and she knew she didn't want to spend a single day away from him again.

'I'm more than okay with that. So, when are you moving in for real?'

'For real?' he asked, looking down at her curiously. 'I've been moved in for a while now, I thought?'

'Not exactly. You've been staying with me, moving in is making it your home too, but at the moment, you still have a home in Sydney.'

'That's been what's bothering you?' he asked, confusion colouring his tone.

'Yeah, a bit,' she replied honestly. 'Every time I wanted to bring it up with you before, there was always something going on.'

'As soon as this dig is wrapped up, I'll pack up and give my notice on the apartment. Okay?' he said gently, making her previous doubts feel almost stupid.

'Okay.' She beamed back at him.

Once this dig was over, he'd be all hers and they could finally start their life together.

Thirty-four

Lottie used the time over the next few days to clean out her house. She'd been eyeing her wardrobe space, frowning at the clothing squished in tightly, and realised there wasn't a lot of room if Damian was going to be moving his stuff in. There was nothing else for it—it was time for a cull.

She'd only ever shared a house with flatmates while she was at university, and none of those times had required the sharing of wardrobe space. How did people actually *do* that? she wondered.

An hour later, she'd changed her mind. *This is so satisfying*, she thought after pulling out items and discarding them into piles of keep, give away and not-quite-sure-yet. The give-away pile was growing at an alarming rate, closely followed by the not-quite-sure pile. She filled garbage bags with the donations and piled them at the door, feeling extremely accomplished by the end of the day. When she finally stood back to admire her handiwork, she called Damian in and waved her hand towards the wardrobe with a flourish.

'What am I looking at?' he asked, sounding a little bit confused.

'I cleared out space in my wardrobe.'

'Where?'

'There!' She pointed at the empty space on the far side.

'I get the *whole* ten centimetres of hanging space?' he asked, lifting an eyebrow.

'There's heaps of room.' She rolled her eyes and let out a small huff. 'It was the best I could do.'

'It's a good thing most of my clothes fold into a drawer then, I suppose,' he said dryly.

She really had tried, but the not-quite-sure pile was proving a lot harder to sort through.

'While you've been busy,' he said, eyeing the garbage bags he had to step over as they left the bedroom and went into the kitchen, 'Mike emailed to say he'd got some early findings from the coroner.' He sat down and opened the email, and she read over his shoulder:

> The body had been wrapped in a heavy woollen blanket, which was still partially preserved. That helped protect some of the other evidence that was found in the grave, namely strands of hair—interestingly, two distinct types of hair was found. One type was long and blonde, but there was a second set of strands collected from a small oval locket that appears

to have been clutched in the woman's hand upon burial and which, over time, as the body eroded, settled around where the hand bones of the skeleton were found. Samples of hair and bone are still undergoing testing and analysis in the lab. Whether this is significant to the investigation is yet to be seen.

'Do you think this locket and the hair is going to tell us something?' Lottie asked slowly.

'I guess it depends on what that hair sample comes back with.'

'It's interesting that she was still wearing the necklace, but the locket wasn't on it, it was in her hand. I mean, if it's a locket with something in it, that sounds pretty significant. Maybe it broke off the chain?'

'It's a fairly solid piece, and that chain was pretty thin. I think it would have been damaged if a locket that size was ripped from it, or somehow came off.'

'So what are you thinking?'

'That it was put there after she passed. To be buried with her.'

'By whom? Jack?'

'Possibly. It's the fact that it's a locket with hair inside it, like a special keepsake. It feels like that's something significant,' Damian said. 'My mum has a baby book for all of us and she kept all sorts of weird stuff in it that we still roll our eyes at—our first teeth, handprints and a small piece of our baby hair. She said they were important things she wanted to keep, to remember us as babies.'

'You think it could be baby hair?' Lottie asked. 'Catherine's baby?'

'That's what we're hoping for. I mean, if this locket *was* somehow Catherine's, it could be Catherine's own hair, or maybe even a lock of Alexander's hair. It wasn't uncommon for people to keep locks of hair of their loved ones. But, again, the positioning of it in the grave makes it feel as though it was put in later, in which case, who would have taken the time to do that? I don't know what to make of it. Maybe I'm just clutching at straws, but if they can find something significant about this hair sample, it might be another clue she's left us.'

It did feel very much like this whole time Catherine had been leaving little breadcrumbs of information like a trail for them to follow. Maybe this was another one.

'If it does come back as baby hair, that would mean that Catherine either had the baby with her or *had* the baby at some point after the robbery,' Lottie said slowly. 'But they didn't find any baby bones.'

There were so many variables in this thing. If Catherine had the baby, maybe it was buried somewhere else; if she didn't have the baby, when did she lose it? Was there even a baby? Maybe they'd gotten everything wrong in those letters and diaries and she wasn't even pregnant.

It was all giving her a headache. 'I keep thinking about the rose bush,' Lottie said, changing tack. 'Someone planted it at the gravesite—there's no way it would have grown from a flower left on the grave. But it doesn't feel like something Jack would have done, or had the time to think about doing.

It's the same with the locket. It's almost like your mother with your hair. It feels kind of like something a woman might do for another woman.' *Or a mother might do for another mother.* 'Maybe the locket belonged to Kate.'

Damian shook his head. 'Kate and her family, like most settlers out here at the time, probably didn't have gold jewellery lying around.'

'Most settlers also didn't have Jack McNally as a brother,' Lottie argued back. 'Maybe Jack gave Kate the locket from a previous robbery as a gift. Maybe he gave it to Kate to put in with Catherine, out of respect?'

'Both are things that would fit Jack's profile. He did do random acts of kindness throughout his career,' Damian said, nodding. 'But it all comes back to the fact that inside that locket is a tiny lock of hair.'

'But if it *is* Catherine's baby's hair, it only leads to more questions,' Lottie said with a frown. 'Like, what happened to the baby?'

In the following weeks, life got busy for everyone. Damian was constantly on the phone, dealing with the Catherine project. There were reports to type up and funding to secure for ongoing research—and his book to write, which was having constant updates as new evidence came to light—and handling quite a good deal of local media. The interest in what had been going on had never gone away, and the fact that much of it was still being kept quiet was only fuelling interest.

'Well, I don't know why they can't just leave those people in peace,' she overheard some people say around town and in the shop after news broke about the excavation. 'It's not right, digging up graves.'

Since Damian's involvement in the project had come to light, Lottie had been constantly fielding curious questions about what was going on.

'I think the point of this is that they don't actually know *how* they died. If this is who they think it might be, she went missing and they're trying to work out what happened to her,' Lottie would point out calmly.

While Lottie wasn't overly concerned about disturbing the dead, she did wonder about what would happen to Catherine after they'd finished with their examination. And she'd brought it up with Damian.

'I'm thinking maybe the progress committee can organise some kind of funding or raise money to re-inter her next to Alexander,' she said. 'It has historical relevance to the town and I'm sure they'll find a way to link all this to the festival next year, since it seems to be entwined with Jack's story.'

'If they can't do something, I'm sure there'll be a way to get it done. Although there might be some interest shown from descendants of Catherine's family. They might want her returned to England.'

Lottie hadn't thought about that. Catherine's disappearance would have been a story passed down within her family for generations, much like Emeline's story had been in her own.

'How sad that she'd come all this way to be with Alexander, and even *now* can't be buried with him.'

'One step at a time,' Damian said, planting a kiss on her forehead. She hadn't realised, when she'd first heard about Catherine just how attached she would become to this woman.

She stared down now at the notes she'd been going through for her book over the last few days, pulling it out after a long break. Her mum had been right—it was time to get back into it. But as soon as she had sat down, she'd realised it was all still just as confusing as before. Ever since discovering the connection with Catherine and the ring, it had taken on a whole new bunch of chapters. What had started out as a chapter on the ring and the curse had developed into a whole saga involving Catherine, Alexander, Jack and Emeline. It changed everything and had left her with more than a little bit of a headache.

'I'm really struggling to figure out how to move forward with my book,' she said, closing the laptop and leaning against the kitchen counter as he turned back to his computer.

'Oh?' he asked, opening his emails.

'I mean, it was just going to be a little book about the women in my family, but now there's this whole other story. My original storyline isn't even true anymore. The entire origin of the ring is nothing like the story we were told.'

'That's true.' He nodded, squinting at the screen as he read through an email.

Lottie chewed on the inside of her lip as she watched him. 'I'm actually a bit stuck.'

'You'll figure it out,' he said reassuringly.

'But that's the problem! I don't know how to figure it out. I don't know where to go from here. Can you maybe take a look and give me a few ideas?'

'Babe, I'd love to, but I've got a ton of work I need to get through and I'm still trying to write my own book. Why don't you just go for a walk or put it aside for a bit? Something will come to you eventually.'

'That's it? That's your advice?'

Her tone obviously managed to cut through his preoccupation, and he looked up from his screen. 'What?'

'I'm telling you that I'm really struggling and you're too busy with your own stuff to really care. As usual.'

'Of course I care,' he said, frowning across at her. 'But I'm also on a deadline and—you may have noticed—I'm having the same issue with my book. I can't finish it until we get everything back from the coroner. I can only give you the same advice I'm giving myself.'

'That something will come to you eventually?' she replied with a slight snap in her tone.

'It will. That's part of the writing process. Ideas eventually come to you, usually when you least expect them.' He turned away from the computer and reached for her hand. 'I know I've been preoccupied, and I'm sorry. I promise, once all this is out of the way, I'll give you and your book my complete attention. Okay?'

Well, now she felt like a whining child. She knew his work was important and why should she expect him to drop everything to help her with her book, when it was nothing more than a project and he was a successful author with his own book to write? Not to mention part of an important archaeological team working on one of the most exciting discoveries in years.

But it really was beginning to feel like she was constantly putting her own dreams on hold to support his. She was spending far less time at the shop than she normally would, closing a little earlier some days to come home and spend time with him, not to mention the days she actually shut the shop entirely to go to places with him.

Those were all her decisions, and she'd been happy to make them, but maybe it was time to prioritise herself for a while.

Thirty-five

The day of the coroner's inquest and handing down of the report finally came, and Damian was heading down to the city. This was a big filming day, the opportunity to wrap up the findings and finally bring closure to Catherine's disappearance.

For Lottie, it was bittersweet. She would miss the time she'd spent with Damian researching and discovering things about this woman from a historical angle, but also as a woman. What an incredible person Catherine had been. She'd stood her ground and married her childhood sweetheart in a time when women were still very much obliged to take on whatever their family deemed the most lucrative union. She waited for her husband to prove himself to their families and then travelled, alone and pregnant, to a strange, wild land. Then went through the trauma of witnessing her husband and multiple men murdered, had her treasured ring stolen and then somehow died and was hidden away, alone, for all those years in the bush, forgotten.

'It won't be long. A few days at most,' Damian told her when they kissed goodbye.

'I'll miss you,' she said miserably. She really wasn't sure how she'd survived being an independent, modern woman all those years before she'd met Damian. Suddenly, she felt like an abandoned child whenever she thought about him leaving. 'I love you,' she said, and then realised that was the first time she'd actually said it out loud.

He must have realised the same thing, because she felt him still before easing back to smile down at her. 'I was wondering which one of us was going to bring that up first.'

'It's weird, because it just feels like it's always been there, right from the very beginning.'

'I feel the same way. I've loved every minute we've spent together. Working on this project with you has been ... incredible. *You're* incredible,' he said, kissing her. 'I love you, Lottie Fairchild. I'll be home soon.'

Lottie watched the big black bike head out of town with its lone rider, her lips still warm from their kiss, and felt an uneasy sadness. She should still be on a high. They'd finally gotten out the words she'd been saying in her heart for months now. She was just feeling left out because she wasn't going with him, she reasoned, shaking it off, before heading back inside to prepare for her day.

'I hate to say it,' Cher said as they took their seats at the first chamber meeting since the festival, 'but I've almost missed this.'

Lottie sent her friend a sidelong glance.

'No, seriously. It's the only chance I get to sit and not make any decisions because, well, *Daphney*,' Cher muttered.

Lottie smirked. To be honest, she'd kind of missed the meetings too. They'd been well and truly over the top leading up to the festival, but when things weren't so chaotic, meeting nights were a great chance to get out and socialise. Her life was fairly social, working in the store, but she didn't get to sit and talk with other people who were having the same challenges and issues that running a business in a small town often produced. They were all too busy running the businesses. Nights like these gave everyone a chance to share their problems, both business and sometimes personal, with a group of like-minded people who had also become friends.

'If it's any consolation, I think you've worn Daphney down.'

'I doubt it,' Cher scoffed lightly.

'Ah, hello? The phone call?' The day the news spread around town that a body had been located in bushland, everyone had gone into a panic. 'You were still on tour and Daphney came into the store, convinced it was you because no one had seen you in days.'

'I bet she was bitterly disappointed when she found out it wasn't me,' Cher replied.

'I think she was genuinely concerned about you,' Lottie said, glancing at the woman in question as she abruptly clapped her hands together and brought everyone to attention. As they settled in for a run-down of the festival stats and Daphney's personal, lengthy feedback on all aspects, Lottie considered that maybe she hadn't missed these meetings as much as she'd thought.

Late the next afternoon, Lottie came in the back door of the kitchen with an armload of timber for her fire to find that her mobile was ringing on the kitchen bench.

'Hi,' she said breathlessly as she dived to answer it after dumping her load of firewood in the basket at the door.

'Hey. I thought you might be tied up in a meeting or something,' Damian said.

'Sorry, I was just outside. I miss you. When are you coming back?' During their last conversation, he'd hoped to have a date he'd be wrapping things up down there and coming home.

'Uh, still not sure about that,' he said.

'How're things going down there?' She missed the sound of his voice—who was she kidding, she missed everything about him—but hearing him now made her miss him even more.

'Yeah, you know. Crazy,' he said seemingly offhand, but she detected something odd about his tone.

'Is everything okay?' she asked slowly.

'It's . . .' He paused before he let out a long sigh. 'This whole thing has really blown up.'

'Blown up?' she asked, uncertain if this was a good or bad thing.

There was a pause on the end of the line before Damian continued. 'The documentary,' he explained, speaking quickly, like he had to get it all out. 'Everyone wants in on the new findings and the whole Catherine and Jack McNally angle is sending people crazy. Mike's got interviews lined up and we still have a heap of filming to do. A new investor has come on board, which means the whole production now has a massive budget to play with, so Mike's got this whole new vision. He needs me to go on tour with him,' he ended, sounding miserable, which threw her momentarily as she tried to digest the news.

'On tour?'

'We've got a number of universities and historical groups booking in talks and the filming hasn't even finished yet. So there's like another six months of work to do on it.' He stopped for a moment and Lottie felt a trickle of uncertainty begin to run through her. 'The thing is . . . I need to be down here to get it all done.'

The uncertainty turned to dread. 'For how long?'

'I won't be coming back up there like I planned. At least, not just yet.'

And there it was. The bomb she'd somehow been expecting to drop.

'Oh.'

She wasn't sure how she was supposed to respond. She couldn't manage to get anything else out as her mind began whirling, realising all the plans they'd made were not going to happen. 'So . . . you're not moving.'

'No, not right now. It's not practical. I need to be here, and commuting from Banalla doesn't make any sense. It's just for a little while, until all this is sorted out.'

'Oh.' Why couldn't she come up with anything better than that?

'I know it's not what we planned. It's just . . . I can't turn down these opportunities. Mike's got these connections and it'll launch my books and my career . . .' He stopped talking and she heard the sadness creep into his voice. 'I feel like I'm letting you down, Lottie. I know I am,' he corrected quickly. 'I wasn't expecting things to take off the way they have. This isn't normal. It's like an unexpected lotto win, but for my career.'

'I understand,' she said softly. And she did. He couldn't turn down these opportunities that had landed in his lap. They may never come around again. It just hurt to realise they came at the expense of *their* new life, the one she'd been picturing in her head.

'This doesn't change any of our plans,' he said, sounding like he was trying to reassure her. 'I still want to move to Banalla. I still want to make a life with you. All this is just a small hitch in the timeline.'

'It's fine. Really,' she said with forced confidence. 'You need to take advantage of all this. You've worked hard.'

'Are you sure you're okay with it?' he asked. 'I've kind of sprung it on you.'

'It's a bit of a surprise.' *Understatement of the year.*

'I honestly never expected it to have such a huge reaction. Nobody did.'

'Then you need to run with it.'

'Look, I gotta go. Mike's here. I'll call later tonight.'

'Okay,' she said and opened her mouth to say goodbye, but the phone had already disconnected. He was clearly in a hurry. She tried not to take it personally, but failed miserably.

She forgot about starting the fire and wrapped her meal in plastic before putting it in the fridge—she wasn't hungry anymore. She just wanted to curl up under her blankets in her lonely bed and cry. Despite Damian's words, she knew that *everything* had just changed.

The days that followed Damian's announcement were hard. Lottie put on a brave face and told herself it was just a minor setback, but deep down she wasn't convinced. These opportunities were amazing, but she suspected Damian wasn't being exactly realistic. Sure, things would die down after a while over the whole Catherine discovery, but if his goal was to help promote his writing future, then this was only the beginning of bigger things. Once his career took off, living the quiet life in Banalla would no longer be something he'd be interested in.

The phone rang as she served a customer and she glanced over, somehow knowing it was Damian calling but unable to excuse herself from the conversation mid-sentence without being rude. When she eventually got away, she called back, but he didn't answer. It was a frequent occurrence. He was on a busy schedule between travelling and talks, and their chances to say a quick hello were limited.

There were times when they did manage to catch each other and talk, and while she always felt close to him during the calls, as soon as they hung up, the distance was there once more.

'Meet me in Canberra,' he said one night while they were talking. 'I'll be there for three days. It'll give us a chance to spend some time together.'

She considered the idea for a moment. 'I can't really close the shop for that long,' she said eventually.

'Can't you find someone to open for you?'

She thought about asking her mum, but she was currently away with Gordon. 'Not really.'

'It's only for a few days,' he reasoned.

'People count on the shop being open when they come all the way up to visit. And I count on those sales.'

'Yeah. I guess,' he said sounding disappointed.

After they'd hung up, Lottie continued to ponder the conversation. She was disappointed too, but she'd never asked him not to do something related to his job. In fact, she'd always been understanding and supportive, keeping her disappointment to herself. How many times had she closed the shop early or for the whole day to do things with him? She knew it was frustration talking—she just missed him so much—but each time she allowed a little niggle of resentment to creep in, it gnawed at her belly and made her more miserable.

'You should have been there, Lott,' he said one night, slurring his words slightly after he'd come back from a dinner with a number of colleagues and one too many drinks. 'They're treating us like we're celebrities! Even the older professors who normally look down their noses at us 'cause we're not in their league, they're falling over themselves to shake our hands. It's crazy. Mike's taking it all in his stride, but it's insane how big this thing is. We were even signing autographs on campus yesterday. *Autographs*, Lott,' he chuckled.

It was hard to picture this version of him as the quiet, down-to-earth Damian who'd been so awkward telling her he was the author of the book she was reading all those months before.

'Sounds like you're having fun,' she said dryly.

'It's not a crime to enjoy some of the success, is it?' he shot back, his tone sharpening.

'I didn't say it was. I've just never heard you drunk before.'

'I'm not drunk,' he insisted. 'I'm buzzed.'

'Okay,' she said calmly. 'It's really late. I have to get up for work in the morning, and you should probably sleep off your buzz before your flight.'

'It's like you don't even want to talk to me anymore,' he said grumpily.

'I'd love to talk to you, it's just a pity you didn't have time to call me before you went out tonight, at a normal time, instead of at,' she pulled the phone away from her ear and squinted at the screen, 'two o'clock in the morning.' *Seriously?* she thought.

They hung up and although she was tired, she had trouble falling back to sleep. She'd texted him earlier with no reply, and now when he wanted to talk, he was cranky because she'd been asleep.

The weeks dragged on and, despite their best efforts, they could never manage to coordinate their schedules.

The phone calls dropped from a few times a day to once a night, then once every few days. In the beginning, his calls were always full of interesting things that had happened through the day—people he'd met and the places he was visiting, but gradually they became shorter, and were mostly filled with small talk.

'Are you happy, Lottie?' he asked out of the blue one night.

'I'd be happier if you were home,' she admitted.

'I feel like each time we talk we're just going through the motions,' he said. 'Like you're not interested in anything I'm doing anymore.'

'I'm always interested. I have been from the start.'

'You don't ask about any of it.'

'I always ask how your day was,' she protested.

'You don't seem really interested, though,' he huffed.

'You don't ask me about mine at all,' she pointed out. Which was true. It was like once he'd left town, he'd forgotten all about how special he'd once found the place.

'I figured you'd tell me if anything exciting happened.'

'It's Banalla! Nothing exciting ever happens.'

There was a long pause before he asked, 'Is this working?'

Her heart skidded to a halt. She opened her mouth to protest and tell him that of course it was, but nothing came out. The silence on the line felt heavy, like a gathering thunderstorm hanging between them.

'It's okay,' he said softly. And although she desperately wanted to disagree—to brush it off and pretend everything would be okay—in her heart, she knew that things weren't okay. They were drifting further and further apart.

'It's not,' she said, but her voice cracked and the tears she was trying to hold back suddenly poured forth.

'I know,' he soothed. 'I'm sorry I put us both through all this. I wish I hadn't. But . . . I'm in too deep to pull out of it. There are so many moving parts, between the books and the documentary, the speaking engagements. I can't drop out now.'

'I don't want you to,' she sniffed. 'This is your big chance. You were right to take it.'

'But . . . I didn't think it would be this hard.'

Even though part of her was desperate to deny it, to tell him he was wrong, that they could survive this, the other, more sensible part of her knew that if they continued the way they were going, there would only be more frustration and, eventually, bitterness. She didn't want to end things like that.

Even if the truth was that she still loved him, and nothing hurt more than breaking up with someone you were still truly in love with.

'So that's it?' Cher asked. She had turned up on Lottie's doorstep with a sympathetic shoulder and a lot of wine. 'It's over?'

Lottie refilled her glass and sat back in her chair. 'Yep.'

'Just like that?'

'Yes,' Lottie said, eyeing her friend sternly. 'It's finished.'

'I can't believe it,' she said, looking deflated. 'I thought he was the one.'

'Well, apparently, he didn't get the memo.'

'What an idiot,' Cher said, shaking her head.

Her broken heart wanted to agree, but she simply couldn't work up the enthusiasm. He *wasn't* an idiot. He was simply making a sensible choice. Unfortunately it came at the cost of their future, and all the plans she'd been busy making were now nothing more than a long-forgotten daydream.

'I have a good mind to give that boy a call,' Cher continued.

'It wasn't his decision to call it quits,' Lottie told her. 'It was a joint decision.'

'But . . . why?'

'Because he needs to be free of guilt about his future, without the burden of me back here, waiting.'

'You are *not* a burden,' she replied furiously. 'That man was lucky to have you.'

Lottie smiled sadly at her friend. 'Yes, he was,' she said with a little slur in her voice. She studied her wineglass and frowned, momentarily distracted as she tried to remember how many she'd had. 'Anyway, as my last act of kindness, I let him off the proverbial hook.'

'I like this analogy,' Cher said, her eyes brightening. 'We'll just cast the net further out. He's not the one that got away, he's the one you threw back!' she said, warming to the theme.

'Catch and release,' Lottie said, toasting the air with her almost-empty glass.

'Absolutely,' Cher said touching her own glass to Lottie's. 'There's plenty more fish in the sea.'

Lottie's moment of drunken rebellion suddenly crumbled and she felt tears begin to well. 'But I don't *want* any other fish,' she howled, placing her glass on the table and dropping her head to rest on her folded arms.

'Oh, sweetheart,' Cher said, rubbing Lottie's back as she sobbed. 'Men are bastards.'

Thirty-six

While Lottie's love life was a crumbling ruin, the same could not be said for her mother's. Hannah and Gordon looked like they'd been a couple for decades instead of mere months, and Lottie could see a noticeable difference in her mother. She'd always considered her mum pretty Zen, considering all the yoga and meditation work her lifestyle embraced, but then Gordon came along and she was suddenly a hundred times more laid-back and happy.

She really was happy for them, but she found herself sometimes making excuses not to go to her mother's for dinner because it hurt to remember that she used to be happy like that not so long ago. Some days, she really couldn't be bothered to hide behind a bright smile and fake how fine she was. She wasn't fine. She wasn't miserable exactly; she was just . . . lonely. She missed Damian. She missed the life they'd been excitedly planning and she was struggling to find the earlier peace she'd been more than happy with before Damian had rode into her life and swept her off her feet.

Almost six months had gone by and she was having a lot more better days than sad ones now, but the place where he'd been was still very much a healing wound.

She'd been sent a copy of the coroner's report once Catherine's remains had been examined. DNA testing had proven it was indeed her, and that she'd most likely died of complications from a gunshot wound, which they had been able to detect by matching a bullet groove that had been visible on the bones left behind. There was no evidence of child remains in the grave, however the hair in the locket was DNA tested and found to have a parental relation to the hair found on the traces of material and remnants of clothing in the grave. While this established that Catherine was buried with her child's hair, the question remained as to what had become of the baby.

Lottie was happy that Catherine had been found and some of the questions had been answered. At the very least, she was no longer forgotten and alone in the bush.

Her mother had decided to trace Catherine's family in order to restore the ring back to its rightful owners, and while Lottie had mixed feelings about the decision, ultimately it was her mother's ring to do with as she wished. Now knowing the true origins of where it came from and how it got to be in her family, Lottie found herself in two minds about the whole thing. She had her own memories of the ring, which were linked to her gran, but then there was what she now knew had come before that, and she was struggling to hold on to her fond childhood memories.

But Catherine had lost her husband—the man she loved—and ultimately her own life over the ring. Part of Lottie agreed with her mum that maybe it *should* be returned to Catherine's family. Although it was little consolation, after everything that had happened.

The one good thing that had come out of the last few months had been her book. Damian had been right; it had all worked itself out. She'd been walking to work one morning and the solution had hit her. She'd hurried into the shop and sat down at her computer, and her fingers had run across the keyboard in an excited frenzy. She'd thrown herself into finishing it, determined to see it through. The ring was always going to have its own special chapter, but after all the twists and turns in the story it had an even more important part to play in her family history and definitely stole the show.

Once she began writing, the story just seemed to pour through her fingertips onto the screen. She'd written from her heart the story of her family, the resilience of her ancestors and the strength each generation of women had needed to find in order to survive their heartache and bring up their children alone against the backdrop of war, hunger, the Depression and prejudice. Entwined in their history was the story of Banalla, which she'd followed through its early conception as a lawless, ramshackle gold-mining town to the thriving, ever-changing place it was now, proving that, to succeed, you had to be adaptable, resilient and accepting.

After she'd finished writing, she'd nervously given it to Cher and her mother to read and, under their insistence, she'd sent it off to a publisher.

It was never supposed to be anything other than a memoir for her family, but despite being sure it wouldn't be something any publishing company would be interested in, they'd accepted it. She was still trying to get her head around that, but she had time as the book wasn't due to be released until the following year.

The rev of a bike outside played havoc with her heartbeat the way it usually did, but even that was slowly beginning to fade. Bikes rode through town daily, and now she barely glanced up, no longer hoping against hope that he'd walk through her door like he had on the very first day they'd met.

The stomp of feet on the doormat did make her lift her eyes from the bookwork she was doing, a customer-ready smile on her lips that slowly faded when she connected with the gaze across the store.

For a moment, the whole world froze.

'Hey, Lottie.' His deep, familiar voice flowed over her like a cool morning breeze.

'Hey,' she managed to get out finally. There were a million questions racing through her mind, like *What the hell are you doing here?* And *Are you actually* better *looking than you were before?*

'I, uh...' he said, passing a rolled-up paper or something he was carrying from one hand to the other before slapping it idly against one thigh, as he took a few more steps into the store. 'I just got into town and thought I'd see if you were here.'

'I'm always here,' she replied, eyeing him warily. Did figments of your imagination act nervous?

'The shop looks great. You've done some work.'

'I painted out the front.'

'Yeah, it looks good.'

Inwardly, Lottie rolled her eyes. This awkward small talk was not them. 'What are you doing in town?' she finally asked.

'I came back to see you.'

'Why?' She hadn't meant to sound so blunt, but shock had taken over.

'I—' he looked as though he wanted to say something but changed his mind at the last second '—thought you might be interested in something I found out. About Catherine.'

Damn him. He knew exactly how to get her attention. 'Oh?'

'Yeah. It's about Catherine's baby. They didn't find any evidence of it in the grave.'

'I remember.' She nodded, wondering where he was going with this. His beard was a little longer than the closely shaved one he'd worn before but was still meticulously trimmed and tidy. She liked it, she thought absently, wondering what it would feel like to rub her fingers through it.

He put down the rolled papers on top of the counter. 'Look at this.' He pulled out a print of a family tree chart, and Lottie noticed it was the one that Cher had given him from her collection.

'What am I looking at?' she asked, studying the page he unrolled.

'Cher's family research checks out . . . except when we get back up to here,' he said, running his finger up the diagram towards the top of the page. 'I found Kate and the rest of Jack's siblings, their parents from back in Ireland. All that pans out,' he explained, and she almost smiled as she heard the familiar way excitement began to colour his voice. 'Except for this one.'

Lottie followed to where his finger had stopped on one name. Finnegan. It fell in the line listing Kate's children, next to an alarming number of siblings. Cher's great-something grandfather.

'There's no record of his birth in any of the church registers.'

'You said before that sometimes records weren't always kept up to date.'

'Which is true. Only we have *all* the births from Kate O'Ryan nee McNally registered in church records before and after this baby. So it struck me as strange that she'd completely miss recording one child. Even if he had died young, you'd expect there to be a death recorded, but there's nothing. Then he appears years later, listed on birth certificates as the father of two children. And his grave is listed in the local cemetery.'

That *was* a little strange.

'Also, on a curious note, Finnegan translates to "son of the fair-haired",' he said in a deceptively nonchalant tone. 'Which is interesting, when all descriptions of Kate, along with the McNally and O'Ryan family, are of them being *dark-haired*.'

'Yeah, but I don't know anyone who names their child after the *literal* meaning behind a name,' Lottie said, sending him an odd look.

'This is a good point. It could just have been that Kate really liked the name Finnegan and as a baby he could have had fair hair. *But* we do have a hair sample found in Catherine's grave from inside the locket, from a baby who was blond.'

'What are you thinking?' Lottie asked slowly.

'I'm not thinking,' he said with a smile. 'The DNA tests came back positive. Finnegan O'Ryan was Catherine and Alexander's baby.'

Thirty-seven

7 April 1863

The rhythmic sound of loping hooves scattered the chooks as they scratched about in front of the small bark hut, sending them squawking in alarm as they scattered.

Kate O'Ryan grabbed the rifle from where it rested inside the front door and walked outside. 'Inside now,' she ordered in a voice her children had learned never to argue with. Her hand was steady as she aimed the gun at the approaching riders. She'd had more experience than most at handling a weapon and defending her family. She'd had to, growing up as a McNally.

A frown briefly creased her hard stare as she caught sight of a woman cradled in the arms of one of the men and turned quickly into a look of disbelief when she recognised the man as her brother Jack.

Kate rested the gun against the doorframe and hurried across to her brother, gathering the reins and holding the sweating animal as Jack carefully passed the pale woman to her brother Paddy, who'd already dismounted.

'Who one earth . . .' Kate started, but Paddy shook his head briefly, his lips twisted in a hard line.

A small moan escaped the woman's parted lips, and Kate forgot about asking questions as her eyes rested on the woman's protruding stomach. 'Take her inside,' she said. Kate noticed the blood and felt her heart sink. 'Put her on the table.' She moved quickly around her brother to go ahead and make room.

Once the woman had been laid down, she wasted no time in lifting the expensive but grubby material of the woman's once-fine garments to reveal blood-stained thighs and a tight, large belly that moved in time with contractions, changing shape as the baby inside fought to get out. The child was still alive, despite the fact its mother was barely conscious.

Kate shooed the men from the room and got to work. She noted the bleeding wound on the woman's side, but there was naught she could do for that at the moment. The child was her first priority.

She was no stranger to being a midwife. She'd had more than her share of experience, even delivering some of her own siblings from a tender age. Her last child she'd had to deliver herself, with the assistance of two of her older children, almost a year ago, when it came early and too fast for the local midwife to arrive. She recognised a problem when she saw it, and this was one of those times. The woman's pelvis seemed too small for the size of the child's head. She washed her hands with the cooled, freshly boiled water and pressed gentle hands against the woman's heaving belly.

Kate was so intent on feeling for the baby's position that she jumped slightly when a hand clasped her arm, and she looked down into the startling blue eyes of the woman on the table.

'Please save my baby.' Another contraction forced the woman to clench her eyes shut tight. 'I don't care about me. Just take care of my child,' she said in a stronger tone once the pain passed. 'Please.'

'Hush, now. You're going to need all your strength to push. We'll have this baby out and in your arms in no time,' Kate said, forcing a confident smile to her lips despite the fact she was not at all confident of the baby surviving the ordeal.

Kate talked the woman through her contractions and pushed against the taut stomach, trying to manoeuvre the child inside into a better position for birthing. It was pure agony for the mother, but Kate couldn't let that distract her—both the mother's and child's survival depended on getting this baby out. With one last tremendous push, Kate gently guided the substantially large head that finally appeared and watched in relief as the rest of its body slipped from its mother and onto the table. Kate quickly gathered the limp child and cleared its mouth, willing it to breathe and giving a grateful sigh when a loud cry finally came. Kate briefly closed her eyes, giving thanks, before clamping and cutting the baby's cord and placing him on his mother's chest. 'You have a son,' Kate said, and she felt her throat tighten with unexpected emotion as the frail woman lifted a hand and placed it on top of the wailing baby.

'A boy?' she said faintly in a wondering voice. 'Alexander would have liked that.' Her eyes fluttered shut.

Needle in a Haystack

Kate gathered the baby and wrapped him snugly in a sheet before placing him safely on the small bed behind her and returning to the woman. Blood had already seeped through the cloth Kate had placed between the woman's legs as well as pooling by the wound in her side, and despite Kate's frantic efforts to stem the flow, she had no success. Within minutes, the woman had passed.

Kate heard footsteps approaching but she was too drained to lift her bowed head from where she stood beside the lifeless body of the stranger on her kitchen table. The child cried from the bed behind her.

'You did everything you could.' Jack's deep voice came from close beside her.

'Why did you bring her here, Jack?' Kate snapped, jerking around to face him. 'Who is she?' She hadn't asked for grief to turn up on her doorstep today. She didn't even know this woman but she'd just witnessed two of life's most extreme gifts—a birth and a death—and she had no idea who this poor soul was.

'It's best you don't know.'

'I think I have a right to know, don't you? The woman just died giving birth in my house.'

'She was in the stagecoach. We had no idea she would be there.'

Kate felt the blood drain from her cheeks. 'Jack, what have you done?' she whispered. It was not like her brothers to take such an enormous risk.

'It doesn't matter. We got the money. This is life-changing for the whole family, Katie. We can start over, maybe in America. Head over to California and live in big houses. We can have servants of our own. Imagine that, Katie. After all those years of you and Ma

workin' as maids, you can finally be the lady of your own manor,' Jack said, jubilantly.

'You've lost your mind,' Kate said, staring at her brother. 'You've robbed a stagecoach. They'll be out looking for ya. How on earth do you think you'll get to California?'

'We'll have to lie low for a bit,' he admitted. 'But think of it, Katie,' he said looking off into the distance, 'No more highway robbery. No more hiding. We can all start again, make something of ourselves. We're rich.'

'We're dead is what we are,' she snarled, cutting into his delusional daydreaming. 'This woman is nobility. Look at her clothes, her jewellery,' Kate said. 'They'll hang you just for this, don't worry about the gold you stole or the troopers you've killed. A wealthy woman with child died. This will be on you, Jack.'

'How was I supposed to know she was that close to giving birth? I didn't even know she was on board.'

'Why would you bring her here and put us at risk?' she demanded. 'Now we're part of this too.'

'Where else was I going to go, Kate? Her husband's dead. The guards were dead. I couldn't just leave her there alone in the bush.'

'Maybe you should have thought about that before you killed her husband!'

'He gave me no choice.'

'This is pointless!' Kate said, throwing her arms in the air. The crying baby interrupted her frustration and she crossed the room to pick it up, feeling milk begin to leak through her bodice. Just what she needed when her youngest babe was almost ready to

wean. 'We can't let them find the body,' she said after a moment, her mind racing. 'Bury her.'

'What about the baby?' Jack asked.

'It played no part in all this,' Kate said stiffly. 'I made a promise to his mother. I'll raise it alongside my own wee 'uns.' Part of her tried to protest that this baby probably had other kin who would want to know of his existence, would wonder maybe at what had happened to him. But there was no way he would ever be able to know who his real family were. Kate was now an accomplice—her life and the fates of her own children were at stake. Her job had always been to hold the family together and protect them, and that was what she would do.

'There are no witnesses to say you robbed the coach, no one alive to testify that you took a pregnant woman from the scene. If you stay low and quiet, then no one can prove that the robbery was you. Then maybe we'll all get out of this alive.'

'They'll know it was us,' Jack said with his trademark cockiness. 'Proving it won't matter.'

'All the same. Keep your mouth shut and disappear. Go north and stay there.'

'That's what I was planning to do,' he snapped. He'd never liked being told what to do, especially by a woman and his sister no less, but they both knew that Kate was his sounding-board and the one who could always be counted on to solve a problem—most of the time. This, though, was bigger than any they'd ever had to deal with.

'We need to make haste and clean up before anyone gets here. I need clean water fetched and you men need to go dig a grave—not in *the family plot, make sure it's somewhere away from the homestead, where no one will ever find it.'* Kate shooed her brother outside, placed the baby back on the bed and quickly set about mopping up the blood and gathering the bloodstained cloths into a pile. She then sat down on the bed, lifted the wailing baby and let him feed.

Fifteen long minutes later, Jack returned with a pail of cold water from the creek, and she detached the child, placing him in the cradle that had held so many of her own. Swiftly she removed the mother's once-fine clothes, noting the lack of any damage on her smooth, creamy skin—this woman had clearly never had to scrub laundry or forage for food, chop wood for a fire to keep her children warm in winter or toil on the land to grow crops. Even her voice, weak with pain, had clearly indicated an educated and wealthy background. Kate had no great love for the gentry, but she washed the woman on her kitchen table with movements that were gentle as well as quick.

This was a woman and a mother who had been robbed of her life and her child and, no matter what her background, she deserved a proper burial.

After she'd dressed the body in a simple shift, Kate opened the door so the men could enter and then took out a folded blanket from the old, timber box at the base of the bed, handing it over to her husband and brother to wrap the woman's body. The blanket could have been used for her family this winter, but there was no way she could in good conscience let this poor woman be put into that cold ground only encased in bloody sheets. She stood back and watched as Jack gently folded the blanket over the woman's face.

'Wait,' she said, suddenly, snatching up her sewing scissors and crossing to the cradle. The baby was fast asleep, and she deftly sliced a small lock of soft downy, blonde hair off the tiny head. Kate reached behind her neck and unfastened the chain she wore, removing the gold locket her brother had given her years before.

'What are you doing?' her husband asked, alarmed by her intention.

Kate ignored the question, concentrating on placing the hair inside the delicate locket. She returned to the woman on the table.

'Kate—that's gold,' Jack said with a frown.

'I know what it is.' She unfolded the woman's hand as best she could and slipped the locket into her fist before tucking it back in and rewrapping the blanket tightly around her once more.

'That was our insurance,' her husband complained. 'What are ye giving it to a dead woman for? It ain't gonna do her any good where she's goin' now, is it?'

Kate looked up at the two men before her and held their angry gazes with a steely glare. 'That gold was stolen—it weren't ours to begin with. We have blood on our hands today, and I intend to make good with the Lord by sending this woman on her way with compassion. And a piece of her little 'un. If either of you want to stand in the way of that, then you'll have to take it up with God himself!'

The men swapped an uncertain glance, but neither made a move to intervene.

Kate swept up the pile of bloodstained sheets and marched them out to the waiting cart and then stood in the doorway, watching with a heavy heart as they carried the woman out of the house and drove her away.

While the men were burying her, Kate cleaned up the remaining evidence and packed what supplies she could gather for her brothers and the rest of the gang. She knew they would split up and go separate ways to avoid being tracked, eventually meeting up in one of their hideouts deep in the mountain bush. Once it was safe to do so, they would send for Kate, her husband and children.

That afternoon, Kate watched her brothers ride off, rocking the small baby in her arms in a movement now second nature to her, having nursed a child almost without pause since she was eighteen. She looked down at his sleeping face and felt her heart lurch. She would love this baby as fiercely as any of her own and it would never know a day of anguish, grieving for its lost mam.

Less than two weeks later, news arrived of Jack's death. Her brothers had all been slain—hunted and shot down like animals by the authorities—and Jack's body displayed like a trophy.

Many years later, as Kate prepared to walk out the door of her little home for the final time, her thoughts went to all the people in her life whom she'd lost over the years. Her parents, her brothers, two babies and a husband—so many. She was old and grey now—her children were mostly grown up and some had children of their own. Her life had been hard—much harder after Jack's death. Her husband, bless him, had been a simple farmer, but without the extra money Jack and her brothers had occasionally brought in life had become more of a struggle. The hard winters had become too much for her to handle now and she was tired.

'Are you ready Mammy?' her son asked. The horse and cart behind him were packed with a surprisingly small number of belongings—not much to show for the life she'd lived here up in the mountains.

'I just need to do one more thing,' she said. 'I won't be long.'

'I'll come with you,' he said.

She turned, holding up her hand. 'No. It's something I need to do on my own. I'll be along shortly.'

It was further than she remembered and the walk was harder than last time, but the buzz of insects kept her company and the birds sang merrily as she breathed in the smell of the eucalypts. She missed Ireland, but this place had been her home now for more years than her homeland had been.

When she reached the small clearing, she almost missed what she was looking for. It was hidden beneath long, spindly native grasses, with nothing to mark the place except the small rosebush she'd planted last time she'd come up here. The bush had been a gift from her husband, an unexpected extravagance after meeting a silver-tongued travelling peddler in town one day—a piece of the Old World, for their new one. She was glad to see that it had survived.

She took a seat on a large, flat rock nearby and tilted her face towards the morning sun, enjoying the peace and quiet. This was a good place, Kate thought. She hadn't come up here for many years, and for most of them she'd pushed away any thoughts of what had happened that terrible day when her brother had brought a stranger to the house, close to dying and in great pain, yet using her last breath to plead for the safety of her child. But she had never truly forgotten that woman, whose name she didn't know to this day. How could she, when each time she looked into Finnegan's face it was like looking into the same blue eyes of the woman to whom she'd made a deathbed promise?

A slight rustle made Kate open her eyes, and she watched as a small wallaby entered the clearing from the dense bush beyond. It stopped when it noticed her, tilting its small head and fixing its dark eyes on Kate's face intently.

There is a knowing in those eyes, she thought, and a sigh of awareness ran through her.

'I kept my promise,' Kate said, softly. 'I've loved your boy like he was my own and I kept him safe. I'm sorry you never got to see him grow, but no good can come from digging up the past now, so this is how it must be. I'll face my Maker with the knowledge that I did all that I could do, and I did it with a pure heart.'

Kate rose slowly from her seat. The wallaby blinked but didn't jump away as she crossed to pluck one of the small flowers from the bush. She carefully laid it on the ground, over the invisible grave. 'Until we meet again, may God hold you in the palm of his hand,' she whispered. She watched as the little wallaby hopped away, and then slowly made her own way from the clearing without looking back.

Thirty-eight

Good grief.

Lottie was stunned by the revelation Damian had just made. *Days of Our Lives* had nothing on this twisted tale. 'I don't understand . . . *How* is it possible that Catherine's child was hidden in plain sight this entire time?'

'From what we can piece together, Catherine dies and Kate's left—quite literally—holding the baby. She's not going to abandon a helpless child, and they can't take it to anyone because then there'd be questions, and they can't have anyone find Catherine because that would only implicate her and her family in the robbery and murder of six men,' he stated matter-of-factly. 'No one would think twice about seeing Kate with a newborn baby, if they even saw her, given how remote her home was. She'd already had a tribe of kids by then.'

'But not registering the birth was a bit suspicious, surely?'

'Maybe registering it would be *more* risky, if someone started adding up dates. Who knows, maybe, despite being a criminal family, they were still cautious about lying to the church? Religion played a much bigger role in lives back then.'

It made sense. She stopped then stared at him. 'If Finnegan wasn't Kate's child . . .' she started, then felt her eyes widen as comprehension suddenly dawned. 'Then Cher isn't related to the McNallys. She's related to the—'

'Comptons,' Damian finished for her. 'Finnegan O'Ryan is a descendant of Alexander Compton.'

Lottie let out a shocked chuckle. 'Cher is going to be devastated.'

They shared a momentary smile, but Lottie soon felt it slip from her face as reality set in. Damian was here. In her shop. She'd pictured this scene a time or two since their break-up, but in those imaginings, she hadn't been dressed in a pair of old jeans, an oversized T-shirt and joggers, with her hair pulled back in a messy ponytail after she'd spent the day rearranging the store.

'I, uh . . . excuse me for a minute,' she said in a rush, heading out the back to lock herself in the tiny bathroom, feeling sweaty and gross.

She glanced up at the mirror and groaned at the sight, quickly smoothing her hair back and giving her armpits a brief sniff. *This is* not *how this moment was supposed to go.* She took a deep breath before opening the door and heading back out.

'Sorry about that,' she said, avoiding his worried gaze.

'So . . . how have you been?' Damian asked when the silence threatened to turn uncomfortable.

'Good,' she said with a shrug. 'Busy.'

'I heard about your book being published. Congratulations,' he said. His smile almost melted her tattered heart.

'Thanks. I'm not sure how it'll go, but I'm pretty happy that it's finally finished.' Then a thought occurred to her. 'How did you know about the book?'

'Gordon mentioned it.'

'Oh. Right.' Of course. She'd never asked Gordon about him—she hadn't been brave enough—but she should have realised they would have stayed in contact.

'He and your mum are still going strong, I see.'

'Yeah. Like two teenagers in love.'

'I'm happy for them.'

In the quiet of the shop, she heard the old grandfather clock ticking loudly in time with her heartbeat until it became too much. 'Why are you really here, Damian?' she blurted.

'I . . . missed you,' he said finally.

Her heart skipped a beat and she felt a slice of pain go through her. She'd missed him too. Every day. But having him suddenly reappear out of the blue like this was . . . a lot.

'You were the last person I expected to see today,' she found herself saying, facing each other like a pair of strangers. It felt weird to know someone so well, yet feel as though you suddenly didn't know them at all.

'I thought about letting you know I was in town, but then I was worried you might justifiably tell me to get lost,' he said with a grimace. 'So I figured I'd use the element of surprise to my advantage.'

'Well, I guess it worked.' She'd been too shocked to slam the door in his face, even if she'd thought about doing it. 'How long are you here for?'

'About that,' he started, swallowing nervously. 'I got offered a job.'

'Oh.' *Here we go again*, she thought. This dreadful feeling of déjà vu.

'Yeah, as a curator for a new Early Australian Museum that's being planned. It covers the period from the First Fleet arrivals, early colonial settlement, Indigenous colonial history through to the gold rush and bushranger era.'

'Wow, that sounds amazing.' It really did. 'I'm happy for you.' She really was.

'Yeah. It means staying on in Sydney full-time, though,' he said with a long sigh. Her heart plummeted, though she didn't know why—he'd already left once.

'That's great,' she said, forcing a smile and straightening her shoulders. 'Well, I'd better get ready to close and let you get back to whatever you were doing,' she said, turning away quickly as she felt an annoying prickle behind her eyelids. She was mortified that he might see her cry.

'Which is why I turned down the offer,' he continued, making her stop.

She turned back towards him. 'Why would you do that?' she asked cautiously.

'Because I'd already applied for another job . . . and got it.'

What the hell kind of game is he playing at? Lottie simply stared at him.

'I'll be working at the university up here.'

Lottie felt her mouth drop open as she continued to stare at him—her mind racing—trying to keep up with what he was saying. 'You gave up a dream job as a curator at a museum to be a lecturer at *Armidale?*'

He flashed that lopsided little grin at her and Lottie's insides did a flip. God, she'd missed that.

'The hours are flexible, so I can focus on my writing, which was my original plan until everything went haywire and I got sidetracked by things I thought I should want.' He took a step closer to her. 'I know what I actually want now.'

'What do you want?' she asked quietly.

'I want us. I want you . . . if you'll give me another chance?'

'You really want to give up everything you worked for to move up here?' she asked incredulously, still unable to believe what she was hearing.

'I let myself get swept away by all the hype. I lost sight of what made me happy. It wasn't the TV stuff or the media hype. I let all that craziness cloud my judgement and worse, I did it at the cost of losing you.'

'You were always very clear about how much your career means to you, Damian.'

Damian looked at her desperately. 'Here's the thing, Lottie. It didn't matter how much it would help my career, or how many books it would sell, when I didn't have you there by my side to share all that success. *Our* success.'

'We made a pretty good team,' Lottie acknowledged. 'But you only did what anyone would have done in the same situation. I never blamed you for that.'

'*I* blame me for it. I'm so sorry, Lottie. I don't want any of it. I want the dream we started to plan, and I'm hoping you might still too.' He slowly stepped around the counter, cautious hope in his step. 'Would you consider it? Maybe see if you can fall in love with me again?'

Her throat tightened; this time, there was no hope of stopping the tears as they fell. 'You idiot. I never fell *out of love* with you,' she said with a sniff.

He closed the distance between them and wrapped her in his arms, holding her tightly. Against his chest, she could hear his heart beating fast, yet reassuringly, and she knew they'd finally found the place where they both belonged.

'I'm a *what?*' Cher demanded, her voice rising in alarm after Lottie and Damian had sat her down to explain over a drink at the bar what they'd uncovered.

'You're a descendant of Lady Catherine Compton,' Damian repeated.

For a moment, Cher sat stunned into silence, which was no mean feat.

'I'm . . . a *lady*!' she gasped.

'Well, I don't think you're actually . . .' Damian trailed off.

'I have noble blood,' she declared. 'I *knew* it.'

'You're not disappointed about not having a blood connection to Kate anymore?' Lottie asked cautiously.

'Of course, that's going to take a bit of time to adjust to,' Cher said, tilting her head slightly, 'but let's face it, finding out I'm a Compton is a pretty good upgrade. I can't wait till the girls down south find out about this.'

'Do you think you should let this all sink in for a bit before you get too excited?' Lottie suggested gently.

'Maybe you're right.' Cher gasped, placing one lethally manicured hand on Lottie's arm. 'Maybe I *should* wait a few days and get used to it.' She nodded thoughtfully. 'I'll need some time to plan my party anyway.'

'What party?'

'My announcement party! I'm no longer a *madame*. I'm now *Lady* Cherise Dubois,' she said dramatically, trying out the name.

'Oh boy,' Lottie sighed.

Epilogue

It had been eighteen months since Lady Catherine Compton's grave had been found in the lonely bushland far up in the hills. After months of paperwork and negotiation, they finally had the go-ahead to re-inter her in the place she should have been buried more than a hundred and sixty years earlier.

The sky was a pretty periwinkle blue with not a cloud to be seen. The sun warmed the backs of the crowd of locals who'd gathered to attend the service and finally lay Catherine to rest.

Lottie wiped a stray tear from her cheek and sent her husband a small smile as he pulled her close to his side and kissed the top of her head.

'You okay?' Damian asked softly.

'Yeah, they're happy tears. I'm glad she's finally where she belongs.' The baby in her arms wiggled and squirmed at being held for so long, and Damian reached over to take him from her. It had been a crazy year and a half since they'd moved in together, then gotten married, followed by the arrival of their baby, Alexander Loxley. She had a whole new family, complete with three new sisters-in-law and Damian's parents, who all doted on Alex—when they could pry him away from her own mother and Cher, that was. Life was full and busy—but never dull.

'I think Catherine would have approved,' Cher said, dabbing at her eyes delicately.

'It was a beautiful service. You did her proud,' Lottie assured her friend. Since the discovery of her real ancestry, Cher had led the fight to have Catherine's remains stay in Banalla. It hadn't really been much of a fight; Cher had taken it upon herself to fly to England and meet with some members of the Shoebridge family and plead the case to have Catherine laid to rest beside her husband. Using true Cher charm, she'd secured not only their blessing, but also a sizeable contribution towards the burial costs.

'While I was pulling all this together, I decided I'm going to write Catherine and Alexander's love story into a cabaret. Catherine Compton,' she said, looking skywards and speaking dramatically. 'The Lady, the legend, the untold love story,' she announced. 'What do you think?' she asked, looking back at Lottie expectantly.

'I love it,' Lottie nodded. 'If anyone can make that happen, it's you.'

Her mother and Gordon walked up and shared a hug before Gordon walked over to where Damian stood rocking his three-month-old son to sleep.

Lottie watched as her mother and Cher swapped a brief glance but, before she could question it further, Cher cleared her throat and broke into a wide smile. 'This has been killing me,' she confided with a small flutter of her hand in front of her mouth. 'Sorry,' she said, squinching up her nose as she glanced at the graves beside her. 'Honey, your mother and I wanted to give you something.'

Lottie sent a bemused glance to both of them, unsure what on earth these two had been concocting between themselves. She glanced down as Cher handed her a small paper gift bag.

'What's this?' she asked nervously.

'We had to wait to make sure,' her mother started.

'Hurry up and open it,' Cher said impatiently.

Lottie reached into the bag and pulled out a box. A small. Antique. Ring box. Her startled gaze flew to her mother.

Hannah smiled gently, lowering her head in encouragement to continue.

Lottie slowly opened the box and—despite already knowing what she was going to find inside—still caught her breath as the beautiful opal glittered in the bright sunshine. 'I don't understand. You said you'd returned it to Catherine's family.'

'I did.' Her mother's smile widened. 'I gave it to Cher.'

'I can't take this,' Lottie said, pushing the ring box into Cher's hands. 'It's yours.'

Cher clasped her big hands around Lottie's smaller ones. 'Honey child, as much as I adore that opal, I am a diamond gal through and through. That blue washes out my skin tone.'

'Cher, it's worth a fortune.'

'Charlotte Fairchild–Loxley,' Cher said, using the no-nonsense voice that made even drunken patrons sit up and take notice. 'That ring has always belonged in your family. They've kept it safe and loved it for all these years. Your mum gave it to me and now I'm giving it to you—freely and with only loving intentions. May this ring bring you and yours only blessings and love,' Cher said, glancing over at Hannah, who gave an approving nod, and then giving Lottie's hands one final, heartfelt squeeze.

Lottie stared at the ring before looking up at her mother. 'What about the curse?'

'It's gone.'

'What if it's not?' she asked, sending a quick glance across at Damian, who was smiling down at the baby in his arms. She'd never believed in the stupid curse before, but now, suddenly, as a mother and a woman with everything she loved standing right there, the idea of something taking them away truly terrified her.

'It's gone,' Hannah said once more, firmly.

'But how can you be sure the curse was broken?'

The panic subsided and Lottie would have laughed at herself if it hadn't felt so real. *Get a grip*, she told herself firmly. *It never existed in the first place.*

'Are you ready to go home?' Damian called when he caught her looking over at him.

'Coming.' She waved.

'Put it on,' Cher said, nodding down at the ring. Taking a deep, calming breath, Lottie slid the gold ring onto her finger. An avalanche of memories passed through her mind of a little girl twirling in her gran's high heels, holding her small hand up high as she admired the pretty blue opal with its rainbow of hidden colours inside.

'Let's go. I'm starving, and all the morning tea is at your place,' Cher said, heading off towards the carpark.

Damian walked up beside Lottie and slipped an arm around her waist as they stood in front of the newly erected headstone:

ALEXANDER COMPTON, BURIED HERE WITH HIS WIFE AND ONE TRUE LOVE, LADY CATHERINE COMPTON. REUNITED, NEVER TO BE PARTED AGAIN.

'You did it,' she said, resting her head against his shoulder. 'You found her.'

'I had a bit of help along the way,' he said dryly.

'You think it was Catherine who helped?'

'Who knows,' he dismissed quickly, and she smiled slightly. Her gaze slid across to the grave on the other side of the gravel pathway.

Needle in a Haystack

HERE LIES FINNEGAN O'RYAN, BELOVED HUSBAND, FATHER AND SON

Granted, it wasn't a large cemetery, but somehow she knew it wasn't just a fluke that Finnegan was buried so close to his father, the man who'd never had the chance to meet him in life, but who would spend an eternity near him. And now he had his mother there too.

Everything had come full circle at last.

'I love you,' Damian whispered close to her ear, seeming to sense the direction her thoughts had been going.

'I love you too,' she whispered back. The opal on her finger continued to glitter and sparkle like a thousand tiny stars in an enormous universe.

Acknowledgements

Years ago, I was lucky enough to be invited to Uralla to do an author talk, and I made a promise to the then mayor that I would use Uralla in a book one day.

The bushranger legacy is something that has always fascinated me, and Uralla, along with a number of other places locally, has a rich history that traces back to those times, with Captain Thunderbolt playing such a big part in the region's past.

So when the opportunity came around to find a location to set my next book in, Uralla became the perfect place for my fictional town. And I couldn't really write a book set in Uralla without including a bushranger or two . . .

So, taking a few bits and pieces from Thunderbolt, and adding a healthy dose of fiction, Jack McNally became my infamous outlaw.

I can't tell you how much I enjoyed weaving this tale and, although it's pure fiction, I really did grow to love Catherine and desperately wanted her to be found and finally have her story told. I take full responsibility for the fact this was able to happen in record time, and with the benefit of a background storyline! My apologies to all the historians out there who could only wish this many fortunate events unfolded in real life to solve missing pieces of history!

As usual, thank you to my faithful readers; my family, who constantly supports me and cheers me on; my menagerie of farm animals who keep me sane; and my wonderful publishing team who make me look a lot more polished and professional than I fear I really am!

Fiction with heart

Craving more heartwarming tales from the countryside? Join our online rural fiction community, **FICTION with HEART**, where you'll discover a treasure trove of similar books that will capture your imagination and warm your soul.

Visit **fictionwithheart.com.au** or scan the QR code below to access exclusive content from our authors, stay updated on upcoming events, participate in exciting competitions and much more.

See you there!